BORN
SAVAGES

Cactus Kiss Publishing

ALSO BY CORA BRENT:

Unruly

GENTRY BOYS
Draw
Risk
Game
Fall
Hold (Coming Soon!)
Cross (Coming Soon!)

DEFIANT MC Series
Know Me: A Novella
Promise Me
Remember Me

Reckless Point

I love to hear from readers!

Contact me at corabrentwrites@yahoo.com.

www.facebook.com/CoraBrentAuthor

COPYRIGHT

TABLE OF CONTENTS

CHAPTER ONE

REN

Although I'm blinking and sitting upright in the dark bedroom of my Las Vegas apartment with a phone glued to my ear, my brain is still half inside of a dream.

It was a nice dream.

I miss it.

It starred a virile, highly bangable male body and the cage of a Ferris wheel.

The three of us – the body, the Ferris wheel and me – went up and down and up and down again. The cage rattled to the steady beat of thumping club music; a tribal pulse that went faster and faster until the world began to turn kaleidoscope colors and then...

BZZZBZZZBZZZ

The sheer symbolism borders on pathetic.

Plus, the more awake I am the easier it is to remember that I haven't done anything that satisfying in real life lately.

But leave it to Brigitte to decide that two a.m. is a splendid time to make a phone call. My sister is not the type of person who allows minor hassles like sleep, empathy and common sense interfere with her goals. And recently her goal involves getting me to agree to do something outrageous.

I sigh into the air-conditioned darkness, sexually frustrated and trying to block out my sister's metallic voice as my mind searches for the face of my dream prince. After all, the body seemed to be attached to a man and men usually have faces.

In a flash, I see him. I can almost name him. But then he is lost.

Inside my head I'm cursing fifteen furious variations of the word 'FUCK!' and mourning a squandered orgasm.

However, I'm a good sister so I stay quiet. I even keep the phone propped against my ear and sort of listen to the words coming out of it.

"Ren! They are committing to ten."

Brigitte has a breathless gasp in her voice, like she's just finished sprinting back and forth across the floor of her crappy apartment in the most dismal quarter of Los Angeles. My sister reminds me of a twitchy rabbit sometimes, a twitchy rabbit that is highly imperious, very well accessorized and smells expensive.

"Ten?" I grumble. "Ten what?"

I know very well what she's talking about. It's also the last thing I feel like discussing in the middle of the night while a slow throb withers between my legs.

"Ten episodes." She raises her voice. Maybe she believes she can shout her way through my reluctance. It wouldn't be the first time. "And a second season if the first one grabs ratings."

My little sister has lost her ever-loving mind.

But then again, whether she ever had one in the first place was always a question up for grabs.

I yawn and try to focus. "A moot point, isn't it? Spence already said no."

A celebratory giggle reaches across three hundred miles and pricks at my blossoming headache. She breaks into a singsong voice. "Oh no, sweet sister, Spencer said yes. Yes yes yes YES!"

If I were the gasping type of girl I would gasp at the news.

But I'm not and I don't, especially because I don't believe it. Spencer is the last one in the family who would sign on for this, a circus of cameras and lost siblings invading his home turf. He still lives down there on that godforsaken patch of Arizona desert where our father once dragged all of us in a quest for something opposite to the L.A. glare. These days, my younger brother is the only Savage still haunting the sage and the cacti. Whenever I picture him he's got his nose halfway up a rusted carburetor and a shotgun slung across his back, daring any rattlesnake that crosses his path to coil up and fuck with him. That's Spence.

Brigitte decides my dazed silence must be consent. She starts dropping names of agents and producers and all the tiresome litany of Hollywood bullshit that I wish I knew nothing about. But I know too much. Show business is coded into my goddamn DNA. It's what made us. It's what broke us. It's what I want surgically cut from my identity, and what I will keep trying to outrun as long as this last name of mine keeps chasing.

My sister talks on and on. My heart hurts a little to hear the excitement in her voice because I know I'll be the one to crush it. Even though Brigitte has a long history of giving me heartburn she is still my sister, still some part of the red-headed little girl who stubbornly clung to my waist to keep me from going anywhere without her.

Plus, she's got Ava, my other sister, on her side. Ava, who was always so soft and adrift, who's been frantic for anything that looks vaguely like love since we were children. Ava has one now herself, a child. A son who at the age of two is a physical reproduction of his gorgeous asshole of a father. Yet he did manage to inherit his mother's wounded blue eyes. Saying no to Brigitte will sting a little; saying no to Ava feels like kicking a kitten.

My two sisters couldn't be more different. There's Brigitte, brash and tempestuous, ready to grab her birthright with both manicured claws. Then Ava, tender and forever bewildered by the awful things the years have done to her so far.

And finally there is me. Loren, or Ren. The brick wall. Stoic. Stalwart. Detached and cold-hearted.

"Do you feel *nothing*, Loren?" my own mother would howl while she grabbed her own throat with theatrical gusto. "Is there even blood beneath that pallid skin of yours?"

There's no point in answering such questions. I always knew that.

"She likes to see me cry.

She'll tell you that's a terrible lie."

Those words once found their way into a fourth grade poetry assignment for Mother's Day. I swear I have memories of being pinched by her when I was too small to tell anyone about it. As soon as the tears showed up Lita Savage would always back off, a perverse smile lighting up her lips. She was, and is, a person who thrives off the agony of others. A person like that should never ever be a parent.

By now, Lita has nothing to do with me. Or with Ava or Brigitte for that matter.

The three of us, the Savage sisters, are like points of a triangle, all independent and lonely in our separate corners. Bouncing around somewhere in our orbit are my two brothers – rugged Spencer and arrogant Montgomery. They circle us as warily as they do one another.

Montgomery. Loren. Spencer. Ava. Brigitte.

Write all our names in one sentence and it'll look like a grand mash up of an old silver screen marquee. That was probably what Lita had in mind to begin with when she married August Savage. She wasted no time delivering her first genetic insurance policy and kept them coming in quick order. Monty was born exactly nine months after the diamond landed on her finger and I came along exactly ten months after him. The twins, Ava and Spence, joined the crazy Savage cast a year later and the youngest, the one who has destroyed my peaceful night, came screaming into her own spotlight twelve months after that. I don't know the specifics but Brigitte's birth must have taken the gynecological cake for Lita because there were no more siblings afterwards.

In fact, ever since I could remember my parents had occupied separate bedrooms and barely spoke. There was never any question about any of us being Savages though. All five of us, in our distinct ways, manage to resemble dead movie stars.

I'm still half listening to my sister yammer on about production schedules and publicity shoots and other things that don't interest me at all. I'm putting off the moment that I tell her I can't do it. She thinks I don't understand but I understand very well. It's a tasteless reality television carnival that has nothing to do with reality. There are dozens just like it these days. I wouldn't be on board even if they weren't planning on filming down in the dusty hellhole that's the last sad relic of the glittering Savage fortune.

"Ren, are you listening?"

"I'm listening."

My god, I can see it like it's all already been filmed, already been broadcast, already the subject of ten thousand clumsily written blogs. It makes me a little sick that the producers are likely banking on that poignancy, on the 'Look how far they've fallen!' vibe of despair as they film the remnants of a glamorous family bickering over water usage and shuffling around in the derelict mess.

Who the hell would agree to that?

Then something Brigitte says catches my attention and it all makes sense. Now I know why my own sisters have shoved their dignity into a sock drawer. Spencer too, apparently. My younger brother must be more desperate than I thought.

"*How* much?" I ask.

"Five grand. Each. Per episode, Ren. So that's five grand times ten. Quick, do the math." Her tone is jubilant. She knows she's won. I never realized it was possible to hear someone smirk. "Think you can beat that as a cocktail waitress out there on the Vegas strip?"

Her words have a sharp edge. They taunt. They are supposed to.

I answer back just as sharply. "I'm not a cocktail waitress."

"You're not far off."

"I deal blackjack to frat boys, party girls and sad sacks with deep pockets who sometimes get the mistaken impression that I'm for sale too. And you know damn well I can't beat that take in six months."

I pause and swallow, wishing I had something fiery at hand, something on the high end of the alcohol proof scale. I could use some fire right now. Whatever fight I had seems to be evaporating. Maybe a different tactic would work. I clear my throat and put on my best voice of reason.

"Bree, I can't help but feel that you're diving right into the dark water without any idea how deep it is. You don't know what you're asking for."

"Stop," she scoffs. "I'm not asking for anything I'm not willing to do myself."

I picture her waving a petite hand in the air and rolling her eyes. No one needs to tell Brigitte what is best. Complaints are unwelcome here. She's never liked her nickname, Bree, and is in the habit of demanding that everyone draw out the second syllable of her full name with a chic, foreign-sounding lilt.

"This is a great opportunity," insists *Brijeeeet* and she suddenly sounds whiny, agitated. *Goddamn her,* she's probably thinking. *Selfish jerk.*

She really does need me to cooperate though. The deal for the show only stands if all five of us sign on.

When I don't answer she sighs with exasperation and her pitch escalates. She only has so much patience for playing nice.

"Dammit Ren! Don't you ever get tired of being a fucking joke? A punch line? An 'Oh god, look what happened to those Savages!' kind of sneering sympathy which isn't really sympathy at all. They gloat. They *laugh*. We're fucking *funny* to them. You know it's true."

I soften. Only a little. The permanent dent in our status hurts her the most. I've gotten used to it. A long time ago I figured out that no matter the circumstances I wouldn't have chosen that insane life. It was never my fate. But Brigitte isn't over it. She never will be.

"Bree," I start to say but she's on a roll. She hasn't made her point yet.

"Down the rabbit hole we went," she howls. "The Savages, in one sad scandalous lump. Took us only a generation to go from America's sweethearts to American baggage. And I'm not talking about the boutique shit. I'm talking about a low end department store kind of baggage made of dog hide and imported from some part of the world where people are forced to live in six foot tin kennels and work in the goddamn baggage factory twenty-two hours a day."

I've stopped listening somewhere in the middle of that garbled monologue. I don't know where she comes up with this crap. It was probably vomited from the mines of some focus group stuffed with Armani suits.

"Don't you ever get tired of being a fucking joke?"

"Hmm," I grunt when she pauses for breath. I'm startled to find myself actually considering it. Mostly I'm considering how much I'd like to tell my florid-faced overseer at the casino that he's rubbed his knobby hard-on across my ass for the last time.

Not that I'm destitute. Living in Vegas can be done cheaply and my single bedroom is comfortable enough for me and a semi-annual guest or two, which is about all I can brag about besides faceless bronzed muscle dreams. Any extra money I come across I immediately send Ava's way, no matter how much she tries to argue that I shouldn't.

The thing is, the world has largely forgotten about me and I've blended into the scenery here. Anonymity is comfortable. If you've never been attached to celebrities you wouldn't understand. My sister's demands would destroy that comfort. I know how it works. Even if the show is only marginally successful we'll be stalked. We'll be wild prey on the loose in America. They would find us as we tiptoe out of a steakhouse, slither into traffic court, and stumble from the dentist. The weapons would be anything capable of basic photography. We would return to being the curious oddities that the world would like to own.

We would be....*Famous*.

Brigitte's voice grows small and uncertain. My silence is hurting her, deflating her ambitions. She begins to sound the opposite of confident. She sounds like a little girl begging her big sister to let her borrow an expensive dress.

"*Please*, Loren," she wheedles. "I need this. We all do. Spence is barely hanging onto the ranch, Ava wants to give her boy something better than a slum life and I can't even get a screen test for a B level slasher flick. People hear my name and they sneer for god's sake. They do! You can tell what they're thinking. 'The Savages, aren't they all dead yet?' This is probably the only shot we're going to get and I know it might be tacky and vulgar. I know that! I know they will edit the shit out of everything we say and make us look even more ridiculous than we are. But it will also put us on the map. Loren, we'll be those faces who get showered with several grand just for showing up at some wannabe's party in Malibu."

I close my eyes. My sister is counting on the fact that I don't have it in me to refuse her. She might be right. "Monty?"

She pauses. "Not yet."

"Does that mean he doesn't know or he's refusing?"

My inscrutable big brother has been keeping himself out of reach since he took a ten-month tour of the California correctional facilities. Assault, complicated by cocaine possession in large enough quantities to be considered intent to distribute. But Montgomery Savage doesn't tolerate being needled in a shoddy bar by some random asshole with a beer gut so he answered with his fists. Unbelievably stupid, considering what he had in his pockets. His sentence could easily have been much longer. And it would have been, except some big name ambulance-chasing celebrity attorney who'd gone to prep school with my father had taken the case pro bono. That was the last time a Savage had been newsworthy and Monty has been keeping quiet down in San Diego since his release. All the gossip says he's shacked up with some has-been soap opera cougar. He refuses to confirm whether or not it's true.

But Brigitte evidently hasn't run her plans past the eldest Savage sibling. She exhales dramatically. "Montgomery has expensive habits and a deep affection for his baby sister. Besides, Monty isn't stupid. He'll understand that it's a better option than whoring himself out indefinitely to some withered, graying snatch and her dusty Emmy collection."

I wince over the imagery. "Better we all whore ourselves out in prime time living rooms across the nation, huh?"

Brigitte lets out a little hiss. "Cut it out, Ren. Negativity etches permanent wrinkles you know."

"Yes, Lita. I know."

She ignores the insult, pretends I'm not mocking her by comparing her to our mother. "This is a legitimate business venture. An entire brand will be forged. The Savages. We can remake ourselves."

"Those aren't your words."

"So? That doesn't mean they are untrue."

I'm out of bed now, pacing the room. It's a small room so it only takes three short strides to get from one end to the other. My apartment is sparsely decorated in a sleek contemporary modern style, courtesy of Ikea. There is a bed, a dresser, a couch and a small dinette. It's neat and clean and boring. It suits me well. After switching on the single overhead light I perch on the edge of the memory foam mattress, the last vestiges of sleep gone. There's no use in pretending that I'll be returning to my Ferris wheel fantasy nap after Brigitte finishes with me.

"Look, I need some assurance that Lita stays the fuck away. I won't even talk about it unless that's a sure thing. No maternal surprises for dramatic effect, like we're sitting down to dinner and she rings the motherfucking doorbell. I don't want to hear a word about her or I swear I'll walk."

Brigitte is ready with an answer. "Oh god, she knows nothing. She hung up the phone when the producers tried to call her. She doesn't want anything to do with us. Apparently she's still playing house with the stroke patient she married, probably busily researching the best way to make him choke on a pillow."

"I'm serious, Bree. It better be written into the damn contract. No Lita." My headache has grown. I scrabble around in my nightstand for the bottle of Excedrin and swallow two pills without any water.

"I swear it, Ren. On my honor as your sister. I'm not all that excited to see her ever again either."

My mouth twitches. Brigitte sounds so earnest. Brigitte is a fantastic actress. "You might have spent a big chunk of your honor when you appropriated my sole pair of Manolo Blahnik's and broke the left heel."

"You've a memory like an elephant. That was years ago. I apologized. I swear I still have some honor remaining. Consider it yours."

"Does it have a name?"

"What, you mean the show?"

"Yes, I mean the show. What do they plan on calling it?"

"Born Savages."

I should have swallowed the pills with at least one mouthful of water. I can feel every centimeter of their slow slide. For a second they pause. I imagine they are caught somewhere close to my heart.

"Clever," I cough. "Who spent years getting an expensive degree for the right to think that up?"

"I think it's cute. It works. I told you who's producing it, right? Gary Vogel. He's behind all the classier projects, the ones broadcast on the Biz Network that are centered around *real* names, not these cheesy game shows that cast common folk nobodies. He's got the Kingston sisters signed on to live on a goat farm in Vermont during shearing season. Stop laughing! It will be quite artistic from what I hear. And get this. Gary happens to the producer for Bastion Brats."

I groan. "You shouldn't have reminded me. That thing is a tawdry disaster."

"It's one of the highest rated shows in the country. Wait, didn't you used to be friends with Bitty Bastion like a million years ago in grade school? Before her exotic journey into twelve rounds of rehab, that is. Anyway, Bitty and Becky already have their own talk shows and the rest are swimming in more offers than they can keep track of. If those moon-faced morons can get that far, think of what *we* can do."

"I'll bet Gary told you that."

"Does it matter?" She sounds excited again.

When Brigitte was a little girl she used to bounce maniacally on her toes whenever she got nervous or excited. It was endearing then. I picture her doing the same thing in her dumpy apartment. It's still endearing.

"So you're in, right Ren? I knew you wouldn't hang us out to dry. Ava's such a pessimist. She was terrified to even ask you."

Once I say it there's no taking it back. "Just the five of us, right? No other Savages."

I can hear the smile in her voice. "What other Savages could there possibly be? We're the only ones anyone is interested in."

"Okay."

"Clarify that 'okay', please."

"You know you've got me, Bree. I won't help you with Monty though."

"Monty will be easy."

"Monty is the opposite of easy."

"Trust me. I'll have Monty signed and sealed before you can say the word Arizona."

Outside a siren wails and then surges into the distance toward some unknown disaster. "Arizona."

The word brings out strange feelings in me. Of a place, of a time, of a boy….

"What other Savages could there possibly be?"

The question has haunted me long before my sister ever casually uttered it.

CHAPTER TWO

OZ

In this group two, are beginners and two are not. The woman worries me. She blinks weirdly fast and chews on the inside of her mouth while casting quick glances at the man beside her. They're a couple, plainly still in that early uncertain phase. She's too freaking eager to please him. It's obvious to me that she's not the underground type of girl. She's the kind that breaks a nail flipping the tab of a beer can. I can do that; sort women out with ease. I'm almost always right.

The other pair is a father/son set from Nashville who tell me they've been caving a handful of other times in these rich Smoky Mountains. They are fine. They are the eager, appreciative types that I love guiding through the caves.

The woman – Leah is her name – grunts as she struggles through the small break in the rock. We're trying to reach a cavernous room filled with complex formations, a caver's paradise. But we have to hold on a minute because Leah's plentiful tits don't like the narrow pass. She shimmies a few inches deeper into the rock and grunts again.

"Fuck," she spits and immediately seems alarmed that such a foul syllable came from her mouth.

The father and son titter just inside the room but Leah's boyfriend looks mad. He throws her a scornful glare.

Right then and there I know what he's about and I don't like him. He's one of those self-righteous bastards. You know the type, hugging his moral superiority like a security blanket or his mother's left nipple. Meanwhile I'd bet my last bag of trail mix that the guy has done eight times as much dirty shit as the rest of us combined.

Well, that is if I don't count myself. There's no way this dude with his oatmeal face and orangutan limbs could beat me in a matchup of belt notches.

But I'm starting to feel sorry for Leah and her squished boobs at this point so I offer her a hand. She grabs at it gratefully and I haul her the rest of the way out of the rock.

"You made it," I say with token enthusiasm, trying not to sound too happy because she could get the wrong idea. Women do that a lot. If it's not the right place and time I always try to head it off, big tits or not.

"Oh jeez, thanks Oz," she gushes and pats her chest, making sure that the girls are still intact. Or else she's trying to direct my attention to their glorious shape. But her biggest problem is that it's tough to look sexy with a sweaty face and trapped in a full body yellow jumpsuit.

Anyway, I've always sworn off banging my customers. There's enough hot ass waiting up above without having to shop for it down here. Plus there's something sort of tasteless about guiding a girl through the dark like a trusting lamb and then getting her on her back. Seems predatory somehow.

That doesn't mean I've never done it. I have. Once. You won't catch me admitting it out loud though.

"Hot damn," says the kid in awe as he adjusts his headlamp and gets a good look around the room.

I smile. This is the reaction I always hope for. I want them to feel enchanted, captivated, bowled right the fuck over that shit like this exists beneath their feet. It was how I felt the first time I ever stepped into a cave. I still feel that way every time I go underground and see things that the world above can never equal.

This place is called the Round Room and it's at the very center of the honeycomb of underground passages that comprise the Guard Cave deep in the picturesque hills of Tennessee. I've been in and out of the whole labyrinth so often that I don't even need a map. Despite the fact that I've been inside some of earth's most stupendous caves I never tire of the sight of the Round Room.

As we edge our way in, I caution the group to take care because the rock formations can actually be quite fragile. The place is a wonder, a fantasyland of conical shapes that extend from the ceiling and bubble out of the ground. It's such a strange sight that if you squint you might believe you are no longer on earth.

The kid's dad is hunkered down and adjusting his headlamp as he examines one of the stalagmite cones. He lets out a low whistle. "How long did you say it would take for something like this to form?"

"A hundred and fifty years," says his son, obviously proud that he remembered a few of the details of my long spiel before we started the tour.

I shine my light on the rigid, imperfect cylinder rising out of the ground. It looks like a gargoyle's penis.

"Per *inch*," I correct him. "Takes about a hundred and fifty years of constant drip for enough mineral residue to collect into an inch of stone."

"Wow," breathes Leah and she's at my side with her arm brushing against mine. Her honorable semi-boyfriend who hates the word 'fuck' is somewhere in the darkness; discarded, rejected, at least temporarily.

The boy is full of questions. He's a bright kid, maybe sixteen or so. He asks how many caves I've been in, how long I've been doing this, what's the most awesome shit I've ever seen. He listens carefully when I answer.

Fifty-eight separate locations on three continents.

I've been with the tour company for nearly two years and before that I was a freelance guide for photography excursions in the southwest.

And finally, the most awesome shit I've ever seen actually wasn't inside a cave, but I can't talk about it in front of strangers. I can't talk about it at all. Instead I just flip off some remark about the unique limestone caverns of Britain and the kid nods with satisfaction. He is named John, just like his dad, and he wears his enthusiasm proudly. I already know he'll be a lifelong caver. He's at the point where he'll never look at the upper world the same way again. I reached that point a long time ago.

John Junior is disappointed when I tell everyone we need to move on but time doesn't stand still down here, no matter how much it seems otherwise. The tour is only supposed to last until five and it'll take a good hour to squeeze Leah and her unhappy tits back through the narrow passages.

By the time we get back to the surface the bad boyfriend has changed his attitude. He's probably realizing that he's on his way to sleeping alone tonight and that Leah likely has a few better options. He's now helpful and attentive, circling an arm around her possessively as she grins and blushes. But I don't miss the way she looks back at me with a kind of puppyish longing just before he firmly leads her away.

John and John Junior shake my hand and say what a damn good time they had, and that this was the best caving expedition they've ever been on. I tell them there's plenty more caves around if you don't mind investing a whole day to hike deeper into the hills. I hand out my business card and tell them to give me a call if they're interested. I really do mean it. I wouldn't even charge them for the trip.

Once I'm alone I just stand there for a few minutes and breathe in the honeyed feel of mid summer. By early October the green on the hills will disappear, replaced by a wild explosion of autumn color. I expect I'll be around to see it. I've been lingering here far longer than I'm used to hanging around a single place but I'm enjoying the break. With my apartment in the nearby small town of Jacoby and my job as a guide, it's been peaceful, a little dose of serenity in a restless life.

The harsh calls of some nearby wild turkeys interrupt the quiet moment. I shoulder my pack and take a quick tour around the cave entrance to ensure that not so much as a gum wrapper was left behind to stain the landscape. Then I cover the half-mile walk back to my truck in five minutes before deciding to swing by the office, figuring Brock will be around.

Brock Gardner is a former nature photographer who suffered a broken spine when he fell from a steep cliff in New Mexico while trying to get some money shots of eagles in flight. We were already friends and I'd been scheduled to guide for that weekend trip, but a painful stress fracture in my right foot kept me off the trail and put Brock at the mercy of some novice who didn't understand his own equipment. Brock's harness hadn't been fastened properly and when he leaned back to switch the camera lens one of the critical lines snapped. He only tumbled for about fifteen feet but the jagged rock he landed on cut right through the eighth spinal vertebrae and that was that.

If you ask Brock about his wheelchair and useless legs he'll tell you the whole story with a matter of fact quality, like he's talking about horse racing or lacrosse, one of those things people find interesting but don't get all busted up about. That's just Brock. He's a no bullshit kind of guy who couldn't swallow pity if you tried to choke him with it.

Brock had grown up in these mountains. When he made me an offer I was glad to follow him out here and take a job at his fledgling adventure tour company. He's a good guy, and one of the few people on earth who knows a thing or two about me.

"Cheeseburgers," Brock announces. He tosses me a greasy paper bag the second I open the screechy aluminum door of the singlewide trailer that serves as company headquarters.

I catch the bag and sniff at the contents, my belly rumbling expectantly in response. "You hauled your wheels to town just to buy me lunch?"

Brock grins and shakes his head, closing the silver lid of his Mac. "Nope. Ashley stopped by with the goods. That's one cute slice of tender blondeness, Oz. Poor girl looked so crestfallen by the news you weren't around I thought about inviting her to sit in my lap as consolation."

"Maybe you should have," I grumble and slide into a rickety folding chair as I open a paper-wrapped burger. I'll have it swallowed in two bites.

"Well then maybe I will," he says cheerfully, "if you're sure you're pulling back from the table."

I grab Brock's water bottle and wash the burger down with a hard gulp.

"Have at it." I wipe my mouth with the back of my hand. "Honestly, I never sat down at that table. I just paused and grabbed a few mouthfuls of the appetizer on my way out the door."

Brock laughs. He knows I don't lie.

Ashley is a local girl, a waitress at the only twenty-four-hour diner in Jacoby. She's cute as hell but lives in the low tide pool of human intelligence. Even though we had some fun sweating it up at my place a few times, at the end of the day I want more in a woman than a pretty face and a wet pussy.

"Harsh," Brock says when he's done laughing.

I shrug. "Truth."

So what the hell do I want? Not much, just mind-blowing sex with a brain attached, a woman who's my match in words and action. Anyone can fuck, but I want to feel like I can't wait to hear what comes out of her mouth almost as much as I can't wait to be inside her body.

I want something I once had for a short, vanished season and haven't been able to replace. I doubt I ever will.

"Oz." Brock snaps his fingers loudly. "Oz man, you're a million miles away.

It's stinking hot in the trailer. I pull off my t-shirt and wipe my face with it. "I'm here. I'm just digesting, that's all."

Brock is studying me. He's used to my casual attitude toward women so this fresh scrutiny has nothing to do with Cheeseburger Ashley. I meant it when I said he could take a crack at that if he wants to. Wouldn't bother me at all.

"Got a call today," he finally says.

"For me?"

"No." He pauses. "California area code. Guy on the other end had one of those golden money voices that could probably convince a priest to shoot his own mother. He wasn't looking for Oz Acevedo."

My stomach does a sick little flip even though this isn't unexpected. In the information age where everyone knows the location of everyone else's last shit deposit, how long did I think I could hide?

Brock doesn't need to say it but he does anyway.

"He thought he might be able to find a man named Oscar Savage here."

I stare down at my knees. "He won't."

Brock's voice is sympathetic. "I know. I told him as much but he knew I was lying like a dog. He asked me to pass along his contact info just in case *Oscar* made an appearance."

I wish there was something stronger than water around. I don't even ask. Brock is an old school teetotaler. "Did he say why Oscar should be interested in talking to him?"

"He said it was a family matter."

My head whips up and I meet Brock's curious green-eyed gaze. "He said *that*? Family matter?"

My friend nods and then grimaces as he's hit with one of his frequent back spasms. "He did."

When he's done twisting his body sideways in the wheelchair, Brock hands me a bright yellow post-it with a name and phone number scrawled in black marker. I shove it into my back pocket and he tries to interest me in a fifty-mile drive to Gatlinburg for a better meal than cheeseburgers. When I shake my head he doesn't push the issue.

"There a tour set up tomorrow?" I ask on my way out the door.

Brock nods. "Yeah, a quartet of old biddies who want to hike to the standing stones to perform some kind of female goddess worship." He watches me. "New guy can take it if you'd rather have the day off."

I cough. "Maybe."

I feel like that damn post-it is burning a hole in my back pocket.

Brock bobs his head. "Just let me know by 6 a.m., okay Oz?"

"You got it."

I try to calm myself while driving the five miles back to my apartment but my heart is hammering. I have the urge to peel rubber and be reckless on the winding country roads. Too many kids ride their bikes around here though.

When I get home, old man Johnson is out on the sagging front porch with a shotgun in his lap. That's his usual position so it doesn't bother me. I throw the truck into park and stalk across the front lawn toward the narrow staircase that leads to the converted living space on the second floor. I start talking to myself without realizing it until I hear my own words.

"Family matter? What the fuck?"

Old man Johnson seems startled by my grumbling. He swivels his egg-shaped body around to stare at me. He's a sad, strange fellow who's lived in this clapboard eyesore his entire life. He charges a cheap monthly rent and stays out of my face.

"Evening, Hal," I say as my foot hits the bottom step.

Hal Johnson scowls and swivels back around in his chair to face the menace of the empty street.   That's fine because I'm not in the mood for a chat anyway.

It's not until I reach the top of the staircase that I realize I have no desire to be inside, brooding and sweating in that empty apartment until I get tired. I hop back down the stairs and take off in the truck, leaving Hal Johnson to stare silently after me.

I gun the engine once and take off for the hills I left behind a little while ago. I don't have anywhere specific in mind. I just want to be out there, on the loose.

By the time I reach a place that looks like it leads somewhere suitably wild and nameless, the sky is growing dark. I grab my pack out of the truck bed before heading into the darkening hills. Maybe I'll just hang out in the woods all night. I've done it before.

The surroundings are familiar. I've been this way at least once. My sole bragging right in life is an uncanny talent for navigation. You could drop me anywhere on earth without a map and I'll figure out how to get back to where I started.

After a few minutes of walking my foot knocks into a fallen tree. Abruptly I throw my pack down and sit on the trunk.

"A man named Oscar Savage."

Quiet reigns all around me. Every living thing for a quarter mile radius has halted, breathless, awaiting the next action of this intruder, a man who sits on a hollow log in the coming darkness and stares at nothing.

Suddenly a battle for survival erupts somewhere in the brush off to my left and a small creature squeals in pain or fear. The nature of the conflict is savage, as wild things so often are.

Savage.

It's a word that implies brutal ferocity.

It's also a name.

But it's not a name that can ever cross my mind without thinking of her. She's bound to it as closely as she once was to my heart.

Five fucking years and I should be able to move on. I should accept that I'm not the same person anymore and it's for certain she isn't either. I should learn how to connect with someone else at this point. I should forget.

Of course I can do none of those things.

My cell phone reception is shitty this far into the woods. I'll need to drive back to town in order to make a call. Which I have every intention of doing. Right now.

Because it's a family matter.

And because I used to be Oscar Savage.

CHAPTER THREE

REN

Most people possess at least a few scraps of unique family lore.

Stories.

They filter down for several generations if they are interesting and are lost sooner if they are not. Usually they are not. Usually the only people who might raise an eyebrow and care about the dusty skeletons hanging out in the closet are the ones who share blood with either the old corpse or whoever stuffed it in there.

The Savages are different. Everyone knows everything about us. Since the explosion of the World Wide Web all you need to do is type our last name into the nearest search engine and you can learn more than you ever wanted to.

You can see that it started in the 1920s.

Charles and Mary Savage were Hollywood originals. She was a socialite from Minneapolis and he escaped a long line of cattle ranchers in the Nebraska Sand Hills. If they'd just stayed where they were they would have gone on to live quiet, ordinary lives and been long forgotten.

But they didn't.

They landed in Hollywood at a fortunate time and became darlings of the silent film era. Their days of stardom were short-lived, ending with the popularity of sound in motion pictures. Mary had a high, reedy voice that grated like nails and Charles was a low talker with a chronic lisp. So instead they became powerful investors and iconic pillars of the film industry for the rest of their lives. They are widely credited as being among the early founders of the motion picture industry.

My great-grandparents weren't happy people. They suffered a turbulent marriage punctuated by infidelity, alcoholism and the birth of three children. Maybe that's why they never smiled for photographs.

Charles was hit by a taxi in 1952 while jaywalking. He died in the gutter of Hollywood Boulevard amid a throng of curious onlookers. He might not have minded. Reportedly Charles loved nothing more than a rapt audience.

Mary on the other hand hung around for more years than most human beings do, long enough to meet her grandchildren and great-grandchildren. My parents dragged us to the nursing home in Pasadena a few times to pay homage. I remember her as a miniature ancient woman who wore a wig of absurd blond ringlets. She yelled all the time, screeching *"Get off my stage!"* if you walked too close. I was nine when she finally died. A series of reporters came around to talk about her but no one was sad. After all, she was ridiculously old and her mind had been gone for decades.

My grandfather, Rex, was among the next generation of Savages. His older sisters, Anne and Joan, were more celebrated for their lifetime feud with one another than for their films. They traded husbands and lovers and publicly ridiculed each other, much to the delight of the fledgling tabloid industry.

Joan inherited her mother's longevity and is still alive – broke and reclusive and living somewhere off the rocky coast of Oregon. Every once in a while her name will be trending on the search engines when a bored reporter seeks her out for an interview about places long gone and people long dead. Even in the twilight of her life she's still obsessed with her dead (*"That pasty witch was ALWAYS jealous of me!"*) older sister.

Rex Savage, my grandfather, was the golden boy of his era. Tall, dark-haired and powerfully built, he was full of testosterone and charisma. An incorrigible ladies' man who starred in a long line of pictures with names like *Desperado Gunslinger* and *Cowboys on the Horizon,* he was the archetypal Hollywood movie star and Hollywood was more than happy to have him. Sometimes when I catch a glimpse of one of his film stills I can't help but do a double take because he looks so much like my brother Montgomery, right down to the curled-lip sneer. It's fucking uncanny.

Rex met his match in a fiery Irish starlet named Margaret O'Leary. She was his costar in the 1951 hit western *Desert Honor.* It's a rather ho-hum movie about a reformed desperado who shoots a bunch of leather-faced bad guys, adopts two orphans and marries the local schoolteacher. It wound up being the only project they ever worked on together but it was enough.

There was a bad kind of chemistry between the two of them. For a decade they married and fought and split and reconciled over and over, somehow creating two troubled children and a legacy of dysfunction. They had just remarried for the fourth time in 1961 when Margaret was killed in a plane crash during a blizzard in the Sierra Nevada mountains.

Rex was inconsolable. In fact he kind of pitched off the deep end. I guess it's possible he would have turned into a blithering joke anyway, but to hear it told, the tragic loss of his wife and the upheaval of his film career had a lot to do with the downward spiral. His later interviews show a baffled old man with tangled nose hair droning on about how in the year 1965 he'd been abducted by aliens while stargazing at the Griffith Observatory.

Then came a morning when Rex decided it was a good idea wander around his wealthy neighborhood drunk as a frat pledge. He fell into a swimming pool and drowned, wearing nothing but a pair of boxer shorts and a crucifix.

It was rather an ignoble end for a leading man. Everyone says so.

Margaret's films are the only ones I'll sit down and watch if I happen to be flipping channels and catch a glimpse of her brilliant red hair in a midcentury Technicolor world. My two sisters won the genetic lottery that gave them the same coloring, although Ava has been dying hers blonde since she was a teenager.

Not me though. Like my two brothers I inherited the wavy dark hair and near olive skin of Rex Savage.

Speaking of me, it's a good thing Rex and Margaret paused their marital wars long enough to produce a daughter, Mina, and a son, August.

An unauthorized biography written shortly before his death three years ago described August Savage as 'gloomy and morbidly disturbed' throughout his childhood. He would collect dead birds from the corners of the family's decaying

Hollywood estate and leave them in various cupboards throughout the home. Supposedly he even stowed some in his pillowcase and slept on them. I have no idea if that's true or not. Regardless of his strange fetishes, in his day my father had the ruggedly striking Savage profile and he happened to be a decent actor. In the late 1970s he starred in a series of critically acclaimed small budget films that were considered provocative, groundbreaking. In fact he was nominated for an Academy Award for *Fist,* a harrowing story about a young man who develops a disturbing obsession with his elderly neighbor. It's the kind of movie you see once and never want to see again because by the time the credits roll you feel vaguely ill. He didn't win. But it's an honor to be nominated. Or whatever.

My father's career came to a crushing halt in 1984 when a young photographer died of a heroin overdose in his bed. Although there was never enough evidence to charge him with a crime, he was tried in the media. According to their one-sided verdict, the strange, intense actor with a legendary family name had injected the drug into the woman's veins while she slept. There were even whispers that he ah, *abused* the dead body afterwards.

Of all the rumors and bullshit that surrounds our family, that's the one thing I don't really believe. My father was far too confused about everyday life to be capable of harming anyone else. He never talked about any of it but the trial-by-media apparently devastated him and he lived like a recluse for a while. He was probably so lonely and vulnerable by his early forties that when a twenty-year-old radiology student encountered him at a local diner she had no trouble sinking her talons into his bewildered flesh and becoming a permanent appendage.

Here's where *we* join the story.

It would be rather pointless, though maybe therapeutic, to sit here and count all the ways my mother, Lita Cohan Savage, was a heinous bitch. But I have a habit of not thinking about her any more than I have to. She left my father shortly before his sudden death but she and I were on the outs long before that.

About a year ago I was thumbing through a magazine while I waited for a flu shot and paused at a paragraph describing how Lita Savage, once married to the late August Savage, was remarrying.

"Lita is presently estranged from her children and they will not be on the guest list."

Estranged. It's always struck me as an odd word. As if one day the parties in question blinked and didn't recognize one another. The truth is liable to be a bit more ugly and complicated. Like her.

Lita already had one foot out the door when August lost the crumbling deco-style mansion, among the oldest estates in Hollywood. She demanded something better. She demanded blood from a stone.

For once he stood up to her and moved us all out to the desert to the only piece of real estate his meager assets were capable of saving.

My father had always hated California anyway.

I have to believe that when he towed the lot of us out to the old western film set in the heart of the Arizona outback he had good intentions. He said he wanted to remove his children from the cold scrutiny of stardom and give us a chance to live somewhere we weren't known, weren't sneered at.

But at the time all I knew was that I was sixteen and outraged. It was really a bad plan. Eventually he learned that when you take a bunch of bratty teens out of their comfortable lives and deposited them in a dusty oven, miles from the nearest traffic light, something is bound to go wrong.

The place was called Atlantis Star but in a sarcastic twist, Monty and I rechristened it Atlantis Slum. It was run down and isolated, a vague whisper of the bustling studio that existed in the 1950s when Rex Savage (pre-alien abduction) filmed a half dozen movies in the area. Rex had been so taken with the backdrop he bought the entire make believe town when it went up for auction a few years later, after the old western film trend was finished.

These days my brother Spencer is the only one living there, ever since August closed himself in his study and was found dead three days later. An autopsy confirmed cause of death was an untreated rattlesnake bite.

In case anyone's wondering, being slowly overtaken by snake venom is a painful, ghastly way to die. There's no way to know what was going through his mind when he sat there, staring at dark wood paneling, refusing to seek help. About all he had left at that point was the skeleton of Atlantis, and even before he was gone, Spence had pretty much taken over the care of the place, though he'd barely graduated from high school. The rest of us don't see much reason to set foot within a hundred miles of it.

Until now, that is.

Today there is a producer sitting across from me over a pair of wedge salads at the Bellagio. He is smiling. He probably smiles in his sleep.

"So Loren, how do you feel about returning to Atlantis Star?"

Gary Vogel is on the well-preserved side of sixty and has flown to Las Vegas just to take me to lunch. It isn't necessary; I already signed the papers just like I promised Brigitte I would. I get the feeling he's trying me out. He wants to see how tough it's going to be to get me to bare my soul. I squeeze a lemon slice into my water glass and avoid an answer.

"Will you be there when filming begins?" I ask, coyly turning the tables with a question of my own.

Gary Vogel commands a half dozen of the most popular celebrity reality television shows. To him, this is just another one, a typical project. He hails the waitress for the check and offers me an artificial grin that he must practice ten thousand times a day.

"No, I'm afraid that's impossible, Loren" he says smoothly pronouncing my name incorrectly as Lo-REN, like Sofia Loren.

But I am LAW-ren or just plain Ren. No need to be pretentious. I'm not Brigitte.

Gary gives me his best charming executive smile. "But my wonderful assistant, Cate Camp, will be there. You've talked to Cate. Cate is incredible. Cate is my proverbial right hand. Cate will make sure everything goes off without a hitch."

I merely nod at his answer. I decide not to let him know that I'm glad he won't be around when the cameras start rolling, which they will be doing exactly one week from today.

I haven't packed. I don't know what to bring. Production for this season will last for eight weeks. My sisters are already there. I haven't talked to Spencer but he's probably working hard to deal with the intrusion. Monty, like me, is waiting until the last minute.

How long has it been since we were all in the same place for more than a few hours? Four years? No, five years. Five years since that wonderful and terrible summer when the ground shifted and opened a wide, permanent fissure in my heart. Monty was the first of us to leave, abandoning August's strange desert utopia.

No. That's wrong. Someone else left before him.

Gary Vogel is a busy man. He brusquely thanks me for a productive meeting and regrets that he must reach the airport within an hour to return to Los Angeles for a vague but crucial reason. I get the feeling he just wanted to see me for himself. He wanted to see if I was under control, if the infamous Savage volatility applied to me.

A little drama will be good for ratings. Too much chaos will be disastrous for the show. Gary has worried himself unnecessarily, at least on my account. I shake his hand and nod mechanically.

"Thank you for lunch. It was nice to meet you too."

I don't mean it at all.

But I can do this. I can do it for my brothers and sisters.

I can be the backbone they sorely need right now.

If I bend, even slightly, no one will ever see it.

CHAPTER FOUR

OZ

"I don't want your damn money," I keep telling them, but the words don't seem to be ones they understand.

They just ignore me and carry on about funds being wire transferred at the end of production. The big cheese is a gold plated dick named Gary who forces his long-suffering assistant to call and/or text about every twelve hours to ensure I haven't fled to Madagascar. Apparently the earth's ability to rotate on its axis depends upon me showing up for my five minutes of exploitation.

In our first conversation Gary seemed slightly ruffled that I didn't know who the fuck he was but he recovered nicely and even stopped calling me 'Oscar' when I said it would be healthier for him to take the suggestion.

"Yeah," I always answer robotically whenever they call for the guarantee that I will somehow materialize in the desert a hundred miles outside Phoenix the day filming is set to begin.

For a while they bugged me about flying to L.A. first. They would really much rather have me land among the Arizona greasewood in a Lear jet or something, but screw that. I will drive there on my own time in my own wheels and there's nothing anyone can do about it.

"Yeah," I respond once again in the same bored voice when reminded of my confidentiality clause.

Of course I told Brock about everything, but it's not like he'll be phoning the tabloids as soon as I'm out the door. If he does, then Gary Vogel can feel free to sue me for my handful of nearly worthless belongings and the pocket change in my bank account. My financial status isn't as bleak as I'm making it sound. I just don't have much use for acquiring stuff. If there's anything my early life taught me it's that too many shiny things aren't good for you.

Before I head out I give Hal Johnson two months of rent, which he happily pockets. I don't expect there will be a problem returning to my apartment whenever I want to. There's not exactly a thick line of people scrambling to live upstairs to a foul-smelling old man who's got a few checkers missing from the board and likes to use his shotgun on the gray squirrels who tiptoe their way into the front yard.

Brock, however, is sorry to see me go and gets suddenly worried about the whole thing . "So they, the Savages, really don't know you're coming?"

I can only shrug because all I know is what Gary Vogel has chosen to tell me. "I don't think they know."

I'm sure it's true. After all, the whole point is to inflict return-of-the-prodigal-Savage surprise. Gary never asked me too much about my history with the family. That leads me to think he somehow already knows it all. Men like Gary are relentlessly calculating. They have no patience for any bombshells they don't light the fuse to.

Of course I always knew I wasn't to the manner born, not a blood Savage. My earliest memories include a woman with thick bristles on her upper lip and a warped left hand with six-inch fingernails. She used to hit me over and over again and shove me into a closet for long stretches of time that might have been hours as easily as they might have been days. Strangely, being inside the closet was better than being outside of it. That might explain my tendency to hang out underground.

I don't know at what point the lip-haired, club-handed child abuser disappeared, but for a while I slid from one messy home to another. Mina Savage always insisted I was five years old when she 'found' me, although she invented my birthday. She always used that term to describe it though. *Found.* Like I was sitting primly on some urban street corner and just waiting to be discovered by a carefree fairy godmother with Louis Vuitton fixtures.

In truth, Mina went to some trouble to find a kid when she decided she wanted one. She knew she didn't have the patience for a squalling, shitting, diapered blob, so she had her lawyers fan out and search for something more to her liking. Something cute and endearing, something that knew how to wipe its own ass and didn't have any nearby family who might object to creative legalities. Something like a little boy who had already spent years in a system filled with crooked bureaucrats who would gladly face the other way if it meant a they could cuddle an armful of crisp green paper.

Something exactly like me.

I don't mean to sound bitter or to make it sound like Mina Savage was a horrible woman. I'm not bitter and she wasn't horrible. Careless, self-absorbed and perennially confused, but terrible? No.

She was the daughter and granddaughter of legends, born into the fishbowl of fame and privilege. Maybe that burden alone had fucked her up at an early age.

Mina was beautiful, stunning. Men were easily captivated by her looks and her name. They had to get a lot closer before they realized that beneath all that auburn-haired glamor was a messy patchwork of scars, despair and addiction. Mina had already been discarded by three husbands who were glad enough to open up their checkbooks and purchase their freedom.

Shortly after I was swept into her care we left the country. We didn't return for over a decade.

Those years were pretty good for me; a sequence of posh boarding schools and fantastic adventures throughout old Europe. Americans always seemed to be everywhere so it was easy to believe we were in some floating version of our homeland.

Believe it or not, failed politicians, woeful ex-movie stars and a packs of disgraced corporate elites tend to run amok in international lands. Think of it as a contemporary version of Hemingway's Lost Generation.

Still, I remain grateful to Mina for paying attention to my education, even though she seemed to forget my existence for large swaths of time. Whether she'd stashed me in the picturesque Alps or deep in the fabled moors of Yorkshire, I could always count on her to eventually show up in a perfumed cloud and rediscover her motherhood.

I remember being happy to see her. Happy, even though I knew I'd be yanked from yet another cozy situation and taken on a frenetic holiday until Mina found a different cure for her loneliness. Then she would deposit me in another luxurious setting thickly populated with more American castoff kids.

Mina was a hell of a parent when she made the effort. After all, it was Mina who showed me the Ufizzi and the Louvre, Mina who photographed me standing proudly in front of the Colosseum, and Mina who arranged for a tour of the caves of France's Dordogne region when I mentioned learning all about the Lascaux cave in school.

She didn't talk about her family, the Savages. Movie stars and sad stories. All I ever knew of them were the things I had read. The fact that I had aunts, uncles and cousins seemed irrelevant. It didn't occur to me to want to be around them. In fact I didn't give them much thought at all until Mina, bedraggled and exhausted from another heartbreak, dragged me out of a converted castle in the Scottish Highlands and announced we were going 'home'.

I can remember objecting, sputtering something like *"Shit, now? Really? I'll be a senior."*

But when Mina got an idea into her head – adopting a kid, marrying a sheik, dragging a teenager back to the Home of the Brave – there was no getting rid of it.

I found myself riding over an ocean in the private plane belonging to one of Mina's old friends as I moodily destroyed tins of caviar and pouted about the fact that I'd been *this fucking close* to porking the new girl in school, a Russian beauty distantly related to some royal family that'd been shot a hundred years ago in Siberia.

Everything was different that time. But I didn't realize it until Mina left me on her brother's doorstep somewhere in the Arizona desert and then ducked back into the luxury Town Car for the ride to Scottsdale's finest rehab facility.

Two months later I learned the hard way that Mina's failures were much worse than I'd ever suspected.

"Oz?" calls Brock and he's got the Concerned Friend grimace on his face again.

I realize that I've been nervously clicking a pen while my thoughts strayed. I haven't spent too much time thinking about Mina over the past five years. She was a fickle woman with her own set of demons. There's not much point in trying to understand her now.

"I need to get on the road." I reluctantly set the pen down on Brock's desk.

If I push it I can reach western Arizona in two days. Surely they're all there already. Surely *she's* there already. Gary had assured me she would be, even though I hadn't asked, not specifically, not about her. Like I said, Gary must know a few things already. He wouldn't have called me in the first place if he didn't.

After bending down and giving Brock an awkward man-hug in his wheelchair, I notice that he's staring at me with a worried frown.

"You remember who you are, Oz-man" he says, nodding. "Don't let them edit you into something else."

"I will. And I won't."

Flimsy promises. I don't give a god almighty fuck what they do with the footage. They could cast me as King Kong With Testicular Scabies and it would bother me as much as a paper cut.

There's only one good reason in the world for me to go down this road. One. And I don't even know whether she wants anything to do with me. Or if she's even worth the trouble at this point.

Shit.

First love.

Only love.

A strange and turbulent summer that was the best and worst part of my life.

I keep the windows wide open in the pickup as I slowly thread my way down through the cool greenery of the mountain roads. I appreciate it all; the fresh wisps of summer, the fluttering hands of the forest.

Where I'm going will be much hotter, much harsher. There's no place to fucking hide there.

Thinking about her, even the most fleeting of memories, tends to lengthen my dick. That's no way to start a long road trip. So instead I think about the long, wandering years since then; a thousand adventures and disasters that blur together and are all equally trivial.

No good. Today it all leads back to her. After all, nobody who spends twenty-three years on this earth is a blank slate. We are the sum of our pains and trials, joys and heartaches. It's impossible to guess them all. And to really understand anything about what's happening today you have to go backwards first.

You have to understand what happened five years ago....

CHAPTER FIVE

Five Years Ago: Part 1

Almost as soon as they land in New York they are leaving.

The woman surrounds herself with people who are paid to tend to her belongings, offer her drinks, escort her to the decadent lounge where the wealthy are not required to mingle with ordinary people. She is agitated, clawing at the inside of her palms with her fingernails, as is her habit when the universe has gone out of order.

Oscar suspects the city has bad memories for her. His mother is a collector of bad memories. They are finally overcrowding her mind.

He is disappointed to be leaving so soon. He knew this place once, New York. This was where he lived, although he remembers little about it except bad smells and cold alleys. He looks out the windows and sees nothing of beauty; only the industrial background of a major international airport. It manages to look ugly even in the balmy spell of early summer. But he had glimpsed the legendary skyline as the plane descended and badly wanted to see it up close. Briefly he considers leaving the woman here and disappearing into the throngs of weary travelers.

"Oscar," the woman croaks and holds out a thin hand to him as a weak smile tries to take custody of her face.

Much of the time she forgets he exists but now she would like him to sit beside her. He sinks into a plush armchair and tries not to look at her face. It's cracked and drawn, a face of pain, a face that seems even more ugly because for so long it was beautiful.

He decides he must be a complete asshole for even noticing these things.

Oscar searches for things to say to his mother. They *should* have things to say to one another. But she's fretful and distracted. Anyway, his mind keeps going in odd directions, thinking about the strangeness of being in his own country again. Then he starts thinking about the girls he knew from his latest school. Some were girlfriends for brief stretches of angst-filled time. Others were just dirty hookups. Oscar doesn't miss any of them. But he idly catalogues them in his mind because it's something to do while he sits beside a ruined woman, waiting for their plane to refuel.

"You'll enjoy being there," says Oscar's mother as she rubs at her temples and then slides her large sunglasses back onto her thin face. She has acquired a curious, affected accent from all her years of travel. Oscar has no such accent. He's convinced hers is deliberate.

She smiles at him again and he sees his distorted reflection in her dark lenses. "I loved Atlantis as a child. My father filmed seven movies there. You've seen them, haven't you, his movies? Yes, I'm sure I showed them to you. When he bought the place he decided to live there part time and had a house built. None of the artificial buildings they added to the set could tame that wild beauty, just as it couldn't tame your grandfather. I wish you'd known Rex. He was a king. He was..."

Oscar's mother loses her train of thought as she stares off into the past. Her lip quivers. Oscar reaches for her arm. He knows something is wrong with her, something much worse than what's usually wrong with her. It seems as if she is decaying into the folds of her Chanel pantsuit.

She shakes off the gloom, pats his hand and smiles another terrible smile. Her voice is a tuneless singsong. "It's so perfect that August moved the children out there. It's a magical place for children. I'm glad he remembers that. You will see, Oscar."

Oscar has only a vague idea what's she's talking about. His adopted mother, Mina, is a Savage. Oscar knows that when he mentions this fact to other Americans they will usually understand what he means. Mina was never an actress though. She never did much at all except frolic with rich, abusive men and impulsively adopt a child. The Savages were a legendary Hollywood family, although they've been cursed by scandal and heartbreak for decades. Oscar has never met any of them. They don't even really matter to him.

But now he is caught up in Mina's latest odyssey. They will be flying to Arizona, to the old film ranch in the desert that was Mina's childhood paradise. Mina apparently plans for them to remain there for some time, in the place where her brother's family lives.

Oscar objects to it all, but only in silence. He's not a child for fuck's sake. He's a month past his seventeenth birthday and capable as any man. Usually if bullshit even comes sniffing in his direction he smacks it back with two mighty fists. And this is major bullshit, this bizarre trek to another continent, to a lost era.

He could easily have scoffed at Mina and refused her pleas when she made her announcement two days ago in the bleak confines of the headmaster's office. She wouldn't have known what to do if he had.

"Oscar! We are going home! Back to America. You will meet your cousins!"

Home?

America?

Cousins?

These concepts are all strange to him. The headmaster did nothing to dissuade Mina. He was apparently tired of dealing with the parade of heartbroken girls that the charismatic Oscar Savage left in his wake wherever he walked.

Mina had always seemed to hate America. How many times had she insisted to Oscar that the whole nation was nothing but a cauldron of scandal, gossip, and narcissism? Oscar didn't exactly believe that was true. Mina assumes the world of cutthroat celebrities is universal; that it exists in Pocatello, Idaho in the exact same form as it is exists in Beverly Hills.

Oscar could have dug his heels into European soil and refused to leave. Mina would not have known how to force him. But he didn't have the heart to refuse her. No matter how careless of a mother she was, she was the only one he had. He could tell immediately that she was sick. He still didn't know whether it was mental or physical, but she needed him. So Oscar quietly, if resentfully, packed his things and followed his mother out of the Scottish countryside.

Tentatively, Oscar asks if they might remain in New York for a short time but Mina wearily reminds him that their posh traveling arrangements are the result of a favor that is nearly at an end. She will not consider a commercial flight. Moreover, her brother is expecting her out in Arizona. His entire family is expecting her, expecting both of them. According to Mina these Savage people are overjoyed at the prospect of finally meeting a long lost cousin. Oscar thinks about that and pictures them; a herd of displaced socialites squatting in the desert dust and clutching designer bags as their flawless faces expectantly scan the sky.

The flight to Phoenix takes five hours. Oscar looks down into the wide expanse of his country. From the air it appears largely unpopulated. Every once in a while there will be a flash of metal in the sunlight, a hint at a pocket of humanity. They fly over interminable brown mountains that give way to a wide valley. It is a riot of beige neighborhoods riddled with aqua-colored dots that Oscar figures are swimming pools. It looks nothing like the place Mina described.

There is a car waiting, of course. On the ground, Phoenix is a maze of concrete and asphalt that shimmers in the heat. Soon the city gives way to sprawling residential stucco in various shades of taupe. Finally, the long stretch of suburbia ends and they are careening through a cactus-riddled landscape ringed by distant brown mountains.

Oscar grows uneasy as they turn off the freeway and spend miles on a bumpy road that dissolves into dirt. Mina has passed out beside him and the driver is nothing but a silent head.

"Shit," Oscar mutters, and by the time they reach a scattered collection of buildings he's expecting the worst.

Oscar slides out of the door as Mina struggles to pull herself back into the land of the conscious. The brilliant sunshine is so harsh, nearly painful.

He curses again and rubs his eyes, seeing spots and beyond that, an imprint of a ghost town. When he opens them, a girl has materialized. She looks him up and down with a bored expression, then tosses a mane of wavy dark hair. Oscar figures she's one of the Savage cousins. She looks about as friendly as your average fork-tongued lizard.

Twenty yards away is a rambling, one story, rustically luxurious ranch home that was probably once quite something but now just looks like it's seen better days. Beyond that is a splintery church, a rickety barn, a shabby general store with a teetering façade, and a narrow Victorian-style building with a sagging balcony and a wooden sign with the word 'BROTHEL' plainly spelled out in weathered lettering.

"Welcome to paradise, *cousin*," laughs the girl who seconds earlier had looked at him like he was a shit-filled paper bag. Her face is pretty, her expression mocking and even though she's not as filled out as the girls Oscar usually likes he can't avoid taking interest in what he does see.

Then Mina spills out of the car and people suddenly start popping up from everywhere. The dark-haired girl is joined by a blonde and a redhead. Both of them stare at him and giggle like idiots. A teenage boy rides up on an arthritic pony and hops off, generating a cloud of dust. That pisses off a bigger teenage boy who has somehow erupted from the nearest cactus.

"Motherfucker," complains the larger boy and swipes at the rider.

The kid on horseback tips his wide straw hat back and glares. "Stay off the fucking path then, asshole."

A shoving match ensues and there's more cursing, some shouted promises of blood. The pair of them roll right into Oscar's legs.

The dark-haired girl lets out a loud sigh, then stomps over and pulls them apart. She's petite and bird-like. Oscar stands ready to jump in if the boys make a move to rough her up at all but they freeze like a cartoon when she yells, "Stop acting like savages!"

The other two girls find this choice of words hilarious and they laugh harder. Oscar is beginning to wonder if they know how to do anything else.

With one final shove, the larger boy rolls off and stalks away without even hinting that he's noticed Oscar at all despite the fact that he crashed right into him a few seconds earlier. The girl holds out a hand to the other boy, who's grabbing at his hat and moodily shoving it back onto his head.

"Hell of an impression we're making," the girl says with a headshake as she hauls her brother to his feet. She meets Oscar's eyes, stares searchingly for a second and then nods. Right away Oscar can guess that she's the rare sort of girl who doesn't have much patience for bullshit.

"I'm Ren." She jerks her head. "This is Spence. The nasty ape stalking in the direction of the brothel is Monty. By the way, it's not a real brothel so don't get all excited. Like the rest of this place it's just leftover garbage from the heyday of Hollywood's revisionist Old West era."

"Is that so?" says Oscar, trying to take it all in. The crumbling buildings, the gang of rowdy siblings, his mother somewhere in the background.

"Brother!" Mina squeals and kisses the air around the head of a broad-shouldered man whose movies Oscar has seen but whose hand he's never shaken.

At the man's side is a scowling woman with the same dainty build as Ren. Her face says she's on the fading side of forty. She's staring at Oscar.

"I thought he was a boy," she complains unhappily. "You described a boy, not a man."

The girl named Ren makes a face, rolling her eyes. Spence looks like he'd rather just get back on his horse and ride somewhere more interesting. The giggle twins go on giggling. Monty broods on the balcony of the brothel. And August Savage is scrutinizing him thoughtfully.

"Hello Oscar," he says and it's the friendliest greeting so far.

"Oscar is tall," Mina explains as she slumps against the car with a sigh.

"You are tall," August agrees. "How old are you now?"

"Sixteen," Mina answers.

"Seventeen," Oscar corrects.

"Ah," nods August. "That explains it."

The scowling woman grabs August's arm and leads him to the far side of the car. Oscar can hear her hissing. He sees August's hard glare in response.

"Enough," says August and leaves her to glower alone as he returns to his sister's side.

Mina looks uncomfortable as she stands in her brother's shadow. When her absent gaze lands on Oscar it's full of apology. This unnerves him.

Oscar looks around. This neglected collection of buildings in the middle of nowhere is not exactly the heaven that Mina remembers. Except for the Savage family it seems there is nothing and no one for miles. It doesn't appear that will change anytime soon.

"Welcome to paradise."

Now that he's been introduced to a few of them, Oscar can figure out who the rest of the Savages are. The bitchy woman who perches atop her stilettos and regards Oscar like he's a wild animal that's just crapped in her roses is Lita, August's wife, matriarch to the gang of wild teenagers. He knows that sullen Montgomery of the Brothel is the eldest, Loren who calls herself 'Ren' is next in line, then the twins Spencer and Ava. Finally Brigitte, who smirks at him through a curtain of red hair, is the youngest.

Atlantis Star looks like a place people might end up if they are running from zombie invasions or hellfire Armageddon. The end of the proverbial and literal road. Oscar wonders how long they've all been stuck out here and why the hell they came in the first place. It's the opposite of glamorous.

August barks that Spencer needs to help Oscar with his bags. Spencer doesn't seem pleased but he obeys after one more regretful glance at the waiting horse.

"Thanks, but I got it," Oscar growls as he heaves two large duffel bags over each shoulder with a grunt. There was more that he'd left behind in the storage basement at school. He suspects he won't ever see any of it again but that's fine. He knows instinctively that he will never be returning and anyway he doesn't need the burden of a whole mess of stuff.

In Oscar's opinion that's the biggest problem with people like his mother. Too much fucking stuff.

Atlantis, on the other hand, seems to have very little stuff. It's a scorched ghost town in bleak condition. A rusted pickup truck sits in front of the house. Beside it is a silver Lexus.

Spence had shrugged and wandered back to his horse when Oscar refused his help but Ren falls in step beside him.

"You can't walk out of here you know," she says cheerfully. "Consequence is twenty miles away."

Oscar stares at her, thinking she must be speaking in rural American slang terms that haven't found their way across the ocean. "The consequences are twenty miles away?"

"Consequence. It's a town. It has a traffic light and a gas station and a bunch of really unhappy people who barely move between May and October. That's all there is in this area. At least it's something though. I drive the girls out there to catch the school bus to Copper, which is another ten miles past that and the only high school between here and Phoenix. But at least it's summer now so I don't need to worry about it."

"Shit, you serious?"

"Always."

Oscar processes her words. "Why don't you go to school with your sisters?"

Ren plays with the ends of her dark hair. "Online school. Spence does it too supposedly, although I damn well never him sitting down at the computer. We get shitty Wi-Fi out here by the way. A gust of wind knocks it out for an hour. Monty dropped out last year and spends most of his time stealing Dad's old pickup so he can whore it up with whatever female is dumb enough to plant her face in his crotch."

Oscar lets out a chuckle. The girl is weird, but there's something innocently charming about her. "You sure don't hold back, do you? Where the hell are we going, anyway?"

"Over there." She points. "You'll be staying at the little house right behind the brothel."

"Words I didn't expect to hear when I woke up this morning."

"Ha! I'll bet. The house was originally built for the caretaker or something. It's where the boys sleep. Well, sort of. Spencer camps out in the desert half the time even though Lita keeps warning him that he'll get his nuts chewed off by a Gila monster. And Monty just uses it as a fuck den so it might be kind of noisy in there. See that piece of crap in the foreground? We call it the brothel since it used to serve as either a saloon or a bordello, depending on what the script called for. Spence won't be any trouble. But you tell me if Monty gives you shit and I'll talk to him."

Oscar glances up and sees Monty still scowling on the balcony of the brothel. The half rotted wood is completely bowed in the middle and Montgomery Savage seems to be tempting fate as he looms there with hulking menace. Oscar wonders if he's aware of just how closely he resembles his grandfather and decides it's probably something Monty's been hearing his whole life. His dark eyes follow Oscar with a mute warning but other than that he doesn't shift a muscle.

Oscar answers him back with a hard stare. It would be more effective if he wasn't twisting his neck to look up but he's kicked his fair share of sullen ass in his day. If it comes to it he would pit his muscle against Monty Savage any day.

Hopefully he won't be hanging around here long enough for things to go that sour.

"Thanks, Loren," he says, still holding Monty's gaze until Monty smirks, drops his eyes and looks to the west where the sun is beginning to dip low.

They've reached the far side of the brothel. Oscar can't hear the voices of the adults any longer. The other Savage girls have disappeared. He watches Ren in the soft evening shadow and is struck by the sight of her. Even without makeup she has a face that demands attention. At the same time, a ray of sun filters through her loose cotton shirt and shows him the curve of her small breasts. Despite himself, despite the fact that this girl is off limits and he's been inside of girls that could body double as porn stars, he recognizes pure fucking quality when it's in front of him. Something stirs powerfully in his core and he shifts the weight of his luggage.

Ren suddenly gives him an arch look. Oscar wonders if she has supernatural dick sensors and can tell he's getting a little chubby in his pants.

"What?" he says defensively.

She smiles. She has a perfect smile. Perfect teeth surrounded by perfect lips. "Thought you'd be more, I don't know, *European.* That's how we thought of you; Aunt Mina's exotic little European waif." She wrinkles her nose. "You seem like you could be from from L.A. Here's the house. Door's never locked."

Oscar stops. "You said it was built for the caretaker?"

"Yeah, I think so. My grandparents, sorry *our* grandparents, were too busy being fabulous in Los Angeles to spend more than a few months a year out here so they paid some poor sucker to sit around and sweep up the dust. The rooms are really small in there but at least there's central air. My father had it installed when we moved out here last year."

"It looks like one of the rest stops we passed on the interstate."

"It probably doesn't smell any better either." Ren's voice takes on a defensive edge. "Look, I know it's not what you're used to and before we wound up here it wasn't what we were used to either, but it's still better than what a lot of people have."

A vague sense of shame pricks at him. There he stands with his elite education and his pricey clothes while the Savage kids have been reduced to this. But why? Mina had once mentioned that August was very bad with money. He knows Atlantis was passed down from Rex Savage and he remembers his earlier thought about people who'd run out of options.

Who the hell is he to judge anyway? A former slum kid himself. He's become a snobby jerk.

Ren is opening the door. "You could stay in the big house, but then you'd be under Lita's thumb and I can tell you from experience that life is not comfortable there."

"I'm sure this'll be fine," he says, following Ren inside as she fumbles for a light.

"Welcome home," she says and Oscar glimpses beer cans, strewn clothing and some mismatched furnishings.

"Nice," he says, dropping his bags in the tiny living room, figuring that'll do until he finds out where he'll be sleeping. Ren stands over by the light switch. Her arms are crossed and she watches him. Oscar has the feeling she is forming a series of opinions about him right then and there.

"New York," he says, taking a step in her direction. "I was born in New York." He looms over her, satisfied when she squirms. "And I'm not especially waif-like. Or little."

"New York," she repeats and Oscar can tell the news surprises her. "I didn't know that."

"Seems like it would have been easy enough to find out if you cared to look into it."

She smiles again and damn if that devilish grin doesn't do all kinds of crazy shit to him. "I guess I never cared, Oscar. Still, seems like the kind of thing you ought to know about your *cousin*."

He leans into the wall just to the right of her, resisting the urge to touch a stray lock of dark hair that's fallen into her eyes. "Usually my buddies call me Oz. And I'm not really your cousin, Ren."

"That's right, you're not. Do you want to be?"

"Hell no."

She nods. "Good."

He can't tell what she means by that. It isn't a straight flirt. This girls isn't full of all the games and plots that occupy other girls. Somehow he already knows this. He also knows that no matter what kind of strangeness has transpired in the last two days and no matter what this girl's fucking last name is he wants to grab her and commit a series of dirty acts right here in the cramped living room.

Ren cocks her head and does a strange thing. She reaches out and tips his chin up. It isn't sexy and isn't supposed to be. It seems almost like a sorrowful gesture. Why the hell would Loren Savage feel sorry for him?

"Are you thirsty?" she asks, brushing past him and heading for the galley kitchen.

He follows her. "Depends. What kind of poison you offering?"

She flicks the tap and begins rinsing out a crystal wine glass. "Water. You want something stronger you'll have to beg it off the boys or steal it from August. Actually if you ask him he'll probably just give it to you." She fills the glass and extends it. "We have water filtration even out here beyond civilization so you're safe to drink from the tap if you don't mind the dusty taste."

Oscar accepts the glass, his hand briefly brushing against hers. The fine crystal was likely born to hold things more sophisticated than water. He takes a long drink and fills the glass again while Loren leans against the counter. Besides her flowing shirt she wears cutoff shorts and her tanned, bare legs end in scarred turquoise cowboy boots. Oscar finishes the lukewarm water and raises an eyebrow at her.

"No," she says. She's smiling again.

"I didn't say anything."

"You're thinking a few things though, Oscar." She sighs and shakes her head, her wavy black hair falling forward and brushing over the tops of her breasts. "You boys, you amaze me. You never even try to hide it."

"Didn't know the Savages were telepathic."

"We're not. You're just transparent."

The accusation bugs him. It bugs him enough to mess with her a little. He stands toe to toe with her.

"What am I thinking about, Ren?"

She blushes and looks at her boots. "S-sex." She stumbles over the word.

Oscar laughs out loud. He laughs so hard he nearly drops the glass. "With *who*?"

Now she's flushing crimson. Her self-assurance evaporates and she shifts uncomfortably.

"Well, weren't you?" she demands with irritation.

This is the most fun he's had in days. He drops the laughter and assumes a look of utter solemnity. "Nope. Right hand to god it hasn't crossed my mind. Not even for a second."

She believes the lie. She bites her lip. "Dammit, I'm sorry."

"I guess I can forgive you for your obscene assumptions."

"Seriously, I'm sorry."

Oscar is studying her. She crosses her arms over her breasts and refuses to look him in the eye now. He can't picture her in the glittering world of the rich and famous, but then she doesn't quite seem as if she belongs here in desert exile either. She might not completely belong anywhere.

Like me.

"How long have you been out here?" he asks. "I mean, I know you guys haven't always lived out here. Mina said you used to live in a mansion in California."

She answers slowly. "Fourteen months. The estate was foreclosed by the bank. An investor from China lives there now. I'm sure you know my dad's career is long over and little by little he's lost his inheritance. Lita's never earned an honest penny in her life but she's long dreamed of pushing us into the business." Ren makes a face. "I took a ton of screen tests and hated it. The lights, the cameras. It was awful. But

Ava's had some bit parts in sitcoms and Brigitte landed a role in a kids' movie. That's when August woke up and pulled the plug."

"You mean that's when he moved you to the middle of nowhere for some reason?"

She nods vaguely and skirts around the question. "My dad's always had this thing about dynasties. He's a student of history, obsessed with it really. If you ever want to know about which family ruled England during the fifteen hundreds you can ask him."

"The Tudors," interrupts Oscar.

Ren shrugs. "I'll take your word for it. Anyway, my dad loves to point out that every dynasty ends, figuratively at least. It doesn't mean everyone drops dead, but there comes a time when the sun stops shining on them and that might be a blessing." Ren frowns and lets out a short, pained cough. "He didn't want us in the business. He said it had to end, that we had to be given a chance at other choices." She looks around with a wry expression. "Of course, there was also the fact that we were virtually destitute. August has gradually sold off whatever remained. Lita just about crapped out steel nails when he moved us out here, but it's probably the only fight August ever won." She looks at him and gives out a little crooked grin. "You get all that? That's the history of the modern Savages."

"There are worse histories to have."

"I know. I'm not complaining. It's not terrible. It just *is*."

"True. And, if August is ever in really dire straights, I'm sure my mother would help him out."

A cloud passes over Ren's face. "Mina-" she starts to say, and then stops.

Oscar wants to hear it. "What?"

She shakes her head. "Nothing."

He drops the subject. "Hey, you sleep up in the big house?"

She nods. "Yeah. This place is small and I don't really want a front row seat to my brother's many conquests. Where Monty digs up all these trashy girls I'll never know. Anyway, August still needs to clear out some rooms where a bunch of my grandparents' junk is stuffed. As soon as he gets around to doing that I won't have to share with Ava and Brigitte anymore. My sisters have their good points but sometimes inhabiting the same space with them is indescribably awful."

"I'll bet. So I imagine Mina isn't staying in the brothel. She'll be bunking up with you?"

Ren gives him a strange look. "No, that's not the plan."

"Care to clue me in what the plan actually is? Seeing as how Mina yanked me out of school, hauled me to another continent and then dissolves into weeping or weird reminiscing whenever I ask her about it."

"Oscar," she says.

A weird sense of foreboding rolls through him. He'd heard a noise. Not now, about ten minutes ago, as soon as they'd come through the front door. He hadn't even registered it at the time. He registers it now.

"Fuck," he spits and heads for the door.

Even before he's outside, before he rounds the corner of the building and looks out at the gravel clearing, he knows. The sounds could have been just the driver of the car departing. But it wasn't.

The rest of the Savages are nowhere in sight but August is still there. August is ready to tell him what he doesn't even need to hear.

"Your mother," August says.

"I know," Oscar answers in a hollow voice.

"She left."

"I know," Oscar repeats.

It seems that August wants to explain. He shifts and runs a palm over his sweaty forehead. Oscar notices that he suffers from a slight tremor in his right hand. "Mina's exhausted. She went somewhere she can get some rest. Somewhere she can get some help. She wants you to spend the summer here, among family." August moves to pat Oscar's shoulder but his hand falls away as soon as his palm brushes Oscar's shirt.

"She's coming back," says Oscar. He says it because he really wants it to be true.

"Of course she is," August nods. "She'll be back at the end of the summer. In the meantime, you have a home here with us." He gives Oscar a curious, pitying look before turning away and disappearing into the house.

Oscar stares at a cloud of dust in the distance. It gathers particles of the desert floor to its side and spins for a few seconds in a perfect funnel formation. Then, just as abruptly, it widens and evaporates.

"You hungry?"

It's Ren. She followed him and she's standing at his side.

Exhaustion, August had said. Addiction. Anguish. Mental breakdown. Oscar has never spent too much time trying to puzzle out Mina Savage. It's always been impossible. She's been running from herself for so long. Why did she drag him into her world in the first place? Maybe he filled some lonely spot in her heart. Maybe she needed another human being who needed her in some way.

Ren moves closer to him. He can hear the kind sympathy in her voice. "Lita can't cook for shit. I'm making barbecued chicken wings." She touches his elbow. Gently, like she's unsure whether it'll crack like eggshells between her fingertips.

He looks down at her and has no thoughts about how good it would feel to get her naked. He only thinks what a relief it is to drop the fucking façade of Oscar Savage. The tough guy, the callous heartbreaker, the owner of a name he didn't earn.

"I'll help you," he says.

She raises her eyebrows. She's pleased though. "You can cook?"

"No. Teach me."

"All right. I will."

And so he follows her lead toward the house. They share a glance. Her brown eyes are full of curiosity and kindness. Oscar couldn't say what his own eyes might show. The shock of Mina's abandonment has already receded. This won't be his dream summer but he's okay with being here.

Ren's shoulder brushes his accidentally and he's glad she's here. On one of life's more fucked up occasions it means a little something to find a friend.

CHAPTER SIX

REN

Sometimes I think about how nice it must have been in the old days.

Not the horse-drawn carriage, shitting-in-the-backyard kind of old days.

Just a few decades back, before the perpetual intrusion of modern technology.

Don't want to hear about something? Turn off the television.

Don't want to read it? Close the newspaper.

Avoid grocery stores and their tabloid-littered checkout stands.

Leave the radio off in the car.

Ignore the phone. Allow it to ring and ring until the caller's ears bleed from the sound of silence.

Voila. Ignorance. Bliss.

It's not so easy anymore.

When I reach reflexively for my phone before I'm fully awake a vague alarm hums somewhere in my fuzzy brain. Too late. Along with everyone else in my generation I'm accustomed to checking on the state of the world before I brush my teeth. My eyes have already caught the top newsfeed headline, along with the first three lines of the article.

"Savage Family Values: In yet another naked attempt to capitalize on celebrity bad behavior, the troubled Savage family is joining the reality television circus. Famed only for their genetic link to dead Hollywood stars, this current generation represents the worst-"

I do not click on the article. I do not need to. Over the last few weeks I've plodded through at least a dozen similar ones, summarized as follows: *The talentless remnants of a famed family have sold their pride and their privacy to Vogel Television Productions. Premiering this September, the cast of Born Savages present themselves for your mockery and contempt every Wednesday night at 8 pm.*

A flutter of dread wanders through my belly. It's become a familiar companion lately, along with an eerie sense that I am standing on the spot next in line to be struck by lightening.

Because I always had trouble with sidelong glances and chronic whispers I left my casino job the day after the press release broke. For the most part I've been holed up in my apartment and engaged in a repetitive loop of Netflix programming.

It's really not as sad as it sounds.

Unless the situation involves crouching before your MacBook; un-showered, withered bologna sandwich in hand while episodes of The Walking Dead swallow up time.

Yeah, I just might have become a little pathetic.

I'm all packed. The apartment is being sublet to a seasonal Cirque du Soleil acrobat for the next two months. I'm wondering if anyone in Gary's circle will whine about my wardrobe. I have jeans. I have t-shirts. I have two pairs of expensive shoes that were gifted by sympathetic designer ages ago, a trusty old pair of brown cowboy boots, and three pairs of everyday Converse. I am aware that if a gene responsible for fashion sense exists, it seems to have skipped me.

The knock on the door comes just when it should. I've been sitting on the edge of the futon with my legs pressed together for the last fifteen minutes awaiting the sound.

The man standing on the other side resembles a mole that has been thrust into unfamiliar sunlight. He blinks at me. Then he attempts a crooked grin.

"Loren Savage," he says cheerfully as if we are old friends.

With a grunt he shifts a thick strap from his shoulder and cringes as the attached heavy camera equipment lands on the floor with a thud. "I'm Rash. I'm sure Gary explained everything to you already." He extends a thick hand.

Despite my better judgment silently warning that I ought to think twice about skin contact with anyone nicknamed 'Rash', I shake his hand. He smiles, exposing a row of teeth the size and hue of corn kernels.

"Nice to meet you," I say and withdraw my hand. My voice is robotic. I still haven't budged from the doorway.

Rash's mud colored eyes attempt to sweep beyond my door-hogging post and into the apartment. "What do you say we set up here for a brief interview before heading out on the road?"

"An interview?" I'm caught off guard. The way it was explained to me, the camera man, this Rash person, will accompany me on my journey to Atlantis in order to capture my homecoming in all its glory.

However, no one said a word about a pre-departure interview. I would have remembered.

I clear my throat. "Actually I'm ready to head out now. If we're going to get there by evening we should really get moving."

Rash glances at his watch, or pretends to. "We've got time."

"No," I argue. "We don't."

Rash steps back and surveys me. There's no hint on his face about what's going on in his head, but I would guess that he's wondering just how difficult I plan on being. After a long moment he nods to himself and shrugs. "All right. You're the boss."

"Actually I'm not. But thank you for the gesture." I retreat inside and grab a suitcase in each hand while Rash quietly observes me. "My Civic isn't very roomy. Hope all your equipment is more portable than it appears at first glance."

"Loren," he says in a fatherly voice. "Look, I'm not your enemy. I understand the lens can be intimidating at first and I won't switch the camera on until you're ready."

I stare at him for a minute. The man appears heartfelt but he's on Gary Vogel's payroll. His job involves gathering footage that may be edited into something interesting, decadent, controversial or any combination thereof. Gary Vogel's shows do not tend to be placid documentaries about earnest people living ordinary lives. Not for the first time I wonder how I'm going to make it through these next few months.

"I appreciate that. I won't hold you to it though. You have a job to do and so do I. So let's get on with it."

I've already turned my back and started a last minute mental inventory of my belongings when Rash clears his throat. When I turn around he's holding out a small black box with a wire attached to it. "Microphone," he explains.

I accept his offering and turn it over in my hand a few times. It's not heavy. I know it isn't. Yet the weight of it in my hand is oppressive.

Rash deftly illustrates how the wireless lavalier microphone works. The end piece may be simply taped beneath my clothes for now.

"When we get to the set we'll have Angel there," he says. "Angel can show you a few common tricks for keeping the piece functional and unseen." He holds up a roll of medical adhesive. "For the moment, just secure the transmitter beneath your blouse and keep the box in your back pocket."

Rash works a few miracles and manages to get my luggage and his ponderous equipment packaged into my silver Civic.

It's a surreal feeling, driving out of Las Vegas beside a stranger and heading in the direction of possible infamy.

For his part, Rash does his best to make me feel comfortable. He chats lightly about his wife and teenage daughters back home in Los Angeles. His nickname has stuck since childhood due to frequent bouts of psoriasis. He does not ask me any questions, and for that I am grateful. Soon enough I won't be able to avoid them, the questions. I won't be able to dodge giving out answers.

There's not much of a geographical distinction moving from the brown, dusty landscape of Nevada into the brown, dusty landscape of Arizona this time of year. Rains might have been more plentiful than usual over the spring because patches of wild greenery are visible beyond the shoulder of the Interstate.

We pause in the hardscrabble town of Kingman to gas up the car and grab some fast food for lunch. Rash speaks affectionately about his wife and how her vegan sensibilities would be outraged by the double patty hamburger in his hand

He doesn't seem to mind that our conversations are largely one sided. He points to sparse ruins that glint far beyond the road, hints of places people once squatted before leaving for unknown reasons. Whether they were boom towns rising from the promise of gold, silver or copper, they were used and then forsaken.

I squint behind my sunglasses and try to ease the ache in my wrists by loosening my grip on the steering wheel. I feel it pressing on me with each passing mile; the memories, the expectations, the very visceral fear of becoming a national (hell, even an international) laughingstock. When I glimpse a battered sign for the town of Consequences my nerves begin to dance with one another beneath my skin.

Rash notices. "You all right there, Loren? You look a little shaky."

"Not shaky. Sun's getting to me. And please call me Ren."

He unzips a black canvas case. "Well Ren, looks like we're coming down the home stretch here." He pauses, drums his fingertips against the canvas. "You mind if I record for a few minutes?"

I don't answer. I've had weeks to prepare for this yet my insides are liquefying. Who the hell was I kidding? I can't do this.

"Ren?" Now he's concerned. He's back to the fatherly voice, the one I imagine he uses when he's trying to figure out his own daughters.

"Fine," I manage to say. "It's fine."

Rash slips the camera out of the case. "Boss'll have my ass if I don't get something."

"I know. It's your job. Record away."

I'd been imagining that when the camera was turned on, every inch of my skin would recoil. But it is surprisingly mundane, and painless.

"I assure you that once the first spell of self consciousness fades you don't even feel them. You forget they are there. You forget you are acting." – Margaret O'Leary

Years ago I was wandering the aisles of a used bookstore in a shadowy corner of L.A. and nearly tripped on a box of movie magazines from the 1950s. I sat right down and turned brittle pages, unsurprised to immediately find an interview with my fiery screen goddess grandmother. I memorized that quote on the spot.

From the time I could talk, Lita would drag me to readings and screen tests. She was a natural stage mother; ruthless, overbearing to the point of cruelty. She just needed an offspring to exercise her ambition on. I was never a good match for her goals. When shoved before the yawning maw of a black camera lens I stiffened. Whatever graceful qualities existed in those prior generations was lost on me. I'm no actor. I never will be.

"Tell me about where we are," says Rash in a gentle voice.

My eyes don't leave the road when I answer. "We are right outside the town of Consequences. Twenty miles from Atlantis."

"Atlantis..." Rash prompts.

"Atlantis Star. Once a grand movie set synonymous with large scale western films, then the private retreat of the Savage family. It's now just an exhausted has-been." I grab my soda from the cup holder and take a long sip. The ice cubes have melted and the taste is flat. "It's kind of like us I guess. But that wouldn't be really accurate either. Becoming a has-been means something somewhere was accomplished. We're never-been's. That's us."

I hear myself talking and try to shut off the words. They were meant to sound casual, lighthearted, a simple rendition of history. Instead the more words that emerge the more bitter they become.

Rash says nothing when I close my mouth and concentrate on the road. He pans the camera over the dusty town of Consequences, aptly named when one of the area's early residents was discovered to be a bank robber and murderer on the run from eastern justice. Rather than await due process, town vigilantes hung him from a cottonwood tree in the town square. The last time I was there, the stump of the ancient hanging tree remained as a ghoulish monument. I'm sure it still does.

Rash might sense my agitation. He doesn't push me for the time being. Instead he busies himself with panning the lens over the landscape and does not bug me anymore. It's nearly irrelevant anyway. We're within a few miles of Atlantis. Soon there will be plenty to talk about and no getting away from it.

There are no signs that lead up to Atlantis. After all, it's not a town, not a tourist attraction. It's the crumbling refuge of an era, of a family. The old fake brothel is still the tallest building. Before I see anything else I see the sagging balcony adorned with the French-style wrought iron embellishments. The vertical wooden sign running down its side is all but illegible.

A memory suddenly surfaces as I follow the narrow dirt road that branches off from the asphalt. If you didn't know exactly where the road was you might miss it.

The memory in question is six years old. We'd left Los Angeles before dawn. Lita produced copious hysterical tears and gave everyone a headache while August cheerfully piloted the Lexus deep into the neighboring state. Monty and Spence rode separately in an old pickup my father had purchased so they were spared five hours of our mother's complaints. After a little while she stopped resembling anything coherent and sounded like the 'Waa Waa Waa' speak of Charlie Brown's mother. Ava worriedly twisted her hair, recently dyed blond, around her index finger and stared out the window. Brigitte watched movies on her laptop and ignored everyone. For my part, I was hard at work trying to process everything. I watched mile after mile of nothing pass by while my mother seethed and my father drowsily pointed out landmarks to a disinterested audience.

I'd been to Atlantis once before, when I was very small. My father had hauled us along for one of his frequent day trips to check on the place. All I could remember was that everything was sharp and hot. The grounds were lazily kept by a man August had hired to clean up once every few months.

Lita had nothing but contempt for the place. *"Why the hell do you hang on to that godforsaken eyesore?"* The real estate wasn't worth much, never was. Perhaps it was just old fashioned sentimentality that caused my father to keep it. Or maybe he figured some day he would need it.

Whatever his reason, I know August Savage had high hopes when we crossed the desert that spring afternoon. He was sure he'd made a decision in the best interest of his children.

Maybe that's why I can forgive him fairly easily while I will always feel like spitting nails over the mention of Lita. He wanted what was best for us. He just went about it the wrong way.

In the end my father must have been horribly disappointed by the way things turned out.

As I get closer to the smattering of tired buildings that are all that's left of the Savage estate, I see unfamiliar vehicles, expensive ones. Leaning against the side of the crumbling church are a pair of cameraman who smoke cigarettes and laugh about something private. One is young, tanned, with a wisp of black hair hanging in his eyes. He carelessly pushes it back and I stop breathing. But then the man moves his head so that I can see his profile more clearly. It isn't the face that haunts my dreams and squeezes my heart.

It isn't him.

I'm glad. And then I'm not.

We'd been out here for over a year when he arrived, full of attitude and sexual confidence that fascinated me from the start. What happened between us was beautiful.

But how it ended was sad and so terribly painful. I haven't seen him since then and I don't know where he is.

Two years ago I scrounged up enough cash to hire a cheap private detective who worked out of a hotel room. Oscar has good reason to hate me and I had no intention of showing up in his life to ruin whatever peace of mind he's managed to find, but I wanted to know that he was all right. The detective was unable to find any trace of him.

Of course I wasn't really surprised.

Oscar was always the most independent person I've ever known. If he wanted to shed his name and disappear he could have. And apparently he did.

Rash has returned the camera to my face. I set the car in park and notice that I am already being watched stealthily from yet another lens. My grandmother was wrong, very wrong. Every second those mechanical eyes are trained on me, I will know it.

"Welcome!" hails a woman. She's a bottle blond and has obviously been under the knife a few times. I'd guess her to be around forty but she's been smoothed out so much it's tough to tell. This is Cate Camp, the so-called 'right hand' of Gary Vogel. I've talked to her before and it usually leaves me feeling tired. Luckily, for now she backs off after a quick greeting.

I scan the scene for my brothers and sisters. Of course Brigitte is easy to spot. She's about twenty yards away, leaning against a rotting wooden horse post. She's deliberately failing to notice my arrival, lost in her own vision of herself flipping her red hair behind one shoulder and gazing pensively in the direction of the stubby Harquehala Mountains as the hot wind lifts the hem of her skirt. It's the sort of pose one might see on the cover of a romance novel. I have no doubt that's exactly her intention.

"Ren!"

Ava bounds out of the house. She moves pretty quickly considering she's balanced on ridiculous heels with a toddler on her hip. I catch Bree shooting a quick frown of annoyance that her calculated non-greeting has been disturbed.

Ava sets the little boy down and tries to nudge him forward but he balks and clings to her legs. I wouldn't expect him to come to me. He turned two this past March and I hadn't seen him since December.

My sister looks tired, older than her twenty-one years would indicate. That wasn't always the case. Years of hard partying, a bad relationship and unexpected early motherhood have taken a toll. She is still pretty, always pretty. Her face holds the round contours and wide eyes of innocence. The blonde hair doesn't suit her complexion though. It never did. She smiles at me and opens her arms. I hug her and pat my nephew, Alden, on the head. For the first time I am happy that I agreed to this lunacy.

Our younger sister abandons her thoughtful perch. She pauses long enough to allow a faint breeze to ripple through her short dress and then careens toward us as if it's been a decade since our last encounter.

"Loren!" Bree shouts and then collides in a whirlwind of limbs and hair. She manages to produce a few tears, overkill even for her. Still, for a moment I clutch my sisters without a care for cameras or spectators.

"Where are the boys?" I ask as Bree fusses at her hair and Ava hoists the baby back onto her hip.

"Boys," answers Brigitte with a sigh. She flounces ten feet in the opposite direction and peers toward the mountains, shading her eyes, clucking her tongue. She talks more loudly than she needs to. "I've scarcely seen our wayward brothers at all."

"Spence is out riding," Ava explains. Little Alden squats her at feet before tipping over as he pokes a curious finger into the dust.

"Figures." My bare arms prickle in the heat and I absently run my fingertips across my skin. The cameras are watching. Silently, morbidly. That's how things will be now. Even movements so inconsequential as swatting an insect away and answering my sister become something of interest to be captured, broadcasted, dissected. I'm not complaining. After all, I'm not here against my will. But I'd grown used to a blissful lack of attention. I feel it shattering by the second.

"Spence never minded the heat. Don't you remember? Keeping him indoors was always kind of like caging a coyote." Ava says this with a smile.

She and Spence are twins but as different as fire and water. Yet somewhere in the forgotten era of floating side by side in dense amniotic fluid, they formed a resolute bond. Spence had always been strangely hell bent on keeping Atlantis, either because of his own love of the place or as a posthumous honor to our father. But he is as proud as he is steadfast. Even though I do not expect to hear the words from him, I'm sure Ava's hardships have something to do with his decision to play along with this show.

As I glance around I notice that the barn has been renovated. Knowing Spencer, he probably did most of the work himself. The unpainted wood is appropriately rustic and although not large, the low-roofed structure appears serviceable for at least a half dozen animals. Beyond it I can see the sturdy metal posts of the corral to the east.

During our family's life in Atlantis the only horse on the grounds was an old mare named Pet that August had acquired from a local rescue organization. She was a bad-tempered animal with no patience for anyone other than Spence. And perhaps old Pet was perceptive enough to pick up on the tension between her loyal caregiver and his older brother. She tossed Monty like a ragdoll any time he tried to sit on her.

"What about Monty?" I ask suddenly. "I thought he was supposed to be here already."

"He's here," frowns Ava and then bends over to prevent Alden from ingesting a sizeable rock.

Brigitte has had enough of staring pensively at the distant mountains. She flicks her lion's mane of startling red hair over one shoulder and sashays up to me.

"Monty is being antisocial," she says airily and tosses a glance of disdain toward the brothel, which looks more woeful and neglected than it did the last time I saw it. Spence must have thought restoring the brothel was of little practical value. Tucked behind the fading building is the cozy former caretaker's quarters where my brothers used to sleep.

"He's in there?" I ask.

"Yup."

"Is he alone?"

"I guess. See that semi-hot cameraman checking out the stable? He and Montgomery haven't really hit it off. Elton, that's the camera guy's name, got a little too close early this morning when Monty was bidding farewell to yesterday night's entertainment."

The incident doesn't sound unlike Monty but I'm still a little startled. "He brought a woman out here with him?"

"No. He drove to Consequences last night and somewhere along the way found some sorry little piece of low self-esteem to keep him company for a few hours. You know Monty, he's not above using the Savage name to get something he wants. For all I know he promised her a starring role." Bree makes a sweeping gesture. "Anyway, he pushed her into a cab this morning and she was kind of upset about it. Monty and his notorious impatience were already on edge and poor Elton trying to do his job didn't improve matters."

"That doesn't sound good."

"It wasn't. Luckily Elton knows when to stay quiet or he might have gotten his head clubbed."

A groan escapes me as all the misgivings I've nursed about this project bubble to the surface. Montgomery and his defiant volatility. No matter what the reward is, how the hell is he going to make it through several months of being observed and recorded like an Animal Planet subject? How will any of us make it?

Careful. They are listening. They are watching.

I am acutely aware of the tiny microphone taped to my skin just above my left breast. It feels foreign, unwelcome. I have the urge to rip it off no matter who is watching.

Brigitte is still complaining about Monty. "He wouldn't even consider living in the big house even though that building over there is a wreck. They had to bring in two generators just to pump electricity in because all the wiring is shot to hell."

Ava isn't saying a word. The look on her face is one I recognize. It's the worried uncertainty that has been her companion her entire life. That's partly Lita's fault; Ava had too tender a nature to be the captivating sex kitten our mother envisioned as her destiny.

I give my sister a small nod of reassurance and her face relaxes.

"Rocks!" squawks Alden as he holds a saliva-glazed object aloft." "Rocks!"

Indeed, it's another rock. Plus, while he was drooling all over everything, my nephew managed to acquire a moustache of Arizona soil.

"Oh, honey, no. Icky yuck." Ava bends over and wipes the desert dust from her son's face.

As I kneel down and remove the rock from his chubby grip he beams at me. I turn the rock over in my palm. "This looks tasty. Mind if I keep it for myself?"

Alden laughs and allows his mother to gather him onto her hip. He's a sweet child. He takes after his mother.

"Where are you going?" Brigitte calls after me because I've walked away without a word.

"Just saying hello to my big brother."

I don't know if the girls can hear me or not because a wide dust devil has descended in a whirling funnel of sand.

Mini tornadoes.

That was how I used to think of them until someone told me otherwise. He always knew what he was talking about when it came to things like that. Dust devils. Rocks. Caves. I can hear the gruff timbre of his voice. I can remember how his words would be curiously offset now and again by an unidentifiable accent, a product of his nomadic lifestyle. I don't believe he was ever aware of it.

I'm still holding Alden's rock and when I squeeze it the sharp ridges cut painfully into my palm.

Our family should have been able to find another way to survive. People have managed far more with far less.

I drop the rock somewhere as I walk. I have no use for it.

CHAPTER SEVEN

OZ

I remember hearing once that in the United States there is more land where there is nobody than land where there is somebody. As I travel across the flat plains of the nation's heart, I can believe this is true.

As I inch toward the western edge of Oklahoma, the last of the summer dusk is settling into night. I've been this way before, on this very section of the Interstate, traveling in the opposite direction, east instead of west.

Over the last five years I've managed to touch most of the major asphalt tongues stretching across the continental U.S. I haven't left the country since the day I touched down in New York beside Mina Savage. Strange, considering I spent such a large swath of my life overseas. Or maybe not strange. Maybe I've just been thirsty to know the country I was away from for so long. I can't explain it. Maybe on some level it was even because of Ren.

I could keep driving for another six easy hours but suddenly I don't want to. Roadside signs promise food, gas, lodging in the town of Sayre so I pull off on the next exit. The surrounding land is flat, with scarcely a ripple. No mountains, no shores, no forest, no subterranean palaces.

This is the kind of land that holds no surprises. What you see is all there is, miles and miles of it. The simplicity appeals to me. Right now, anyway.

As I'm gassing up the truck, I catch a strong whiff of barbecue and my stomach lurches in response. There's a free standing restaurant about twenty yards off and it looks like it's seen better days; the harsh prairie winds have licked the red paint off in places and the sign 'Aggie's BBQ' is slightly askew above the narrow entrance, like it might land on someone's head one of these days.

A pair of thirty-something women stand in the parking lot sucking on cigarettes and murmuring to one other as they watch my truck swing into a spot only a few feet away from where they stand. I feel their eyes searching me as I head for the door and I point my head down because a conversation isn't really part of my plans right now.

The restaurant is dark and appropriately smoky for a barbecue joint. I order a rack of ribs with a soda and devour it quickly in a small booth with seats lined in orange vinyl that might have been cool forty years ago.

The shuffling, wheezing fellow who took my order yells something indistinct back to the kitchen and then begins grimly running a greasy rag over an empty table in wide circles.   The air conditioning is either non-existent or broken; the heat borders on oppressive.

All in all, Aggie's BBQ has the feel of a lost part of the universe where time isn't relevant.

I chew my food as Johnny Cash croons mournfully from somewhere unseen, recognizing Folsom Prison Blues only because August Savage had a penchant for vintage country music. Every time I walked into the big house at Atlantis an antique record player would be belting out music from a corner of the living room. Somehow it was always on, even if there was no one in sight.

All of a sudden I feel a ripple down my spine and a wild gust of wind rocks the building enough to make the walls creak.

The old man wiping the counter pauses long enough to squint out the dirty window. "Nothin'," he scoffs, "not a storm."

I don't know if he's talking to me or not so I tear off another mouthful of tender rib meat and stay quiet. This area has got to be prime real estate for tornadoes so I would bet the locals are used to looking skyward every time a few clouds decide to hang out together. I've seen one of the telltale funnels myself once, tagging along with storm chasers a few years back at the Kansas/Missouri border. The clouds gather and link arms before they animate and whip up a nightmare to send to the ground. It's horrifying and fascinating, nothing like the harmless compact whirlwinds of dust that dance across the desert.

"No, not a mini tornado. Dust devil. Read about them in one of your father's books."

"Doesn't look devilish to me, Oscar. Looks happy. Playful."

Funny how scraps of conversation can revisit out of nowhere, things you might not even realize your mind knows until something else triggers the dormant memory.

Just like that I'm no longer in a stifling barbecue joint somewhere on the Oklahoma prairie. Instead I'm standing beneath a scalding desert sun and beside an incomparable girl, a girl I was never supposed to have and swore I wouldn't take but did anyway. I don't even need to close my eyes to remember how she shaded her face with her palm and squinted at the frisky dust tunnel in the foreground of the Harquehala Mountains.

Playful, she'd called it, and then her sweet, full mouth tilted up as she glanced at me sideways. I hadn't kissed her yet and I didn't kiss her then. But in that glance she told me she understood what I'd already accepted.

It was only a matter of time.

I *would* kiss her. I would push all barriers aside and I would get inside of her every which way. We would say *fuck the consequences* together and then suffer the mortal wounds of our own stupidity when we learned that reality is far messier.

In reality, *consequences fuck you.*

"Hey, buddy." The shapeless, rasping old man who took my order is looming over me with a grimace. He puts a hand to his back and I realize the sour look isn't for me. He's a man who spends his days walking through pain and the fact has permanently wrenched his face into a scowl.

"You forgot your drink," he grumbles and sets a plastic-lidded cup next to my plate before he trundles off with a dirty dishtowel slung over a drooping shoulder.

After hastily finishing my meal, I toss the trash and nod a farewell to the proprietor. I don't imagine Sayre is a real hotbed of tourist activity, particularly not at the onset of summer, so there are probably limited lodging options.

I could sleep in my truck, of course. I'd done it many times. But tonight I don't feel like risking any attention from local busybodies.

It doesn't take long to find a place with a flashing vacancy sign. It's called The Oklahoman and its mid century paint peels from its face but it looks non-threatening enough. There is a malarial-looking woman behind the pressed wood desk in the lobby. She frowns when I tell her I don't have a credit card but cheers right up again when ten twenty dollar bills land in front of her nose. She touches the money with a ragged fingernail, glances around and then tosses me a card key.

"Room Eighteen. It's right over my head so keep it down."

"No problem," I tell her and flash a smile because she seems like the kind of woman who doesn't get rewarded with smiles every day. Her lips twitch but she merely stands there and observes me with caution as I head back to the car.

I'd packed haphazardly, with the bulk of my clothes shoved into two black plastic bags and stuffed beneath the passenger seat. In the end I decide I don't feel like picking through my crap in the dark front seat so I grab it all and head upstairs.

There's a couple engaged in a tense standoff on the opposite end of the upper balcony. They exchange hissing murmurs which sounded complicated and then abruptly the man scoffs, "Fuck this shit," before lumbering down the spindly staircase.

Meanwhile, his woman leans over the wrought iron side and whisper screams "Wayne! WAYYYYYNE!"

I've had enough of people today so I get indoors and toss my bags in a corner. It's early and I'm not tired at all.

There's a 'How goes it?' text from Brock so I tap out an answer and then switch the thing off. Unlike virtually every other member of my generation, I don't wear my phone like an arm. I feel better when I'm not connected.

I really wish I'd packed a few books. It's rare for me to be without a book. Maybe I ought to pick up one of those e-reader things so I can just click on whatever catches my attention.

The television only offers a handful of channels and two of them are showing World War II movies. Another one seems to be some sort of public access outlet where a group of women sit around a chipped tile table and mispronounce the names of expensive wines.

I'm about to give up and pass a few minutes beating off when I flip to the last channel and notice it's one of those celebrity shows featuring news about people with gummy grins and collagen lips. Not that I care two pubes about whether Ark Deveroux abandoned his pregnant wife for his nineteen-year-old costar, but I happen to catch a few words of the marquee traveling in slow motion across the bottom of the screen.

"Born Savages, featuring the descendants of the legendary Hollywood family, begins filming this week in a remote, undisclosed location."

I wait to see if the bubbly host will run a segment about it, but there is nothing else said and the show closes with a fish-faced selfie of some actress I'd never heard of who'd apparently appeared in a campy adaptation about teen werewolves living in Miami before she wound up in rehab.

I shut the television off. If I want news about the Savages I know where to find it. If I want to get a glimpse of Ren I know where to find that too. There have been some weak moments over the past few years where I typed her name in to a search engine only to be cut to the bone by the fact that she grows more beautiful with each phase of the moon. I've sat there in front of a laptop, stupidly drinking in every graceful movement she makes as she's unknowingly tailed by some weirdo who had slyly shadowed her around during her casino shift and then posted it to YouTube.

Even in that short glimpse, Ren's pride was written all over her. She moved with sure purpose and didn't make time for distractions. She never was and never will be the kind of woman who craves the glare of the spotlight.

So why this? Why now?

Everything I've ever known about Loren Savage screams that something had to have veered terribly wrong for the proud, intelligent girl I once knew to agree to the cheap fucking sideshow that this thing is destined to be.

Ren hates cameras. Ren hates attention. Money wouldn't be enough of an incentive for her. I can't make any sense out of it. But maybe that's because I never really understood her as well as I thought I did.

The lights cut off. Abruptly, as if they are candles snuffed by a cool breath.

Now I hear it outside, the wind. It's probably a chronic companion to the land here, more so than the desert and its variable moods. The brown valley that cradles Atlantis Star is full of almost tranquil stillness, where sometimes it seems even a loud exhale will disturb the scene too much. Other times the furies of nature threaten to lift every grain of sand from the desert floor.

Strange that in the scope of my transient life I spent so little time there yet it somehow remains the centerpiece of my heart. It's the place that lives in my dreams and keeps me company in the darkest, most forbidding of caves.

There are heavy footsteps roaming the balcony outside my door. A man's voice howls into the wind as the utter blackness of the stormy night prevails. He mutters a drunken slur and retreats.

"I'm sure. I'm sure. I want this."

"Damn, I love you, Ren."

I go from being all cool and composed to being so hard I ache. I've got my pants down and my dick in my palm in a flash.

Sure it eats at me a little, the knowledge that I'm getting off on the memory of a teenage girl, but we're not kids anymore and if I had something better I'd use it. Every other female I've ever put it to before then and since then, they just all run together in my brain like they're really all one pussy attached to replaceable heads.

But I remember every second with Ren, the way she curled her fingers around the back of my neck and gasped when I pushed deep inside the tight place that hadn't ever been breached before. I kissed her. I told her things I meant completely. I made her promises that should have come true. Once I was in there I never wanted to leave.

It was more than that though. It was a soul-to-soul connection that I'd never known before, haven't even glimpsed since.

It was consuming.

It was shattering.

It was something that was forbidden in that time, and in that place.

I stroke my own shaft and pretend it's her soft hand on me. I close my eyes and make believe her hot mouth explores slowly, licking the sweet spot just south of the head. That's how I come, hard and violent, with the vision of unleashing myself inside her mouth, my hands gripping her head and not letting go until she swallows it all.

The wind grows stronger. The thin walls of the motel rub against one another and groan from the strain. It sounds like a strange sort of sex ritual, lacking rhythm or pleasure. I wonder how many of the other rooms are occupied, how many other errant travelers wait in the darkness. A town this close to tornado alley would have a storm siren but I hear nothing.

Impatiently I smear my own essence on my bare thigh and listen. The wind begins to lighten just as my thudding heart starts to slow down. Eventually the sounds recede to a vague crackling of dry leaves and an occasional growl of thunder. There is a stirring of people as they resume their night. A few congregate on the balcony outside, murmuring and laughing over a private joke.

The lights are still off. I hop off the bed naked and turn all the switches off so the lights won't blind me when the electricity resumes. After a quick shower in the pitch darkness, I return to the narrow bed, strip off the towel and sink into the lumpy, well-used mattress.

I'll see her tomorrow. Every cell in my body vibrates with that certainty.

I don't know what she's done since I've seen her last and I don't care. Right now I can barely remember the details of my own life these past five years.

They are irrelevant.

All that matters is getting to her even if I have no clear plan for what comes next. It doesn't matter if every fucking camera-toting gossip in the country wants to watch it happen or if she screams at the sight of me and tries to run in the opposite direction.

It's happening anyway.

CHAPTER EIGHT

REN

Monty isn't in a friendly mood when I find him. That's not surprising. My older brother has been sunk too long in his own bad temper to shed it on a whim or for a camera.

He greets me with a weary nod as if we see each other far too often for his taste. Then he gestures that I ought to follow him inside and shoots a warning glance toward a skulking cameraman in the background.

"Fuck you," he sneers at the man. "Told Gary I'm not fucking with that shit until tomorrow."

He slams the door at my back and looks me up and down with his arms crossed. "They got a piece on you?"

His voice is even more gruff than I remember, as if life has scratched it up a bit and added a few pounds of gravel. There's a tattoo on his neck. Not a good one. It's a stark tribal shape that might as easily mean something as it means nothing.

"What?" I answer, a little startled because it sounds like my brother is asking if I'm carrying a gun.

Monty raises his eyebrows. They are roguishly sculpted things that have a mood all their own. Anyone would assume a little manscaping is to thank.

But Monty doesn't cultivate his looks. He doesn't have to. Whatever advantages he has are a Savage legacy. His looks, among other things.

"A mic, Ren. They fit you with a microphone?"

"Oh." My brother averts his eyes as I reach fumbling fingers into my blouse and extract the device taped to my skin. I'm holding it in my hand and wondering how to mute it when Monty hisses between his teeth, grabs it, and severs the wire with a prompt snap between two fists. He lets it fall to the scruffy old parquet floor and we stand there staring down at the pieces.

"That was violent," I comment and look up, surprised to see Montgomery Savage grinning. If I wasn't so stunned at the sight I would probably applaud.

"How the hell are ya, Loren?"

"I may have misplaced my mind but that's probably a good idea considering what's about to go down." I pause, looking my brother over more carefully. He's bulked up but not in a soft way at all. He is a bristling wall of muscle and scarcely bottled wrath.

If I weren't his sister I would run across the street to avoid him.

"I'm glad you're here," I say with honesty because after all, I *am* his sister and right now we are a family in sore need of allies.

Monty clears his throat with a small nod and I know that's the best acknowledgement I'll get.

We don't hug. Ava and Brigitte are huggers. The rest of us are aloof nodders.

He starts walking toward a portable fridge in the corner of the room and seems to expect I'll follow him. He fishes out a few Blue Moon beers and hands one over. He sucks back his whole bottle before I can even twist the cap off and take a sip.

My brother stares moodily out the window with a frown. The barren valley at the foothills of the Harquehala stare back. At least the cameramen are warily distant at the moment. Instead of pressing a lens against the glass panes they are nowhere in sight.

Monty seems to know my thoughts. He shoots me a wry glance. "Guess we should enjoy our last few moments of obscurity."

I snort. "Is that what you call this?"

"What do *you* call it?"

"Popular indifference. We are noteworthy when we do something violent or indecent."

Monty rolls his eyes. "That sounds like a shot if there ever was one."

"I wasn't talking about you. Come on, Monty. You know I don't cut you down that way. I'm not Lita." I take a swallow of beer. It's warm. Only the bottle was cool. "We're not here to produce some down home family feel good show. We were given this shot because we're-"

"Fuckups," my brother finishes and holds his bottle up in a mock toast before draining the last drop and tossing it across the room into an empty cardboard box that seems to be serving as a trash can. "At least some of us, anyway. You've managed to keep your nose clean. Me? Not so much."

I pause. I haven't talked to Monty much over the past few years. Whatever communication we've had tends to skirt carefully away from subjects like prison and fortysomething sugar mamas. I can see the change in him though. Monty was never full of sunshine and delight. But now there's a steeliness to him that's sharp and a little frightening. He stews in his own skin like a large angry animal. Suddenly my heart hurts for him, for Monty, my big brother, even though he would be the last man on the planet to ask for pity.

"I'm sorry," I mumble miserably. I'm confronted by my own selfishness. I've removed myself from my siblings, remaining at an emotional and physical distance all because I was nursing a hurt that I've never been able to face.

It seemed like the only way to heal my soul was to stay away from the things, the places, the people, that reminded me of what I'd lost.

Anything reminiscent of Oscar.

"Hey, Ren," says Monty with some gentle concern. He's peering at me and I don't realize I'm crying until dueling tears spill down my cheeks. My brother sighs and plucks the beer out of my hand, setting it carefully on the counter.

Monty coughs into one hand and sighs again. "It's not your fault. You've always done the thing where you try to carry all the family's shit on your shoulders so we don't have to. I know it's fucked up for you to be back here. And I know why."

"Do you?" I'm surprised. We've never talked about him. The day he left was the last day any of us spoke his name out loud. "It's just history. All of it. It only messes us up if we let it."

A crooked grin crosses his face. "Who's messed up? I'm fucking spectacular."

I grin back. "Sure you are."

He shrugs. "Easy confirmation. Just ask anything on the west coast with a set of tits."

"That's a lot of tits, Montgomery."

"I could stand to meet some more. As soon as we wrap up this circus I plan on working my way east until I hit an ocean or something."

"That'll keep you busy for a little while."

"Maybe."

A shadow of pain pulses beneath my left eyebrow. An old enemy, prologue to a migraine. My hand goes to my forehead, pressing the spot. If I take two Excedrin within the next fifteen minutes I might be able to head it off in time.

Monty opens a narrow cabinet beside the kitchen sink. After knocking a few other things aside, he finds what he's looking for. He tosses a bottle to me and I'm glad to pop it open and swallow two of the pills that rattle around inside as my brother watches.

"It'll be okay, Ren," he says quietly and touches my shoulder in a rare gesture of brotherly affection.

And that's Monty; impenetrable, solitary, but capable of rare flashes of gallantry. I remember once when I was nine and he was ten. We were in the middle of a childhood war. Usually such conflicts were Monty vs. Spence or Monty vs. Lita or Monty vs. Everyone. But we battled one-on-one every now and then.

Monty had been pissed for weeks because I'd accidentally left the water on when filling the tub in the hallway bathroom beside his bedroom. Water spilled over the top of the old claw foot tub, flowed across the threshold and found a shoebox full of the vintage video game cartridges he'd left on the floor just inside his room. They might have been salvageable if Monty had the patience to consider such a thing. Instead he screamed and ranted and set the box afire in the backyard barbecue pit. If it was Spencer's fault he would have clobbered him without mercy but even when in a rage Monty would never hit us girls. He glared and brooded, held his nose whenever I walked into the room, ignored me more than usual at school where we were in the same class because he'd been held back in second grade. I shrugged it all off irritably because I understood my brother well enough to know that sooner or later he would move on to a different grievance.

And then came the Faberge egg incident. It was the most valuable object in the crumbling mansion where chandeliers hadn't operated for decades, fixtures were cracked and ants marched in dogged lines along the ivory-colored stucco walls.

The egg was an emerald green, encrusted with exquisite pink roses, a gift bestowed on our screen goddess grandmother by some minor European royalty. It used to sit in its own display case in the center of the second floor library, one of the few remaining treasures that hadn't yet been sold off.

By that time our father, August, had pretty much given up on most things; his career, personal hygiene, and fighting with his bat shit crazy wife. He was forever retreating to the moldy attic room where he could pet his vinyl record collection and write sprawling incoherent memoirs about his life. He would have one more battle left in him – the Battle of Atlantis Star - but it was years from surfacing. Maybe he was storing up the energy for it.

In the meantime, Lita was free to practice her brand of roughshod parenting, which involved nightmarish casting calls (*don't improvise, why the fuck did you improvise?? NEXT!*), chronic body shaming (*my god, suck in that baby fat, you look like a pregnant fourth grader!*) and scattered episodes where she would howl that we were all disgusting brats before running off to places unknown for a few days or a few weeks at a time.

Anyway, I had a habit of dawdling in the library and staring trance-like at the glittering antique. You can't appreciate a thing like that unless you get close. Close enough to understand the intricate artistry that was spent on its creation.

I would stand there, chewing on my thumbnail, and imagining that I was really the resident of a dazzling realm with no ants crawling the walls or dirty floors beneath my feet, no confusing legacies to grapple with or cruel mothers to avoid.

In that world I was Loren the Beloved, twirling in pink tulle, eating as much ice cream as I pleased and tiptoeing around a gleaming castle. The egg winked at me from its golden pedestal, beckoning, promising.

I needed to get closer.

If I got close enough to touch its surface then the magic was possible.

Typically I wasn't a dreamy child and at age nine I was old enough to know magic was a false promise. But I placed my hands around the glass dome of the display case, surprised when it lifted easily, and watched my finger move to the nearest embellished rose with the same hypnotic power that a certain fairy tale princess would understand when she touched a sharp spindle.

I didn't mean any harm. I would have gladly tossed my greatest treasures into the old fire pit behind Monty's video games before I would have willingly damaged that egg. My mind took a moment to catch up to the horror of the prize object rolling from its perch, sliding across the narrow table and hitting the floor, shattering in several places. I stared in disbelieving shock as broken slivers of pink roses spun out in several directions.

"You are in such deep shit," said a voice and I whirled around to see Monty standing there with a knowing smirk on his face. His laughter followed me as I sprinted back to my room, where there was nothing to do but crawl beneath the bed and cry until nightfall.

One of the other kids happened to walk past the library and raised the alarm about the shattered egg. It would have been a big deal under the best of circumstances but my mother was feeling especially wronged because Ava had been cut from the casting of a prime time family drama.

And so misfortune became catastrophe. Lita might have blamed the staff if there was any staff remaining to blame. I cowered at the shrill, familiar sound of her voice. She was accusing Ava. Ava was crying. Balling my fists and gritting my teeth, I crawled out from beneath the bed. Let her slap me or withhold dinner for a week, let her perversely grin at the other kids and say in her false sugar voice, "Let's play a game. Let's pretend Loren is invisible!"

I'd suffered through all of that before. I could take it again.

My feet were cold on the bare floor and I wished I'd put on shoes. Somehow that made it worse, facing my mother in bare feet. She was shrieking my name from the library.

People would always say Lita Savage was an attractive woman. If I'd I'd been able to separate her character from her face I might have thought so too. Her blonde hair wasn't natural and her features were a smudge too pointed but she turned heads even in a city stuffed with hopeful, plastic beauty. There was nothing beautiful about her face as she turned on me. My siblings were clotted together in the corner of the library, August was blasting an Elvis record from his attic hideaway and I was on the verge of being eviscerated by Lita Savage's fire breathing madness.

I opened my mouth to say the words I needed to say. *Yes, I did it. Yes, I'm sorry.* But they stalled somewhere in my throat while my heart hammered and my mother loomed.

Lita wasn't consumed by love for any of her children but some were tolerated more than others. I was the least of all Savage offspring to her. I knew it. Monty knew it too. That might have been the reason for what happened next. In the midst of the wild scene, of crying siblings and a vengeful parent, he calmly stepped up, that stone-faced ten-year-old kid, and said, "I fucking did it. So there. And fuck you, Lita."

I look at my brother now - my damaged, prideful big brother - and wonder how different his life might have turned out if he'd been born to a normal family.

I could easily wonder the same about the rest of us. Surely gentle Ava wouldn't have been swallowed by the scandalous Hollywood party scene, Brigitte wouldn't be desperately searching for a fame she considered her birthright; I wouldn't be a skeptical escape artist. And Spence...well, maybe Spence alone had enough strength of character to be who he was always going to be. Somehow I can't imagine him as anything other than a modern cowboy haunting an obscure desert outpost.

It doesn't matter now.

We are who we are.

A bubble of anxiety rises in my gut as I realize once again that we have sold our souls with this show. But there's no backing out at this point. Gary and his corporate minions are expecting a train wreck. And the world will see what it wants to see.

"I've guess I should go unpack," I tell my brother.

Monty nods vaguely and stares out the window toward the house. A few hundred yards away I see Spencer riding a brown mare at a lazy walk, seemingly oblivious to the pair of cameras trained on him.

"Need any help carrying your shit?"

I shake my head. "Nah. I didn't bring much."

He gives me a penetrating stare. "You up for this, Ren? I can derail the whole damn thing if you want."

I do. This is a mistake. I know it. Monty knows it. But I think about Ava and Alden, of Bree and her desperate hopes. And I just can't.

"Better not. Gary would sic his cadre of lawyers on us." I gesture out to the yard, where Bree has reappeared and is standing in a wistful pose as the last of the sunlight disappears. "Besides, there are other people to think about."

Monty frowns as he catches sight of our youngest sister. "That there are," he says reluctantly and that confirms what I already suspected; Monty isn't the selfish prick he usually seems to be.

"Stay out of trouble tonight," I warn on my way out.

"Fine," Monty shrugs. "But tomorrow all bets are off."

When I walk outside I see Spence has dismounted and is leading the horse around to the far side of the stable. He sees me but doesn't stop walking.

"Hey, Ren," he says as casually as if we just saw one another this morning instead of over a year ago. Then he swings open the stable door and disappears.

Someone, probably Rash, has already been thoughtful enough to carry my luggage from the car to the house. Speaking of Rash, I don't see him anywhere. The two camera guys who were out here a few minutes ago have disappeared as well. I wonder if they were told to back off for the rest of the night. Either way, all bets are off starting tomorrow, our first official full day of filming.

Bree has returned indoors and the house is silent. I assume my sisters are in there wrangling with their own personal demons. Spence hasn't emerged from the stable and hopefully Monty will brood alone behind the brothel for the night.

The rubber soles of my shoes are quiet on the rough sand as I wander out beyond all the Atlantis structures. The original two thousand acres have been pared down to barely three hundred over the years as land was sold off to the government at bargain basement prices. The surrounding area is all part of a protected natural preserve and new construction is prohibited. Atlantis was grandfathered in and as private property and may remain as such as long as it's owned by a member of the original family. If it was sold to the government for peanuts, the buildings would likely be razed immediately and the landscape returned to the authority of the desert.

A faint breeze lifts my hair slightly as I pause and watch the shadows of the mountains disappear into the invading night. I feel funny, a vague wave of dizzy detachment. Maybe it has something to do with where I'm standing. Perhaps some distant part of my genetic makeup recalls that other Savages have stood here before.

Or maybe it's something else.

How many times had we hiked out here at night, two teens in desperate, frantic love? I might have stepped right in these tracks five years ago, our hands clasped together, my body in a fire to feel his.

I turn away with a shudder and slowly walk back toward the house. The activity has died down now that the crew has departed for the night, having rented out a floor in the only motel in Consequences. On a typical night they'll wrap up around eight p.m. and return promptly at seven the next morning, unless there's something interesting going on.

For the hours in between, there were cameras installed all over the property. I didn't bother to listen too closely when Cate Camp outlined their locations. As I reach the front door where someone has been thoughtful enough to leave the bright porch light on, I expect that I'm being watched in some way.

It's late. I'm tired. I don't know what to expect tomorrow or the day after that but I've already sentenced myself to being here no matter what.

I wonder if this is how a caged animal feels.

CHAPTER NINE

OZ

Being alone never bothers me. I'm used to it. Maybe it's a side effect of those fucked up early years. Or maybe some of us are just born that way. It might not be the worst thing. Caves and caverns, forests and deserts, all tend to make for better company than people. People are messy.

I had left the hotel before the sun came up, pausing at a gas station on the way out of town to fuel up and grab some breakfast from a vending machine. Oklahoma bleeds into Northern Texas and suddenly, without any preamble, I'm in New Mexico. My phone might be buzzing like a hive if I bothered to turn it on.

Let Gary and his team sweat about when or where or how I'll turn up. I said I'd be there. And I *will* be there.

New Mexico, at least the part I'm driving through, is full of muted neutral colors. There's a gentler look about things here than what I know awaits in Arizona.

My back is unhappy about being pressed against the seat of the truck hour after hour. I stretch and hear a pop. It's doubly unhappy because last night was restless. A lot of violent tossing that receded into uneasy dreams of Ren.

Ren straddling me on a public beach, Ren dancing naked in a church, Ren in a YouTube video blowing smoke rings at a desert sky and then winking. None of that ever really happened. But now every excuse I've repeated to myself for the last five years seems flimsy. I've stubbornly remained in my own exile rather than demand the answer she owed me.

But for crying out loud, hadn't she already told me to leave? Hadn't she said the only thing that could make me turn away?

I can remember the way her hair felt between my fingers and the laugh in her voice as she said my name but there's a big gaping hole between the last time I held her and the first night I spent without her, bitterly alone and resolving to stay that way. Everything else I can see with crystal clarity but I usually avoid thinking about those other details.

She'd pressed some money into my hand. I remember that. Like I wanted fucking money from her. Her pig of a mother lurked the background, acrid smoke hung in the air and Monty Savage punched me at some point. I might have killed him if Ren hadn't stepped between us. None of that was important. Not the blood in my mouth or the screaming in my ears. There was just Ren saying something I couldn't hear and then Ren saying something I *could* hear. Something impossible.

"Go."

"No."

"Go, Oscar!"

"You don't mean it."

"Yes I do. We are finished. We are nothing. And you need to leave me alone now."

"Then you fucking say it. Tell me you don't want me. Ren, you tell me that and I swear to god you'll never fucking see me again."

"I don't want you, Oscar. I don't want you. I DON'T WANT YOU!"

Because it's been so long since I've thought about that moment, I can't even be sure it's right. Except the sick feeling in the pit of my stomach tells me it is. There are some gaps, some puzzle pieces that aren't quite interlocking; there's Ren crying, there's August shaking his head, there's Spencer chasing me down and urgently pushing the money into my hand, the money Ren had tried to give me before I threw the wad of bills back in her face. Then there's Spence helping me get a bag hastily packed and stealing the keys to the pickup in order to get me at least to Consequences, where I would have a better chance at finding a ride somewhere else.

Everything still ends with *"I don't want you."*

The hurt feels fresh right now. I know why I've kept that particular memory away. And it was a valid excuse for a while, when I was still a kid trying to carve out a way to survive. I'd hitched a ride to Phoenix and the thousand bucks Spence had pushed on me was enough to grab a room in a decrepit motel and get my bearings.

It's a sad fact that the world isn't awash with opportunities for a homeless teen with no last name. I told anyone who asked that I was called Oz. I wanted nothing to do with Oscar Savage anymore. He was never real anyway. Acevedo became my last name on a whim when I was watching a local news broadcast and the cute reporter chirped her name at the end of a segment about the toxic desert toads that surfaced in the summer monsoon season.

I started looking for work in the area surrounding the huge state university but didn't have much luck without any ID. I got turned down flat everywhere I tried, a few would-be employers snottily informing me that they used e-verify and can't hire those who are in the country illegally. I didn't bother to argue with them.

During the day I would sneak into the university library for hours at a time, enjoying the free air conditioning and turning the pages of dusty old science books that most everyone seemed to have forgotten about. That's where I had a stroke of actual good luck when a man walked by, glanced at the book I was reading, and asked me if I was enjoying it.

"Good," he said, when I warily nodded. "Because I wrote it."

His name was Dr. Lemon and he was a geology professor. He wasn't put off by the vague answers I gave to whatever questions he asked. To him, it didn't matter that I was a rather tough-acting teen with an obvious chip on my shoulder. It was enough for him that I sat in the library hour after hour devouring book after book. He did ask if I had any family who might be looking for me and I said no. Then he asked if I wanted to finish high school and I said hell no. He frowned over that and then searched around in his leather briefcase, withdrawing a shiny brochure. Some friends of his ran a tourism company in Colorado. He told me to wait until the following day and give them a call. They were searching for tour guide trainees.

Sometimes I wonder how the hell I would have managed if Dr. Lemon hadn't done me that favor. Maybe I would have turned to dealing, or worse. Maybe right now there's another kid sitting in a library somewhere reading about acid-eating microbes in South American caves as his empty belly rumbles. Dr. Lemon died of pancreatic cancer about a year after that fateful meeting. I hope someday I'm able to pay it forward, the chance that he gave me.

Miles pass and my mind never strays from Ren for very long. I'm not awfully creative and for the life of me I can't imagine how things are going to go when we're face to face. I keep myself occupied with the radio so I don't have to think about what the hell we'll say to each other when I drive into Atlantis.

"So Ren, what's up? Been a few years, haha. You look hot. Sometimes I think I hate you. And sometimes I think the opposite."

I'm starting to wonder if maybe this wasn't such a good idea, showing up like this. I could have tracked down Ren a long time ago to figure out whether we could wade through the mess of our past. But it would have been harder for her to find me, if she'd even tried. Maybe she *had* tried and then gave up.

Gary's oily assurances that the family has no idea I'm part of the production schedule may or may not be bullshit. I don't give a damn about the rest of the Savage clan; Ren's sullen brothers or her airhead sisters. I know August has been dead for years and Lita can go eat glass for all I fucking care.

Once I told the girl I loved that she'd never have to see me again. That's a promise I should have broken a long time ago.

CHAPTER TEN

REN

I remember reading something once about how in olden times royalty would always be surrounded by people. They had all these well-dressed clingers – usually minor nobility - hanging around at all hours to help them dress, to hand them spit glasses, to inspect their piss, to claw wax out of their ears, whatever.

Even though no one has tossed me a chamber pot when I sit up in bed the first morning of filming, I have the feeling I'm opening my eyes inside of a fishbowl.

It gets worse when I open the door.

"Shit!"

The shriek erupts from my mouth when I nearly collide with a prowling cameraman.

It's the handsome dark-haired one one I'd seen yesterday. He doesn't say sorry. He doesn't say anything. He just trains his lens on my wild hair and puffy face.

I cross my arms over the old t-shirt I'd worn to bed and disappear into the bathroom for a while. At least there are no cameras creeping around the bathroom. Well, none that I can see anyway. I decided not to think about that. I have some trouble attaching my microphone and finally just stuff it inside my bra, winding the cord beneath my shirt and attaching the box piece to the waistband of my jeans.

When I finally emerge, the cameraman is gone and I find my sister Ava in the kitchen scooping some hideous orange goo out of a jar and feeding it to her son. Rash is crouched in a corner with a camera balanced on one shoulder. He looks like he was painted there. I wonder if his knees hurt.

"Hey," says Ava with bright cheer as Alden spits out a blob of orange. I can't say I blame the kid. I'd spit it out too.

There's a large country kitchen table in the middle of the room that I don't remember seeing before. Spence used to have a folding table and one metal chair. It's probably a prop, procured by Vogel Productions. Brigitte had told me that Spence had gotten rid of a lot of the furniture ages ago. Gary's team must have arranged a little bit of interior renovation.

I pour myself a cup of coffee, sit on the rustic bench that fits neatly with the rustic table in the rustically repainted kitchen while Brigitte prances around the clearing in front of the kitchen window amid a cloud of feathers. I gulp down some black coffee. I never sweeten my coffee.

"What the hell is Bree doing?"

Ava wipes her son's mouth. "Feeding the chickens."

"I don't remember seeing any chickens yesterday."

"They weren't here yesterday. A truck arrived this morning with some chickens and a premade coop."

"Ah, another prop." I'm starting to sound downright bitchy.

There's a low whistle from the corner. I turn and face the source of the noise.

"What's that? You calling a dog, Rash? I haven't seen any around. Unless one arrived with the chickens."

"Ren," Ava whispers. "You're not supposed to talk to the crew."

"Then maybe they shouldn't whistle at us."

"It was supposed to be a subtle hint." Rash has lowered the camera and fiddles with one of the dials. The cameras are actually smaller than I expected. I wish this would make them seem less appalling but it doesn't. "I was just reminding you to stay on track. Any mention of Gary or the show and certainly any direct conversation with the crew will need to be edited out."

Edited out. Of course. Reality television, what an absurd contradiction.

"Sorry," I grumble. "I know I'm supposed to pretend this is real life."

"It *is* real life," argues Ava as she lifts Alden out of the high chair. The little boy lays his head on his mother's shoulder and gives me a winning smile, squeezing my heart in a little spasm. For his sake, I've got to keep up appearances.

"You'll get used to it," Rash promises. He removes a white square of cloth from his back pocket, rubs it across the camera lens and resettles it on his shoulder. "Hey Ren, the others have already given their fifteen minutes in the Blue Room. You want to get this out of the way now?"

The Blue Room is an appendage to the original house. It juts out of the back like a square hump and spoils the sensible footprint of Russ Savage's architectural design. It had been Lita's project, a lavish guest bathroom that August tiredly agreed to build and never finished because there was no money. Now it's been refashioned into a confessional booth of sorts, with sea-colored walls and neutral Pottery Barn furniture to lounge on while pouring out the contents of your heart. Of course you understand before you start talking that everything you say will be appropriately modified for the show's needs.

"Why the hell not?" I grumble.

"Camera's all set up in there. Just switch it on when you're ready and answer the questions as best you can."

"What questions?"

Rash or Cate Camp or someone on the Born Savages payroll must have explained it to me already. Nevertheless, Rash patiently explains again. Every week there will be a different list of questions that we are supposed to address during our Blue Room interview. We may choose a crew member to be present for prompts or we can sit there and monologue it all the way. For the life of me I cannot picture my brothers engaging in long winded monologues but apparently everyone's finished their weekly interview except me.

Suddenly I'm eager to get this first hurdle over with so I spill out the rest of my coffee, plant a kiss on my little nephew's forehead and head down the hall. Before I go I wave out the window to Bree. She doesn't see me. She's trying to gracefully wrench her heel out of the mud while a chicken pecks at her lime green toenails.

The Blue Room smells, strongly, oppressively, of freesia. One quick glance around and I see the culprits; a cluster of of those benign jelly-like air fresheners that gradually dry up and wither into a hard crust. It's an unpleasant odor to me because it reminds me of Lita. Her signature scent was an expensive freesia-based perfume and she always wore too goddamn much of it.   I grab the air fresheners in a hug and and chuck them out the door into the hallway before settling into a wide papasan chair. I feel like I'm sitting in a cereal bowl.

There is a laminated piece of paper sharing a table with a camera. I nearly topple out of the papasan chair as I reach for it.   Silently I scan the list of questions. There are five of them and most don't seem so bad.

What was it like growing up in a famous family?

How do you feel about returning to your childhood home?

How would you describe your relationship with each of your siblings?

What was your life like immediately prior to returning to Atlantis Star?

What is the biggest regret of your life?

Surprisingly, talking is easy.   I don't really mind that there's surely some dude holed up in front of a screen somewhere, absorbing every word I say. I've spent my life grappling with my family's legacy and it's almost a relief to say the words. I know there are a lot of people who would roll their eyes over the complaints of a so-called privileged little rich girl but there are a lot of people who don't know shit. They can assume whatever the hell they want. I'm here for the sake of my family. If anyone needs to despise me, or all of us, for the spectacle we're making, then so be it.

It's not until I reach the final question that I find myself stumbling. I repeat it out loud.

"What is the biggest regret of my life?"

He's there, unbidden, unwanted, and my tongue loses the will to function. For a long time I had nursed a secret fantasy that he would find me. The fantasy never got any further than that. How could it? I'd made it cruelly clear that I never wanted to see him again. For all I know he isn't even alive. He left here a penniless, furious boy. The world doesn't have patience for a boy like that.

In the end I leave the question unanswered. Better people than me have tried to put words to the agony of lost love. They usually fail.

After rolling out of the papasan chair and switching the camera off, I stand in the center of the Blue Room for a moment, listening to the silence. Somewhere in the distance I hear the bark of my brother Monty's voice, then the burst of a car horn. I don't especially want to leave the Blue Room. The remainder of the day yawns in front of me like a blank canvas I'm expected to populate one molecule at a time. Not for the first time I wonder what will happen if Gary and friends fail to extract their pound of tabloid flesh. After all, a bunch of wayward siblings wandering around a former movie set and trying to think of things to say to one another doesn't make for compelling programming, no matter whose blood runs through their veins. Just a little while ago Ava had argued with me that this is real life, but people won't tune in for tedious breakfast exchanges or to watch Brigitte skipping around with chickens. They want shouting and hair pulling, scandal and sex.

It's kind of funny to think of your daily life turning into channel surf bait. Picture some bored married couple lounging on opposite ends of a faux leather couch and flipping channels to find a distraction from the fact that they'd rather do just about anything than have sex with each other. Maybe if there's nothing on television one will wander into the bathroom, iPad in lap, playing Free Cell on an endless loop while sitting on the toilet while the other one composes a completely fictitious Facebook post.

I don't know how much time I've been sitting here in the Blue Room. There's no clock. Eventually someone will be obliged to come hunt me down so I decide to save them the trouble.

The hallway is quiet. There are three bedrooms in the old house. I've got one and my sisters have the other two. I heard from Brigitte that during the planning phase of the show there were plans to add a few rooms on to the house but Spence had a fit and wouldn't cooperate. Apparently Gary knows when to pick his battles because he gave up on that one. Spence was gallant enough to give me his bedroom and he's decamped to our father's old paneled study. Monty could spare one of the closet-sized rooms in the old caretaker's place, but he and Spence still don't mesh well together so it's probably better if they stay apart.

After wandering around the house, nearly tripping over another stupid cameraman, and feeling like the walls of the brick house are pushing inward, I step outside into the yard. The sunlight is harsher than a tanning lamp. A fat brown chicken darts in my direction and collides with my legs, causing me to unleash a shrill yelp and jump back about six feet.

"Jesus," Spencer scolds as he stalks past with a saddle slung over a wide shoulder. "You girls will jump at the sight of your own damn shadow."

"Sorry," I mumble, "I'm not accustomed to being assaulted by poultry."

My brother pauses, looks me up and down with the same inscrutable gaze that he was born with. When Spencer looks your way you can't help but feel vaguely inadequate. It's annoying. I don't really need anyone's help to feel inadequate.

I roll my eyes at his silence. "Good morning to you too, little brother."

He issues a Spenceresque grunt and loses interest in both me and the livestock.

"Hey!" I have to trot a little to catch up to him.

He turns around and waits.

"Uh, you need any help?"

There's no expression on his face. I'm sure I'm boring him. "With what?"

I resist the urge to lean over and unleash an ear-splitting shriek right in his face, just to see whether it's possible to rattle his cool cowboy composure at all.

"I don't know, anything. Sponging off the horses? Shoveling manure?"

"Nah," he turns away. "I've got it covered."

"Spence!" I shout. I want to ask him not to leave me here in the dusty yard with nothing to do. Ava can keep herself busy with the baby. Brigitte is surely off somewhere coordinating her next staged camera appearance. I don't want to think about what Monty is doing because it's probably disgusting. I've got to find *something* to keep busy.

"Can you rebuild an engine?" Spencer asks.

"Huh?"

"I've got a '75 Mustang in the barn."

"Oh. Why?"

"Restoration project. The owner lives in Phoenix, was a friend of August's. Which I'm sure is why he sought me out. Lord knows there are closer places he could have gone." The saddle on Spence's shoulder is thick, expensive. It looks heavy. He doesn't even shift his weight though. He holds it there casually as if it's a wad of cotton.

I fall in beside him and he resumes walking to the barn. "Can't help you with that," I say. "But I need to do something." I lower my voice, hoping that maybe the mic doesn't pick up everything, then figuring it doesn't matter anyway. "Please, Spence."

Spencer walks in long strides. The soles of his leather boots make rhythmic crunching sounds in the dirt. At first glance he's not as striking as Monty but there's a rugged surety about him. I've seen the way women drool when he's around. Spence isn't one for relationships though. That might be the only thing he has in common with Monty. He does whatever he wants and shrugs over the fallout. He's a born loner.

"If you want to clean out the stall I'm fine with that."

"Good," I breathe, oddly relieved to be granted permission to mop up horse crap. "What about that?" I point at a tiny red house sitting in the middle of the yard. It sits several feet above the ground on raised wooden stilts and a plank runs from the ground to the cutout door.

Spence curses and glares at the thing. "Chicken coop. They dumped it here with those fucking birds. Pain in the ass to keep chickens alive out here. Now I've got to enclose the damn thing with barbed wire or else the coyotes will be rolling in a bloodbath an hour after sundown."

The chickens, unaware as to the precarious nature of their fate, bob around the yard and peck and the dirt.

"I can help," I offer.

"Maybe," my brother answers.

Spence slides open the barn door and I'm met with a breath of cool, musty air flavored with just a hint of shit. It's a nice barn, as barns go. Spence razed the dilapidated structure that had been eroding since the mid fifties. He built something sturdier and more functional in its place. No one would ever accuse the boxy structure of being aesthetic but it's not supposed to be.   There is wall separating the attached garage where Spence works on cars to pay the bills. Out of the four simple stalls on the other side, three are occupied. There is the soft rumble of an exhaling animal to my left and I'm nudged by a large brown nose.

Spencer heaves the saddle from his arms and holds out a wide palm. "Easy, girl. Easy there, Pet."

"Pet?" I squint in the darkness at the gentle brown mare. "This isn't the same horse."

"Nope."

"But you gave her the same name."

"Yup."

I nod in toward the horse in the neighboring stall. "His name Pet too?"

"No."

Spencer doesn't seem like he's in the mood to talk, which is pretty well par for the course. Words and Spencer have never gotten along real well.

I grab a wide broom off the wall and start sweeping the floor in front of the stalls, even though there's nothing much on the floor for me to sweep. Out of the corner of my eye I see Rash creep silently through the door, camera in hand. I'm startled to realize there are at least three other cameras mounted in the beams of the barn. For a few seconds I'd forgotten about them.

"How are ya, Ren?" Spence asks and he gives me a frank look.

I swallow. "I can't complain."

"You could. But you won't."

"What does that mean?"

"I didn't think you'd show up. I really didn't. Figured this place was full of too many ghosts for you."

"I can handle the ghosts of Savages past."

"All of them?" Spence has turned his face away and I'm not sure I heard him right.

"What?"

He looks me in the eye. "You heard me."

I lower my head. "I did. It's time I got around to thanking you for what you did that night."

"I didn't do nothing. So don't thank me."

A long, silent moment passes and then Spence produces carrots for the horses. Silently he hands a few over, watching as I offer them to the animals.

"And how are you, Spence? I worry about you out here you know."

"I know. You shouldn't."

"Do you have a girl?"

"Whenever I need one."

The earlier gloom has passed and I laugh. Spencer isn't bragging. He just tells the truth and doesn't care what anyone thinks about it, not unlike Montgomery in that way. Both of my brothers are hard characters. At this point they might get along if either of them decided to give a half ass effort. Perhaps that's one thing that will wind up coming out of these odd circumstances. Maybe it will bring us together.

Or tear us apart.

Spencer soothes the horses for a few more minutes and then retreats into the garage. After sweeping up the stalls, refilling the horse troughs and straightening some odds and ends I can't think of anything else to do in here. Despite the fact that there's sweat trickling down my back and a gritty sensation all over my skin, I feel good. There's a certain satisfaction that comes with work, any work. Now if I only I can spend the next eight weeks sweeping out the barn, I might make it through all this.

Spence has his head in the guts of a car and I don't want to disturb him. The sun is hotter than it was when I ducked into the barn. I wish I had some sunglasses as I briskly cover the distance between the barn and the brothel. There's no answer on Monty's door, meaning he's either sleeping something off or he's out somewhere searching for trouble.

After giving up on Monty and walking around the south side of the property, I pause at the ruins of a rose garden once kept by my grandmother. Hell only knows how she managed to keep delicate roses blooming in a fierce climate like this or why she would even have bothered when she and her husband only averaged a few months out of the year here, but she did. I've seen the pictures. Enormous lemon-colored roses that looked as if they were painted with a Technicolor brush.

My nephew is asleep on a leather chair in the living room, curled up like a cat with a small stuffed dog wedged in the crook of an elbow. He's precious, this little boy. I need to make an effort to spend more time with him. I touch his sweet face as I pass by.

I hear Brigitte's voice coming from somewhere, echoing throughout the narrow hallways. She's having a biting argument with someone via speaker phone, interrupting every six seconds to talk over the guy on the other end. The man she's yelling at sounds as if he's had enough of her. Brigitte has a flair for provoking moods like that.

Ava is softly at my side before I hear her coming.

"Did Monty take off?"

"I don't know, did he?" she wrinkles her nose. "I thought I heard an engine gunning a little while ago so it's possible. Where have you been?"

"Capering around in the manure with Spence."

"Spence likes manure."

"Of course he does. Manure doesn't talk back."

Ava laughs lightly and brushes a hand across her sleeping son's cheek. Alden's father was cut from the same cloth we were. Child of celebrities, privileged and fucked up since birth. He'd already been hitting the party scene pretty hard when he and Ava hooked up. Costars on a short-lived family sitcom, they were bad for each other; a wild and entitled pair who behaved as rowdily as they pleased. The paparazzi had a field day with them partying all over Hollywood and Lita, goddamn her, encouraged it. Of course it couldn't last. All Ava got out of it was a broken heart and early motherhood. She told me once what Lita had demanded upon the news of her pregnancy. *"Get rid of it."* Ava refused. After that Lita was pretty well done with her. She'd been done with me for a long time already.

Ava follows me when I head to the kitchen. My hands are dirty. All I can find in the way of soap is an ancient trial sized bottle of dishwashing liquid. It takes me a full minute to realize there's a crew member in the room. It's Elton, the guy Monty apparently had a rough time with yesterday. He doesn't make a sound. He's just parked there in a corner, like an appliance. For all I know he's been glued to the wall.

"You know," says Ava brightly, "I think it would be fun to have a nice family dinner tonight."

"You do?"

Somewhere there are families who habitually sit down together at a certain hour and avoid eye contact as they slice their way into fried pork chops. At least I think there are. I've never actually seen one. Savages don't do sit down dinners. When we were kids we would just kind of forage handfuls of cereal or a bag of chips from the pantry because Lita couldn't even boil water. Even when I learned to cook, meals were somewhat haphazard because no one could seem to sit down in the same place at once.

Ava is rooting around in the cabinets, which are magically stocked with things that seem to puzzle her.

"What do you do with tomato paste?" she asks.

"Glue bananas together," I say but she doesn't seem to hear me.

"I'll make spaghetti," announces my sister loudly, as she grabs some cans and a box of pasta.

I don't buy it. Sure, Ava's calmed down a lot since her party days but she doesn't fool anyone as the domestic type. Last time I visited her she agonized over how to puree carrots for Alden's dinner. Someone must have put the idea in her head that all of us squished around a table for an hour might light some fireworks.

When I open the refrigerator I am surprised to see it as well stocked as most restaurants. No way was that Spence's doing.

"You know," I say, "I bet it wouldn't be too tough to grill up some of those steaks later."

Ava looks down at the ingredients in her hands, sets them on the counter and twirls a troubled finger around a strand of hair. "Maybe I could make a salad or something."

I close the fridge. "I love salad."

Not true. I'm a meat lover, always will be. A bowl of green stuff is about as desirable to me as an enema.

Ava's looking kind of desperate though. I understand. We have instructions. We're supposed to keep things interesting. And if that means making asses out of ourselves in the kitchen and then suffering through an uncomfortable family meal then so be it. My sister looks nervous and for a second I just want to hug her and tell her everything will be all right. My other sister is screaming for someone to go fuck himself and the noise causes Alden to start howling for his mother.

Ava rushes back to the living room and when I get there a minute later she's got her little boy in her arms, rocking him back and forth while his small hands grip her shoulders. The sight of them, mother and son, makes my heart hurt a little.

When have I ever loved anyone like that? Have I ever really loved anyone at all?

Of course, I love my brothers and sisters. The affection I had for my father seems vague at this point. Lita was impossible to love.

And beyond that...friendships weren't strong, the relationships short and unfulfilling. I've said them before, the words. I've said "I love you" and meant it completely. But that was a long time ago, when I was someone different.

I try to picture what he would look like now. He was nearly a grown man when I knew him. His arms, he had the strongest arms. Once they carried me a distance that had to be well beyond a mile.

Spence had commented on the ghosts here, my ghosts in particular. My brother is perceptive. Or perhaps I just wear my heart on my sleeve. Oscar stays inside my head whether I want him there or not.

I need some air, even if it's satanically hot air. There's a knotty wooden bench on the shallow front porch and once I'm outside I plop down onto it uncomfortably. I know I'm being watched.

The chickens run loose all over the yard. I picture unseen predators nearby, waiting for the cover of darkness as the brainless birds bob their heads and peck at the dirt. Suddenly a few of them squawk and some feathers fly loose.

A rather shabby pickup truck rolls into the yard and comes to an abrupt halt twenty feet away. I'm not especially interested in who's in there. It's probably someone from the crew, or maybe Monty. The door opens and a man emerges. He's broad-shouldered and well built; tall, with a shock of black hair. For a moment I don't feel a shred of recognition. Then a buzzing begins at the base of my skull and zooms through my entire body.

"Holy shit," says a voice I recognize as mine. Somehow I'm standing even though I can't feel my feet. I can't feel anything.

He's nothing but casual as he steps from the far side of the truck. He sees me but doesn't seem surprised.

I, on the other hand, am quite surprised. Even though I've fantasized about this meeting six thousand times I'm still stunned. I shouldn't have been.

"Loren," he says and his voice cuts me in half. He knows it. His grin is as devastating as it ever was. I can see in an instant that he's both different and the same. His mouth still tilts into a mocking smile automatically.

But there's a wide chasm of time between us. Somewhere in that deep gulf we went from being soul mates to being strangers. I know nothing about the way this man's body would feel under my hands. Whatever agonies he endured after the terrible night he left, the night I coldly *ordered* him to leave, belong to him alone.

"Oscar," I whisper. I notice the way he stops walking, and the way his face freezes. Maybe he has an entirely new identity and the sound of the old one is unpleasant. Or maybe he's hardened by the sound of my voice. It's probably easy for him to hate me. This could be the start of some elaborate revenge. Obviously it's no coincidence that he's here now. While I've been wondering how I'm going to make cleaning horseshit look interesting for two months, Gary Vogel, knowing more than he ever hinted at, was scheming behind the scenes, ready to drop a bombshell. The only demand I'd ever uttered was 'No Lita'. I should have figured out what else was up for grabs.

"I go by Oz now," he says, rather tersely.

The cameras are here, ingesting every second. I have to say something. I have to do something. I have to *not* fall to my knees or run into his arms. Especially because he's done nothing to invite me there.

"Welcome home," I finally manage to say and it sounds strange to me because this was never home, not really. It's just a place. That's all it ever was. It only matters because of the things that happened here.

Oscar Savage stares at me from ten feet away. He looks me over shrewdly and I wonder if he sees more than a pathetic woman who has signed her private life away.

"Are you staying?" I ask him, clasping my hands behind my back to keep them from trembling.

"I am," he answers and there's an edge to the words, like he's daring me to argue, which I don't plan on doing. He watches me, all six foot two inches of bristling, resolute maleness.

I couldn't move him if I tried.

My mind scrambles to come up with more words, any words, to fill the void. Oscar does nothing to ease the tension. He doesn't even seem to notice that we are being filmed.

There's nothing separating us besides five years of silence that began with a terrible night. So many details remain lost to me, intentionally lost, because I couldn't stand remembering what it felt like to be in love. All I know is that for a little while we were together.

I know it was powerful, tumultuous, intense.

And then it was gone.

He was gone.

I've been keeping all of it buried for so long I don't know how to sort through it now. But I'll have no choice because here stands Oscar Savage, demanding either vengeance or acknowledgement. He's not going to give me a choice about it so I'd better start figuring a few things out.

After all, somewhere in all that buried history is the truth.

CHAPTER ELEVEN

Five Years Ago: Part 2

It seems like hours have gone by and still she waits for the whistle. Never for a second does she doubt it will come. That would mean doubting him.

Earlier tonight her mother was waiting for her when she ran, breathless and disheveled, through the front door. Lita was perched on the edge of an enormous chair backed with ghoulish ivory tusks, a relic from the days of Rex Savage, when people didn't know any better about much of anything. It certainly never occurred to them that massacring a majestic animal for a few trophies was wrong. Ren has always hated that chair.

Lita was tapping her thin fingers on the ivory arm. Dark and gray roots showed through her blonde hair. She made no secret of despising her husband for moving the family out here, for despising her children for failing to lift her out of these circumstances. She observed Ren with a silent sort of disgust before lighting a cigarette. When she decided to speak her words were like bullets. "You better goddamn well watch yourself, girl."

"Of course, Lita. It would never have occurred to me to watch my step if you didn't order it," Ren answered with eye-rolling sarcasm.

She knew how it irked Lita Savage to hear her children call her by her first name. Of course all five of them did it.

After Ren and her mother exchanged a tense look, one of ten thousand such moments of tension over the past seventeen years, Ren hurried out of the room. The air was poisonous wherever Lita was and Ren didn't want her mood spoiled. She was still on a high from being with Oscar.

Now, lying in the dark and waiting to hear something from him, it seems impossible that he's been in her life for less than a month. She can't remember what it was like to spend a day without him in her world. Ren doesn't think of herself as romantic. She's not all silly and swoony like her sisters. Boys say nice things to get what they want and every now and then she lets one of them kiss her. Oscar, on the other hand, still hasn't tried a damn thing. She doesn't know how to ask him to.

There it is. The sound begins low and ends on a high note. Ren smiles and goes to the window.

"Where the hell are you going?" Brigitte hisses from her bed.

Since August still hasn't gotten around to cleaning out his parents' ancient crap from the extra rooms, Ren gets to be stuck in the smallest bedroom with her two sisters. The three beds take up so much room it's tough to walk across the floor without bumping into a freaking mattress. As Bree complains at least once a day, *"This sure as shit ain't the lifestyles of the rich and famous."*

"Can't sleep," Ren hisses back. "I'm just gonna go up to the brothel and see what Monty's up to."

"Bullshit," Brigitte answers, a little too loudly. Ava stirs in her sleep and lets out a catlike whine. Bree lowers her voice. Slightly. "Monty's either out getting busy with some local airhead or else he's drunk on that beer he stole from the Consequences Convenience Store yesterday."

Right outside the window, Oz lets out another whistle.

Brigitte hears. She vaults out of bed and pads over barefoot, pressing her face to the window. But Bree always takes her contact lenses out before bed and Ren knows she can't see anything out there.

"Who's that?" Bree frowns into the darkness.

"An owl."

"Like hell."

Ava suddenly sits up in bed. She must have been just pretending to sleep. She sighs and uses a rare serious tone. "Careful, Ren. I mean it. Lita's hair is already standing on end. I heard her this afternoon, whining to Dad about Oscar."

Ren feels uneasy. "What was she saying?"

"That Aunt Mina better haul her saggy ass back here and retrieve her hellraising little thug."

Ren exhales, relaxing. "Oscar hasn't exactly raised hell. She must be confusing him with Monty."

Bree grunts and crosses her arms. She starts chewing on a fingernail. "She's afraid. Lita, I mean. I'm not sure why. Maybe she thinks you'll wind up bearing Oscar Savage's love child and tarnishing the family name."

"More than it's already tarnished," Ava agrees.

Ren isn't especially moved by her mother's distress. "She's just making noise because she's got nothing better to complain about at the moment. Lita still thinks one or more of us will be her meal ticket back to Hollywood. To her, any exposure is good exposure."

Brigitte sighs as if she's being forced to explain physics to a five-year-old. "Unless it involves the sexcapades of two kids, both with the last name of Savage. Get a clue, Loren. The wrong people get wind of this and we'll look even shittier than we already do. I can see the headlines: Deranged Famous Family Now Inbreeding."

"That's messed up, Bree. We're not even really related for crying out loud."

"You think that will matter in the realm of the tabloids?"

Ren turns away, troubled. Brigitte may seem like a spoiled brat most of the time but every once in a while she manages to hit the nail on the head. Ren doesn't have an answer for her. She's had enough of her sisters for now. Oscar is out there waiting in the darkness, waiting.

"We're just friends," she says, flinging open the window.

"Just friends," repeats Brigitte in a mocking singsong before hopping back to her own bed.

"Just friends," parrots Ava with a yawn and then rolls back under the covers.

Ren is still wearing the same cutoff shorts she's worn all day. But she exchanged her loose button down shirt for a form-fitting tee. The night air smells of rain. Miles to the east the mountains are masked by darkness, an absolute kind of darkness with no moon, no stars. A flash of lighting parries with a groan of thunder as a summer storm approaches.

Oscar is closer than she thought. He catches her as she stumbles on her way out the window. His strong hands linger on her waist longer than they need to and his breath is close to her ear.

"Thought you'd probably be asleep by now."

"No you didn't or you would have come."

"I'd have come anyway, Ren."

They are inches apart and she can't breathe. Is this how it happens for every girl? There's an ache that's nearly painful, something she can't solve by herself and doesn't even know how to talk about. Oscar pushes a few strands of hair from her forehead. They'd spent the day together, as they'd been spending every day together, but it isn't enough. They are like opposing magnetic ends, always finding their way to the same space in the dreary landscape of Atlantis.

Today August had decided he needed some tools and the town of Consequences was the nearest place to shop. Lately the Savage patriarch had become something of a hermit, adopting a scraggly beard and spending most of his time either up in the stifling attic or out in the old barn with Spencer. The barn was built as a set prop; it was never meant to be a true barn and it was in desperate need of a makeover if it was going to start housing more animals like August wanted. He'd hatched some kind of half-baked scheme for boarding horses. Ren didn't pay much attention to the details. Of course Lita had nothing but horror for the whole endeavor.

Spencer tagged along with them this afternoon. Ren didn't mind because Spencer wasn't in the habit of taking an interest in other people. Her younger brother lounged in the bed of the pickup the entire time and stared up at the sky thinking inscrutable Spencer-type things that probably involved being twenty miles away from the nearest human being. She'd let Oscar drive. Within two days after his arrival, Ren had taught Oscar to drive a stick shift and he was actually more comfortable behind the wheel of the old clunker than Ren was. Several times his smooth fingertips grazed the skin of her thigh as he reached for the stick. Too often to be wholly accidental. She didn't flinch. She didn't encourage him either.

Once they were in town, Spencer disappeared into the hardware store. There was a vending machine by the gas station on Central Street where they grabbed some cold sodas and chips. Ren and Oscar wandered around, licking their cheese-covered fingers and laughing together with sticky mouths, not aware that anyone else even existed. For all they knew the entire populace of Consequences had been reduced to ash by some cosmic apocalypse. They sat on the pickup tailgate, side by side with their hips touching while Oscar talked in an excited voice about caves.

Hanging out in the back of a pickup truck in some small town that didn't even warrant a map dot, beside the boy she was falling in love with, Ren felt as far away from Hollywood as she could get. It was a good feeling.

Then a woman resembling a muskrat, tiny and matted, stopped right in front of them. She smelled like she'd perfumed herself with nicotine.

"You're one of those Savage girls," she said in a monotone that hinted at nothing.

"I am," Ren answered warily. Long accustomed to being known for *what* she was - or rather what her family was - than *who* she was, she was prepared to be annoyed. Ever since they'd moved out here to Atlantis they'd been treated with polite suspicion by most of the locals. Most had no memory of Rex Savage or of the golden era of cinema that briefly made the area a place of interest. They only knew a bedraggled family with a famous name had moved into their midst.

The woman shifted her gaze to Oscar. "But you're not one of them boys, are you?"

"He's not my brother," Ren blurted and blushed, irritated with herself for explaining anything to this prying stranger.

"I'm not her brother," Oscar confirmed in an amused voice and he slung a casual arm around Ren's shoulders. "I'm her cousin."

The woman had no more questions after that. She pursed her bloodless lips together and ducked into a paint store.

"Think we scandalized her without even trying," Oscar laughed.

Ren had wished he would keep his arm around her. But he removed it as soon as the woman was gone.

Now though, in the darkness with nothing but the yips of coyotes in their midst, there's something about the thickness of his breathing and the way his hand squeezes her shoulder. Like he wants more and he's considering taking it.

"Come with me," he whispers, grabbing her hand.

Their steps are soundless as the thunder drowns out everything but its own complaints. When there's a lull in the rumbling Ren hears music; crashing, angry music from another era.

"Monty." Oscar nods in the direction of the brothel.

Out of the night comes the brief, piercing howl of female laughter.

"Sounds like he has company."

Oscar snorts. "That he does. And he's sure as hell not shy about keeping it in the bedroom. Or in his pants for that matter."

Ren feels her face getting hot. "A little TMI, dude."

"Believe me, not as much TMI as I've suffered tonight."

"Gross. Just do me one favor, Oscar, and keep it to yourself."

He laughs, nudges her shoulder. He's teasing now, flirting. "I've been keeping *everything* to myself, Loren."

"What does that mean?" She knows what it means.

He raises his strong arms toward the sky and stretches. "It means this whole goddamn desert stay has been one long drought."

This is what he does, this flirty banter that never ends with anything more than handholding. Sometimes Ren thinks he's testing her. Other times she thinks he's holding himself back for another reason, a vague sense of honor or a funny feeling that there's a line that shouldn't be crossed.

Or maybe he just thinks she's ugly.

Ren withdraws her hand, tosses her hair. The storm has receded, passing them by after all. They are beyond Atlantis now. It's a bad idea. You never know what lurks in the desert brush and none of it will announce itself in the darkness. It's the one thing August always warns them about.

"A drought, huh?"

"Yeah. At least I've got my blue balls to keep me company."

Ren sniffs, deciding she's a little insulted. "All those fancy schools and they skimp on etiquette lessons. Mina might be upset when she realizes she didn't get her money's worth."

"What's that mean?"

"Means you talk like a man whore sometimes."

Oscar stops walking. He allows a long minute to pass before speaking. "Thought you figured a few things out about me already. Being a gentleman doesn't come naturally to me, Ren."

"Then don't be one."

She tosses the words off frivolously. When he grabs her wrist it's a shock.

"Stop," he warns. His tone says he's not kidding anymore.

She's defiant. "Why?"

He's closer now. There's a sweet smell on his breath and she recognizes it. Beer. He must have snagged a can or two from Monty. He's got her other wrist and if he moves an inch closer their bodies will press together. He's so much bigger than her, so much stronger. Her head begins to swim.

"Because," he snarls, "if I kiss you, Loren, there's no fucking way I'm going to stop."

He says it like he can't imagine anything worse.

She shakes her hand loose from his grip and reaches for him, touches his face. He turns his head away and spits a curse, something in another language that she doesn't recognize. The humiliation stings.

Ren tears away from him and begins stalking back to the house. All their teasing during the long, hot days of the last month and they've never fought. They've also never kissed. What kind of an idiot is she anyway? They're not falling in love. They are just two bored kids who can't find anyone else around worth talking to. Even if they were to mess around it wouldn't mean shit. Oscar has told her a few things about himself already, about all the girls. To him, she would just be another one. Forgettable.

Oscar doesn't let her get far. He catches her from behind and his arms wind around her body, holding her tight against his hard chest.

"Let me go." She kicks at him.

"Why the hell are you acting like this?"

"Look, I feel like enough of a jackass already. Just leave me alone and maybe Monty can find you a friend to help end your fucking *drought.*"

He spins her around. Roughly. His hands are on her face and then his fingers are all wound up in her long dark hair. He's forcing her to look at him even though there's no light in the sky and she can hardly see his face.

"Damn you, Ren! I can't just treat you like any girl. You know how many there've been? You don't know because I don't even know. Not one of them has meant a thing to me except a good time. I've been bouncing around from place to fucking place since I can remember. I don't even have real friends and the only family I have is a woman who forgets who I am most of the time."

He coughs at the end but relaxes his hold on her. Ren reaches up, finds his lips with her fingers, tracing them.

"I'm your friend," she whispers. "I'm your family."

A small groan rips out of his throat. He kisses her. He's not soft or hesitant like the few other boys she's kissed. All she can think is *my god, my god, my god.* She would sink right into the desert floor if he wasn't holding her up. This, she knows, is how a kiss should be. This is the one she'll compare all others to for the rest of her life.

A sonic boom of thunder cuts loose overhead and the sky opens up. The storm that had seemed to roll back into the Harquehalas has returned with a vengeance. They are soaked to the skin within seconds but their mouths stay glued together. It seems nothing can conquer the power of that kiss. It is cosmic, it is limitless.

Then a streak of lightning lights up a mesquite tree only a few yards away. The feathery branches are briefly lit by a burst of fire and then just as suddenly the flame is drowned by the rain.

The kiss is over. Oscar grabs her hand and they run all the way back to the house. There's a narrow patio overhang along the south side of the building and they huddle beneath it but everything is all right because she's in his arms.

"You should go in," he sighs, running his lips along her neck.

"I will." It's a weak promise. She has no desire to go anywhere.

"Loren." God, her name never sounded as good as it does coming from his mouth. He gently kisses her forehead, her eyelids. "This changes everything you know."

"I know."

"There's no going back. No matter what."

"I don't want to go back, Oscar," she promises, hugging him stubbornly. She doesn't even know what it means. She doesn't know what she's saying. She only knows that she needs him. She feels lightheaded and needs to breathe deeply before she can speak. The words aren't as hard to say as she thought they'd be.

"I lied from the beginning," she whispers. "I don't want to be just friends. I never did."

He strokes her hair. She hears the smile in his voice. "Good."

CHAPTER TWELVE

OZ

Loren Savage was never as tough as she pretended to be. I'd figured that out less than five minutes after meeting her. Beneath that know-it-all shell was a vulnerable girl just aching to be loved.

Which I did. Goddammit, I did. Not that it mattered when the world caught fire and a choice was laid at her feet. I don't know what she really believed or didn't believe. But she turned her back and cowered behind her train wreck of a family.

And now...

I don't know who the hell she is. I just know that the second she sees me she looks like all the blood in her body went somewhere else and she might tip over.

Maybe if she does fall over I will catch her.

Maybe I won't.

Some perverse part of me is glad to see the alarm in her eyes. She probably thinks I'm just here to fuck things up with her stupid show. Ren glances sideways at a creeping cameraman and then looks back at me with what seems like silent pleading.

Yeah, I know they're there, sweetheart. If you think I give a damn you've got another thing coming.

I'm pretty good at playing it cool when it suits me and right now it suits me to act like I'm just here for shits and giggles.

"Are you staying?" she asks.

The tremor in her voice does something to me and it crosses my mind that I ought to cut the crap and just go to her. If I could touch her, just once, I'd know right away whether or not I'm wasting my time. Problem is, I'm not ready to face it if that's the case. I've upended my simple, solitary life to come out here and expose myself to the world.

For her.

I'm just not ready to let her know that.

"I am," I answer and she tiredly nods like she was expecting that answer but hoping for another one.

There's no time to say anything else because the most irritating feline shriek in the world crushes all the conversation.

"Oh. My. GOD!" it says as its owner flies out of the house in a cloud of red hair and skin. "Oscar Savage! We thought you were dead!"

It's Brigitte, the youngest and most obnoxious of the Savage siblings. I didn't like her five years ago and I don't like her now, especially not when she wraps her ropy arms around my neck and makes me choke on her perfume. She detaches herself after a quarter of a second and starts howling about how she absolutely can't believe it and oh my god she's so glad I'm not dead and oh my god she can't believe that the earth is really round and that I'm still walking around on it.

Ren remains silent, rooted to the front porch, although I notice she has shifted her attention from me. She's now glaring at her sister with angry suspicion. She should. After all, someone told that Vogel character more than he ever had a right to know and by the look on her face, that someone sure as hell wasn't Ren.

"Hey there, Oscar," says a more timid voice. It belongs to a stacked blonde holding a little kid.

I don't know her. I wave half-heartedly. Never mind, I do know her. It's Ren's other sister, the one who was always walking around with her teenage tits hanging out and waiting for someone to notice them.

"Hey, Ava." I greet her with a smile because I don't remember her being awful. Kind of lonely and needy but generally a good kid. The only ones in this ridiculous family I could stand to be in the same room with for five minutes were Ava and her twin brother, Spencer. And Ren of course. The rest of them were generally pains in the asses. Brigitte with her scheming seemed destined to be a carbon copy of her witchy mother. August kind of lost himself in his own hazy fantasies and generally couldn't hold a conversation. And Montgomery, Ren's older brother, always skulked around spoiling for a fight just for the sake of fighting, not because he gave a shit whether he won or not.

Once we've said our awkward hellos, things kind of come to a standstill. Ren disappears into the house without another word, Ava on her heels. Brigitte sighs and wanders purposefully toward the scenic backdrop for some meaningful modeling.

I would grab my bags out of the truck but no one ever gave me any hints about where I'll be staying. Atlantis looks pretty much the same as is ever did, a fake town that some rich guy bought as a souvenir. A sturdy-looking barn has replaced the dilapidated building that I remember. The brothel has crumbled a little more, the phony jail is more rusted, the church seems like it's one sigh away from pitching over into the dirt.

The only really nice building is the main house and it looks like someone has been keeping it up okay. But overall, Atlantis Star doesn't look like the kind of place anyone would brag about so once again I wonder about what kind of ideas that Vogel character has.

I still don't know what the hell the point of this show is. Was the whole pack of Savages lured out to this bad memory just to be made fun of? Gloated over? And are they all so goddamn desperate not to have to earn an honest living that they fell for it?

"Oz!" hails a voice and suddenly there's some middle aged woman with bouncy implants heads my way. She's not familiar so either she's part of the crew or some other long lost Savage.

I was right on the first count. Her name is Cate Camp and she's part of Team Gary. She fluffs her brassy blonde hair, describes her role here as something more than a director but less than a therapist, *Ha ha.*

She actually laughs just like that; *HAHA,* two staccato bursts of artificial personality. She's trying to get me to like her because someone in Reality Television School probably told her if she wins over the cast they'll be more likely to spill a thousand and one of their darkest secrets. Nothing about her interests me but I'm trying for minimal civility until I can figure a few things out.

So instead of silence or profanity I give her a series of one-word answers.

Cate Camp says, "You've traveled a long way."

I say, "Yes."

Cate Camp says, "And you haven't had any contact with the family at all these past five years."

"Yes."

"You spent a summer here and left shortly after the death of your adopted mother."

"Yes."

Cate Camp shows me her un-Botoxed frown lines. She's displeased with me. "From what I hear you left under bad circumstances."

"Yes."

Cate Camp goes for the throat. "And all the trouble was due to an inappropriate relationship with one or more members of the family."

Now I'm done answering her questions.

Cate Camp gets suddenly maternal, patting my arm lightly and lowering her voice even as she silently signals the nearest Camera Creep to get ready. "It has something to do with Loren, is that right? The tension was obvious between you two. She wasn't exactly dancing for joy when she saw you, now was she? No, she looked at you like you were the last man on earth she wanted to see. Oh Oz, nobody could blame you for whatever happened. You were just a kid. And they threw you out into the world like you were nothing, didn't they? After all, you're not really one of them. You're not; you know that. So tell us. Tell us *how that makes you feel.*"

What a fucking joke. She's going to have to be a lot more cunning than that to get a rise out of me. I act like she didn't say anything. I grab my duffel bag out of the truck and look around.

"So what are the sleeping arrangements here, boss?"

Frown lines etch themselves deeper into other frown lines. Cate Camp isn't good at her job. She has no patience for anyone who doesn't immediately cooperate with her. The frown lines would dissolve if I would punch a fist into my palm and spill my guts about everything that happened but I'm about as likely to do that as I am to start square dancing.

She points to a run down trailer-like structure. "Your remember your old quarters?"

"Yeah." I give no hint that I'm surprised. Of course they already know the details of that summer, *all* the details.

Cate Camp snaps her fingers at the Camera Creep so he'll follow me as I trudge off in the direction of the brothel, toward the little house that still sits behind it.

Gary Vogel has a hell of a lot of money backing him up. He could have set the show in posh California quarters. Or at the very least he could have sprinkled some of those resources over Atlantis Star to make the place slightly less dilapidated. But what the hell would be the fun in that? I have a bad feeling it's all intentional. Of course it is. There's nothing more American than a sordid tale of celebrity ruin.

The structure that squats behind the brothel is the old caretaker's house. It was all right when I stayed here. The air conditioner wasn't really enough to deal with the thin walls and living with Monty was like rooming with a wolverine. But other than that, it was fine. It actually doesn't look much different and a wave of nostalgia sweeps over me. I've passed through dozens of places in my life and rarely thought of any of them as home. Something about being back here leaves me feeling a little out of sorts though. I suppose I knew that would happen all along. If this place didn't mean a thing to me I wouldn't have come.

No one answers my polite knocks. There's a camera trained on me, of course, but I've already decided not to even think about that. After all, I have no intention of watching whatever kind of strange brew they turn into a so-called show.

The doorknob turns in my hand and since I don't feel like standing out here in the heat all day I have no qualms about going inside.

"Hello?" I call.

Someone spiffed up the inside of the place. I know Spencer lives at Atlantis full time but the leather couch, hipster wall prints and turquoise accents don't seem like things he would choose.

No one answers me but in a few seconds I can see I'm not alone. Well, I'm never alone now. The Camera Creep comes slithering through the doorway after me and I know there are fixed cameras installed all over the place. I was told that the crew tails us in shifts for about twelve hours a day and the fixed cameras pick up anything else that might be exciting. Maybe I should have asked Cate Camp if they're everywhere, even in the bathrooms, but then again maybe I'd rather not know. If someone really finds it interesting to watch me brushing my teeth and taking a shit, then we as a people have probably fallen off the evolutionary abyss.

It's not just the Camera Creep keeping me company. Not six feet in front of me is Montgomery Savage. He's sprawled in a chair. He's got no shirt on, a web of dark ink on his body and his pants are open. His bleary eyes try to shift into focus. Then they widen. "The fuck are you doin' here?"

"I'm not here," I say, dropping my bag. "You're dreaming."

Monty utters a grumpy string of curses and rolls out of the chair, finally straightening up and glaring at me like he's an angry bull and I'm standing here with a red blanket screaming 'Toro!' He's pretty ripped, more than he used to be, and it's obvious he's been roughed up by life. But I would bet that I could take him down if I needed to. I'd rather not though. We're not fucking teenagers anymore.

Luckily, Monty seems to settle down after a few seconds. He pats his pockets and finds a pack of cigarettes there, lighting up and looking me over coolly.

"Jesus," he says with a short, humorless laugh, "I wonder who else will come crawling out of the fucking woodwork."

"Yeah, I'm glad to see you too, Monty."

He puffs on his cigarette while I look around. Monty probably isn't going to make things any easier, or more pleasant. I'd rather just stay out of his way.

"So is there anyone else home?"

Monty shrugs. "Spence is jerking off in the creosote somewhere. The girls are probably in the big house."

"I saw them already."

He raises an eyebrow. "Is that so?"

I look him in the eye. "It is."

The last time I spoke to Monty Savage we had a difference of opinion. I thought he ought to mind his own goddamn business and he thought I needed to get acquainted with his fists. I wasn't about to be taken down by some Hollywood pretty boy no matter whose brother he was so I gave it right back to him, like I usually did. We both came out of the scuffle rather worse for the wear with no clear winner. He'd gotten in the last parting shot though.

"You go near my sister again and I'll fucking kill you."

A few hours after that all hell broke loose and whatever I'd thought I was to these people didn't matter. They were more than ready to toss me in the dumpster. Even Ren. Maybe she had her reasons but I've never understood how they could have led her to do what she did. People didn't connect the way we'd connected and then lose it all just like that.

Anyway, whatever else I have to say about Monty, he cares about his family in his own way. That's why I decide to hold my tongue and not fire back some snappy retort that would piss him off. If I'd ever had a sister I probably wouldn't like any guy who messed around with her either.

"I guess you can take the back room," Monty says, turning his back to me as he runs a hand through his black hair. "I wondered why someone got it all cleaned up. I guess I should have known."

"Thanks," I mutter and start to head down the narrow hallway.

"Hey, Oscar."

I turn around.

Monty Savage is giving me his best and most dangerous scowl. I have to admit it is effective. "If you're here to cause any trouble for her, you and me are gonna throw down."

I'm not in the mood to cave to him. Or to give any assurances. Let him stew for a while and wonder what I'm up to. So all I say is, "I expect we will."

It's the same room I stayed in five years ago. It's small and square and someone decorated it in retro southwestern style. I close the door in the face of the Camera Creep but I'm sure they have other ways to watch me.

Even though it's hotter outside than it is inside I crack open a window. There is all kinds of nervous energy running through me even though I get nervous about as often as I turn my head and cough.

Ren was obviously shaken by the sight of me. Part of me wants to go barreling into the big house right this minute and make her even more uncomfortable. Another part of me feels kind of sorry for the way her face paled and her hands trembled. I'll give her a little space, for now. But only for a little while.

Because I'm here. And she's going to have to deal with me whether she likes it or not.

CHAPTER THIRTEEN

REN

Ava chatters away about the gourmet spaghetti she's going to make for dinner even though dinner is hours away. She grabs mismatched pots out of the kitchen cabinets and let Alden smack them against the terra cotta tiles.

There is no mention of the fact that Oscar Savage has materialized. It should be a subject worth discussing even if she knows nothing about what happened between me and Oscar five years ago. And I'm sure she knows something. She's trying to distract me from the full tilt freak out that threatens to erupt.

"That sounds good," I tell my sister when she mentions driving into town for a bottle of wine. When I look up, Ava catches my eye and gives me a tiny smile of sympathy. She opens her mouth to say something but then glances at the nearby camera and shuts it.

I rub my eyes and see a medley of rainbow color. When I stop rubbing, I see his face. He's no longer just a painful memory spasm.

He's here.

He's right out in the yard talking to Cate fucking Camp, likely plotting the next shocking plot twist. At least it doesn't look like he's going to follow me into the house. For the time being anyway.

If Oscar had wanted to find me he could have found me long ago. I was never hiding.

Why now?

Of course I already know the answer. Oscar is here for the show. He's here because someone thought this would be a nice unseemly addition to the story. I'm sure he's being paid handsomely for showing up. With some bitterness, I think about how his arrival could not have been scripted better.

"Shit," I whisper, so softly it could be mistaken for a sigh.

Alden scurries over and drops a stainless steel pot in my lap. He offers me a delightfully impish toddler grin and announces, rather oddly, "Imma bat!"

Ava's still gathering kitchen implements and trying to hide the fact that she's furtively looking over my shoulder to see what's going on outside. Meanwhile, I'm at war with myself.

On one hand I want nothing so desperately as for Oscar Savage, Oz, or whatever he's decided to call himself now, to climb right back in his pickup truck and return to whatever pocket of the world burped him out. But then the other hand holds out a big stop sign. Because the second I saw him, some shriveled, long dormant piece of my heart swelled.

This is something I can't help. This is something that happens despite the fact that I know very well he's been paid off.

Ava's watching me worriedly and trying to corral her son as he starts galloping around the kitchen island carrying a wooden spoon. She looks like she's scouring her mind for something to say to me and I wish I could let her off the hook. Really though, we're not the sort of sisters who pour our hearts out to one another. And even if we were, I simply have nothing to say at the moment.

Then the heavy wooden front door swings open and a second later Brigitte comes flouncing in, all apple-cheeked and bright-eyed. Even though I know I shouldn't, even though I can see myself in my mind's eye already in a television promo clip grabbing my sister's arm in a vice-like grip and hissing in her face, I do it anyway. It's all I can do not to slap her when I demand, "What the *hell* have you done?"

She's startled, her face frozen in angelic innocence. If a cartoon balloon materialized above her head it would read *"Who, me??"*

"I haven't done anything, Ren," she pouts and lets her soft blue eyes fill with tears. She looks down at my fingers clamped on her arm, likely wondering what kind of mark will emerge on her delicate skin and how she can capitalize on it.

I let her go.

"Damn you," I choke out.

"Ren," whispers Ava with hurt bewilderment. She always has and always will defend Brigitte. Ava is not a good judge of character. Beyond her reputation as a hardcore party girl, she's really flighty and naive. But she doesn't have the kind of self-serving nature that our little sister does. She wouldn't have sold me out in exchange for a few close ups. And the boys wouldn't have blabbed about me and Oscar, not for any amount of money.

But all bets were off when it came to Bree. She might have inherited a little too much of Lita.

I stalk back to my bedroom, ducking in there only long enough to grab my keys and purse. My sisters are exactly where I left them in the kitchen. Bree is traumatized by the way I manhandled her and Ava is patting her injured arm with maternal comfort. It makes me want to scream.

"Imma bat!" Alden announces winningly when he sees me.

Even though I'm not feeling especially cheerful I'd have to be heartless not to smile at him. None of this is his fault. He was just born in the middle of it. I smile at the little boy. "You sure are, buddy."

"Where are you going?" Ava calls as I head toward the door.

"Town."

Bree practically knocks the kid over as she lunges in my direction. "Wait, Loren," she calls a little too loudly. "We need to talk. I'll come with you."

"No, you won't, *Brijeeet.*" I slam the door without looking to see if she's got her fingers on the doorjamb. I need some time with no sisters and no brothers and no wronged, angry ex-lovers.

However, apparently I can't have some time without cameras. At least it's just Rash who trails after me. If Cate Camp shows her face right now I just might gouge her artificially inflated boobs with my ignition key.

I get behind the wheel and wait for Rash to follow me in there. He has stopped though. He's standing about ten feet away from the car and he's got his camera off his shoulder and stares down at it with a frown. He looks up and winks, then jerks his head briefly in what seems to be a 'Get out of here,' gesture.

I get it now. He's actually being decent, pretending to have technical difficulties. He's trying to do me a favor. Rash does point to the dashboard though and I notice the tiny camera now mounted to it. I give him a thumbs up and get the car pointed toward Consequences. I think about tearing the camera off the dashboard and chucking it to the side of the road but I don't. In the end I just crank up Katy Perry tunes and sing in a very loud off key voice, feeling perversely gleeful that someone is going to be forced to sit through the footage of my rotten performance.

It's good to be out alone. The ever-present feeling of slow suffocation relaxes a little. Mercifully, Oscar was nowhere in sight when I pulled away from Atlantis. His truck, however, was just where he'd left it in the large clearing between the house and the brothel. So he isn't gone, just hidden.

The Consequences Convenience Store is just as I remember it. Beside the door they have the same air freshener carousel with probably the exact same merchandise that was hanging there five years ago. An older man wearing a red smock and a tag that says 'Kenny' is dusting off a shelf of fishing gear, which doesn't make any sense because there's no fishable water within a hundred miles. He doesn't look up when I enter.

The booze is still in the back, exactly where it's always been. Monty used to make raiding the CCS, as we called the store, something of a hobby. He was always brazen and foolish about it so I don't know how he managed to never get caught.

The pickings are rather slim here. I'd meant to bring back some wine but even I know a seven-dollar bottle probably isn't go win over anyone. I grab a bottle of red anyway and snagged a six-pack of beer on my way to the cashier.

Once I'm done at the CCS, I drop the bags off in the car and take my time, dawdling around Consequences even though there's little to see. It's not that it's the crappiest place on earth. It's just kind of a dull void. One that's been loosely sprinkled with people who seem half asleep.

There's too many memories here though. That's the whole damn problem with this godforsaken wrinkle in the state. It was hard enough to keep Oscar at bay and out of my head when he was somewhere unknown. But now he's lurking back at Atlantis, waiting to assume whatever role in the Savage comedy he plans on playing. If there was ever a good reason for me to ditch this whole project and drive in the opposite direction until I can't drive anymore, this is it. Gary couldn't physically force me to return. Whatever kind of power Vogel Productions has, they still might run into some legal trouble if they try to drag me back to Atlantis by my hair.

My fingernails are digging into my palms. No, I won't do it. I won't run. There must be some feisty blood left in me somewhere. Maybe I can call on the spirit of Margaret O'Leary to spare some of what made her so hot-tempered and indomitable. If I'm weak enough to be chased away by a ghost of old heartbreak, then I'll never really make much out of myself. I'll be another sad drifter, perhaps like Aunt Mina, always confusedly searching and always coming up short.

Let Oscar Savage do his worst. Whatever scripted part he means to play can't be any more painful than what we've already done to each other.

No. Lie. What I did to him.

Oscar walked away from me because I told him to. And as I watched him disappear, a boy alone cast out like garbage, I silently pleaded for the world to be kind to him. I begged him to forgive me, to forgive all of us for being too flawed and cowardly to stand up for anything. My own father had stood by with vague confusion and didn't say a word because he was too drained to notice anyone else. And then Oscar was gone.

It's too late now. I don't even know who he is anymore. I don't know what kind of revenge he has in mind. I just know that I'll be taking at least a few cans of that six-pack to bed tonight. I need the edges to be numbed just a little. Hopefully it will be enough. I need it to be enough so that when I close my eyes I don't dream of him, that I don't dream at all.

CHAPTER FOURTEEN

OZ

I've been here for a week now. A week in this surreal landscape of cameras and crew members and a cast who play-act their daily lives for a fucking paycheck. Ren avoids me and so far I've allowed her to. I've kind of been skirting around the whole damn lot of them since I arrived, eating alone and refusing to set foot in the big house.

Yesterday I helped Spencer out, fixing some of the sunscreens that had been knocked loose by a dust storm the other night. Spence seems to regard my presence as nothing out of the ordinary. At least he doesn't walk around with his head up his hostile ass, like Monty does. But Spence hasn't asked me what I'm doing here and I haven't volunteered to tell him. I offered him a hand with some work, which he stoically accepted, and that was that.

Gary Vogel himself has yet to put in an appearance, although he's got that insufferable disciple, Cate Camp, following me around. She lurks around corners and coughs up nervous suggestions about what I should say and what I should do and where I might want to think about saying and doing it. I don't tell her openly to fuck off. I figure silence is enough.

I watch Ren when she doesn't realize I'm around. She never really relaxes. She wanders warily around Atlantis looking for something to do and escapes to the nearby town several hours a day to uselessly roam around there.

Something's been lost to her these last five years. There used to be an innocent kind of confidence in the way she carried herself. The kind that said even in the midst of her crazy family she at least knew exactly who she was. I'm still furious with her. I still want her like hell, maybe now more than ever.

Last night I found myself wondering what she would do if I stood outside her window and whistled, just like I used to.

The temps are still pretty cool early in the morning so I take a hike toward the Harquehala's to watch the sunrise. One of the bumbling Camera Creeps tries to follow me but I don't have much trouble leaving him behind. About halfway up a vague trail I search for a flat rock bench that I know is there, close to a cave opening that I also know is there. A few turkey vultures circle overhead for a while and then move on. As the sun climbs to reach its rightful place in the sky I decide I'm done tiptoeing around this Born Savages bullshit.

The heat is starting to turn fierce. I jog down the rugged trail and nearly topple the huffing and puffing Camera Creep, the skinny one who's smoking behind the brothel every time he gets a break. I smile to myself as he curses and does an about face, trying to keep up with me. Let him try all he wants. I'm not waiting around for an audience.

The front door of the big house is unlocked so I stroll casually inside. That pretentious little snot, Brigitte, is sitting in the front room on an ugly chair adorned with grisly animal tusks. She looks up from her tablet where she's probably scouring the internet for news of herself.

"Oz!" she exclaims with round-eyed surprise.

"Where's your sister?" I answer shortly.

She gives me an empty-headed look and points down the hall. "She's in there."

I barrel through a swinging set of doors that I vaguely remember lead to the kitchen. Ava is in there, setting a bowl of applesauce on the table in front of her kid. The hand that holds the bowl freezes midair and she stares at me.

"Imma bat!" squeals the kid.

Ava sets the bowl down and rests her hand on the boy's blonde head. "Yes, honey, I know."

Brigitte has collided with my back, making an 'oof' noise. I swivel around to glare at her.

"I meant your other sister."

"Oh, you mean *Loren*?" Brigitte says in a stupidly loud voice like she's got a bucket full of sisters and is easily confused. The years have not made her any less annoying.

"Ren's in the barn," Ava interrupts, watching me curiously as her little boy jumps from one ceramic floor tile to the next. "At least that's where she said she was going."

I mutter a terse 'Thanks" under my breath and head straight through the side door. I hope Ren's bratty sister doesn't follow me. I'll have to forget how to be polite for a few minutes.

Ava's apparently doing the work for me though. I hear her say, "Don't," in a warning voice and as Brigitte starts sputtering I let the door close at my back.

Once I'm outside I nearly collide with Monty. He smells like an ashtray and has his shirt off so all the female world can admire his chest.

"Where's the fucking fire?" he growls and I brace for trouble. But he just shakes his head and sidesteps me.

Suddenly Cate Camp's blonde head peeks around the side of the house. She looks from side to side like she's a secret agent and then her raspy voice hisses some orders into her mouthpiece.

The barn is new and smells of paint. Ren is standing in the middle of it, holding a giant hose. It takes approximately two microseconds for her face to change from surprise to alarm when she sees it's me. I'm done biding my time with her though.

"I think it's time we talked," I say with supreme coolness.

She blinks. She looks at her feet and swallows hard. "Okay. What do you want to talk about?"

You. Me. Heartbreak. Your fucked-up family. This ridiculous show. Five years of silence. Take your pick, sweetheart.

But none of that comes out of my mouth. Instead I laugh at her. "I don't know Ren, why don't we talk about major league baseball standings?"

She turns her head the other way, says nothing.

There's a giant push broom leaning against a nearby wall. I grab it and start carelessly moving it across the floor. I sweep a large circle around her feet. "Or we could talk about gluten free dietary alternatives. That's absolutely relevant. What the hell do you think I want to talk about?"

She still says nothing so I keep talking.

"I know. We could discuss that old Savage-endorsed adage that tabloid publicity is the best publicity." I get right next to her and her breathing quickens. I reach out and tug ever so lightly on the sleeve of her shirt. "Of course once upon a time when you had the chance to test that out you crawled back into your den like a gutless rat."

"I don't blame you for feeling that way."

"Good. I do hate to be blamed for things."

"Oscar..." she says, her voice trailing off, her eyes full of pain.

"I'm not looking for an explanation, Loren. After all this time I don't really fucking care."

Her eyes flash. "Well, good for you. But you seem to be going to a lot of trouble for someone who doesn't care."

"And for someone who used to hold all this celebrity crap in contempt, you're sure going to a lot of trouble to whore yourself out."

She whirls around, swatting me away, her eyes flashing. "That's not fair."

"Nothing's fair, baby."

"Fuck you."

"Yeah you did."

Ren knocks the broom right out of my hands. It clatters to the floor. "Why the hell are you here, Oscar? Why now?"

I kick the broom away. "That's a real bullshit question to ask me."

She scowls, then adopts an ominous tone. "I can try a different one. How much cash did Gary promise you?"

Laughter erupts out of my mouth. I'm mocking her and she knows it. "Honey, just because *you're* for sale doesn't mean the rest of the world is too."

Her mouth falls open and her face reddens. I've hit a nerve. Good. I'd like to get on every single one of her goddamn nerves with a cattle prod and juice some sense into her.

"You have no idea," she spits caustically and throws the rubber hose clumsily toward my feet like she's all of a sudden going to be tough. But then she backs away as her eyes skate nervously from side to side like she's searching for something.

I get it. She's trying to figure out how she's being seen right now.

"Holy shit." If there was something nearby to punch I would punch it. Instead I glare at her. "The cameras. The motherfucking cameras. That's what you're looking for. You trying on a pose for the best angle?"

"Shut up."

"How about you turn to the side? Give 'em a profile shot. Suck in your stomach and push out those pert little titties. Didn't Gary give you orders? Sex appeal matters when it comes to ratings. You know, maybe old Gary should have paid for you to have some work done to enhance your assets. Need to grab that male eighteen to thirty five demographic."

"Goddammit, shut up!"

She's about to lose it but I don't feel like shutting up. I take a step in her direction. Her breathing catches and her brown eyes widen.

What the hell does she think I'm going to do? Hit her? I've never hit a female in my life.

But she betrays herself when she looks down. She zooms right in on my cock like it's just shouted her name. No, it's not fear that made her gasp. It's something else.

For whatever reason, this girl is deprived as all hell and every inch of her is shrieking for a good, dirty screw. In truth, I'd be game to give it to her, right here and now, but I'm not going to let her off the hook that easy.

"You know," I whisper into her ear, "America would probably get off on some hot and filthy incest."

Her face twists and her body tenses. There we go. God, she's angry. Shit, it's hot.

"You son of a bitch."

"Maybe. No one's ever claimed the job though so as far as I'm concerned I'm Mina Savage's kid."

"The hell you are."

"Eh, a moot point at this juncture. But it'd be good for ratings if we offered the folks at home something to spank their shit around to. In any case, if you're unwilling, there are other options. Speaking of which, I haven't seen Lita around yet."

I'm hitting way below the belt now. The mere mention of Ren's mother is like a slap across her face. There's more than one reason for that.

"Don't you fucking dare," she whispers.

"If you believed that lying bitch then you think I already did *fucking dare* so what's the harm in talking about it after all this time?"

"You bastard, I wouldn't believe Lita if she told me the desert is dry."

"The way I remember it, there seems to have been a few questions. Care to ask them now?"

"No!"

"Fine. We don't need to talk." I lean in so close I can nearly taste her. "I'd really rather not hear your voice when we're getting busy anyway."

She gives me the coldest of glares but she doesn't fool me a damn bit. If I tear her pants open right now and shove my hand down there I know I'd get nothing but a warm, wet welcome as her pussy clenches my fingers like a vice. But her eyes flash again and she scoffs, keeping up the charade. "So this is who you are now. Nothing but trash?"

"I always was, Loren. Your mother told you so, remember? Gutter trash that can and did fuck anything with a hole. You knew it. Don't tell me you didn't get off on that. You loved it."

The way she's looking at me, she might start swinging both fists at my head. What the hell is wrong with me that

I'm hard as iron right now? I'm not thinking about what we once had. Things have gone downhill fast since I walked into the barn and none of that long dead tenderness has any place here.

I want it rough and dirty. I want to bend her over, spread her wide and conquer the living shit out of her.

And I know she'd let me.

But then just like that all the fight fades from Ren. Her shoulders slump. She looks at the ground and bites her lip.

"Loren." I reach out to touch her but stop short. It hurts suddenly because I know she's no fucking actress. She looks miserable because she *is* miserable.

"No," she whispers, writhing out of my grasp. "I can't do this here."

My hand falls to my side. "Here's as good as anywhere else."

She breathes, slowly, in and out. There seems to be a pattern to it, like maybe it's some new age technique that's supposed to clear her head. Maybe I was a jackass for barging in here like this, for blindsiding her on this absurd show in the first place. I'm not sure what I'm hoping for out of all this. But I'm not going anywhere until I figure it out.

"It's not going to be so easy to dismiss me this time."

She nods tiredly. "I didn't think it would be."

She leaves. I let her go. I stand there alone in a dusty barn, knowing I'm being watched and unable to make myself care. I shove my hands in my pockets and my left knuckle is scraped by an object. I withdraw the rock I'd casually picked up on my morning hike. It looks completely ordinary, parts beige and pinkish red. It isn't valuable. If you tumble it in a rock polisher for a month it will emerge with a brilliant red color. I like it the way it is though. Five years ago I had a rock just like this and then I lost it. At the time I didn't even know what it was, just a thing that I'd grabbed as a hasty keepsake because I'd just had the best night of my life and wanted to keep the memory close.

As it turned out, forgetting would have been merciful. I couldn't forget the most important parts. I've spent five long years trying.

CHAPTER FIFTEEN

Five Years Ago: Part 3

"What is that?"

"What?"

"You just swiped something from the ground."

He holds it up for her. She squints in the gray light of pre-dawn.

"It's a rock," she says, puzzled. "Why?"

Oscar drops it into his pocket. "Just because."

Ren hugs him suddenly, fiercely. "I don't want this to end."

He feels giddy. He kisses her upturned face, briefly playing his tongue over her lips. He doesn't know how he's going to stand letting her go in a few minutes when they reach Atlantis. "No night lasts forever."

A sigh rolls through her, a sad one. "I didn't mean the night. I meant us."

"There's no end, baby. Not for us. This is just the beginning."

The chill of the night desert causes her to shiver, ever so briefly. The sun hadn't even dipped over the horizon when they set out hours earlier. Now it is utterly dark. He holds her to his side possessively, running every moment through his head.

No one had seen them go. Oscar is sure of it. The only question mark is Ren's brother Spence, who they glimpsed trotting through the valley on his horse. Even if Spencer had seen them though he wasn't the type to go gossiping about it.

She'd been asking to see the cave for weeks, the one that had always been rumored to exist around here and which he'd finally found on a solitary early morning hike. It wasn't a great cave, barely worth looking at in fact when compared side by side with some of the overwhelming caverns he'd climbed into during his years overseas.

Ren didn't care about that though. She was enchanted by the strange, romantic idea of a secret place. A place that seemed to exist only for them.

The cave was nestled into the side of the mountain with only a shallow outcropping of rock to navigate by. The entrance was a stretched, round shape, kind of like a yawning mouth. Oscar had enough sense to stuff some flashlights in the backpack that also carried bottled water.

He'd be lying if he didn't admit he was making plans during the hike up there. After all, he'd taken care to swipe a few condoms from Monty before heading out. The entry to the cave was narrow but short, ending in a small oval room that smelled of rain and wild things.

It was there Ren sank down to her knees without a word. Enough sunlight filtered in so he could see her, barely. She lifted his shirt, ran her tongue over the hard muscles of his belly and then searched lower. He wanted her to, and then he didn't. He stopped her before she got further. He took his shirt off and spread it on the ground, lowering her on top of it. His heart thudded in his chest even though he wasn't shy around any girl, not ever.

But then, there were no other girls like this one.

She'd never told him it was her first time, but she didn't have to. He knew even before her body proved it to him. Afterwards, they were silent together, skin against skin, until the light began to fade and Oscar started to worry about getting down the trail in one piece.

Now, closing in on home and facing the reality that they will need to separate for a few hours, Oscar thinks that never in the history of people was it easier to walk beside someone.

"What are you thinking about?" she asks, somewhat shyly. They are within sight of Atlantis now. At night it gets swallowed up by the desert, with only a few meager lights to tell the story of its existence. Oscar is thinking about the cave, about her. He's thinking about whether it's possible to know you're making one of your life's best memories while it's happening. He swings an arm around her shoulder.

"I'm thinking about Cowboys and Indians."

Ren laughs. "Why?"

"This is where your grandfather made all those movies, wasn't it?"

"*Our* grandfather." She's teasing.

"Don't fucking start."

"Oh, don't be angry with me, cousin."

"I'm as much your cousin as the goddamn president. And as for Rex Savage, never met the guy and we've got no blood in common."

Ren grows thoughtful. "I guess it's a good thing he died before he got to see what became of us, the Savages."

He peers down at her. "It's not so bad, is it?"

"Depends on who you ask. To August, life is just fine. To Lita, it's catastrophic."

Oscar has to stop walking because he needs to wrap her in his arms. He'd like her to stay there forever. "What about if I asked you?"

A slight breeze lifts Ren's hair and he is hit with the now familiar scent of her cherry vanilla shampoo. It's got him going again. He can't help it. He presses himself against her so she'll feel it too, how bad he wants her.

"Oscar," she sighs, "I've never been this happy before."

"Me either."

"I love you."

"I love you too."

He kisses her, long and deep. He wants more but they are getting close to the big house and anyway she wouldn't be up to it so soon after her first time. It's okay. There will be other nights.

They are coming around the south side of the big house, hoping not to be seen. Beyond the town, there's a rickety fence surrounding some crumbling gravestones. The graves are not real, of course. Nothing about this place is real. It's a fake cemetery where actors wept artificial tears over people who'd never existed in the first place. It was all a tragic fantasy to suit a story. The cemetery has always been left alone, kind of a macabre reminder of the world of make believe. Still, it gives Oscar the fucking creeps and he'd rather be elsewhere.

Suddenly there's soft two-note whistle from the center of the fenced off square. It couldn't be anything remotely supernatural. But Oscar nearly jumps out of his skin just the same. There are far worse things than ghosts that lurk in the darkness.

Instinct causes him to swivel and push Ren behind him, shielding her from whatever's coming. His fists are tight. The whistle sounds again and the footsteps are nonchalant. Oscar relaxes a little. It's probably just Monty. He's enough of an asshole to hunker down in the dark just waiting for someone to pick a fight with.

The left side of Oscar's face is still swollen from the last time they went it at three days ago. Oscar got in more good shots than he took though, so that's something. They've been staying clear of each other since then. That's the way things always go between him and Monty. Either they're bashing each other's faces bloody or they're ignoring each other's existence. Oscar knows there's some deep rage in that guy and it has nothing to do with him. Yet there must be something redeeming about Monty because Ren always insists there is and Oscar would trust Ren with his life.

"Hey," says the voice from the darkness and it's not Monty.

"What's up, Spence?" Ren asks, surprise in her tone. "What are you doing out here anyway?"

By the light of the full moon Oscar can see Spencer Savage has his hands jammed in his pockets. He gives a nod to Oscar and then focuses his attention on his sister. Of all Ren's siblings he's the only one Oscar would tentatively call a friend. The kid's something of a puzzle. He's quiet and serious and has a habit of avoiding people whenever he can. He's all right though.

Spence take his hands from his pockets, removes his hat and yawns. "Just hanging out."

Ren crosses her arms. It's her big sister no-nonsense pose. "You're not going to run off into the desert again are you?"

Spence has a habit of taking off when it suits him. A few weeks back he disappeared for two days and even his hellish mother was worried. When he casually strolled back into Atlantis he seemed rather bewildered by the fuss, shrugging everyone off with the explanation the he was camping and didn't think anyone would miss him. It wasn't a cry for attention, not with Spence. He felt like leaving so he left. Oscar could respect that, although Ren has said she wishes her younger brother needed people, just a little.

"Not today," he answers casually. He looks at Oscar. "Actually I was waiting for you guys."

"You were?"

"Yeah, I saw you head up to the trail earlier. You had to come home sooner or later."

A light in the big house flicks on and then off again. Ren looks toward the house and frowns. "Something happen? Monty steal one too many beer cases and get carted off by the Consequences PD?"

"Maybe. But that's not why I was waiting." Spence clears his throat and fixes them both with a look of sympathy. Considering it's Spence, this seems as abnormal as a jackrabbit playing Tic Tac Toe. Oscar can feel Ren's rising tension. He takes her hand.

"Spill it," Oscar orders. "What's going on?"

The boy scratches at his head and seems to mull over his words carefully. "Look, I don't have a problem with whatever's going on between you, but not everyone feels that way."

"Eh, whatever. I can handle Monty."

"I'm not talking about Monty. He can be a dipshit but he doesn't have a big mouth."

For some reason a cold finger travels up Oscar's spine. "But someone does?"

"Yeah, " Spence admits slowly. "Someone does."

Ren sucks in a breath. "Goddammit, why can't Bree mind her own fucking business?"

"Who says Bree had anything to do with it?"

"Well who the hell else is a hair-flipping tattling little gossip?"

Spence exhales and glares at his sister with rare annoyance. "Jesus, Ren. You guys think you're fucking invisible or what?"

Oscar lowers his head, understanding perfectly. Why were he and Ren kidding themselves that no one around them would notice anything was up? Here they were in an isolated place in the middle of a dull summer and lately they've been all over each other. He'd found a way to justify it, telling himself that they'd broken no laws and no one should raise an eyebrow over two teenagers getting together, not in this day and age. But now he silently curses his own fantastic idiocy. It's not that simple. Not when the two teenagers in question both have the same famous last name.

Spence squirms, apparently regretting his brief outburst. He sighs and runs his hand through his dark hair again. "Look, this is the deal. Oscar, as long as you make my sister smile I won't be getting all up in your shit. But we all know my mother's an evil bitch and right now she thinks she's found something to get bent out of shape about. I just wanted to warn you, that's all." He hops over the low fence and starts to walk away into the night. He spins around once and repeats, almost apologetically, "That's all."

As soon as the night swallows up Spencer Savage, Ren exhales and buries her face in Oscar's chest. His arms circle her body and he imagines himself creating a protective cage where she'll be safe. Safe from Lita, safe from the judgment of strangers, safe from the world.

"It'll be okay, baby." He hears his own confidence, tries to make it real.

"Will it?" she asks in a small voice. It's the first time she's ever hinted at doubt.

"Of course," Oscar whispers. He kisses her mouth, her cheeks, her forehead.

She pulls back a few inches and tilts her head back, peering up at him defiantly. "I meant what I said. I love you. Not like a silly, giggly kind of crush that my sisters fall into every other week. I love you and it doesn't matter what time or anything else does to us. Even if the worst happens and we're ripped apart it will change nothing. I'll still love you, Oscar."

Ren is suddenly crying and he rubs her back, whispers nice things, tries to soothe her. Something about her desperate tone alarms him. Ren isn't like this; she doesn't dissolve into hysterics. The words she choked out were so strange, impassioned.

"I know," he assures her. "I know. I'll still love you too. Anyone who wants to whine about how we're too young or too reckless doesn't understand a fucking thing about us. It'll be okay," he says once again, her face cupped between his palms. "I swear it."

There's no way to know how much time passes as they stand at the fenced edge of the cemetery in the moonlight and hold one another. It's late but the hour is irrelevant. Oscar breathes her in, kisses her occasionally, and wonders what on earth in his history of casual conquests led him to deserve a girl like this.

Finally she pulls away from him, murmuring that she'd better get back to her room before anyone decides to make a stink about her absence.

The porch light is on at the big house. They hear voices, female voices, talking quietly so they circle around to the back. Ren has permanently disabled the lock on her window so that she can climb back inside without alerting anyone. Slowly, she raises the small, square window and cautiously ducks her head inside. She looks back with a smile of relief and Oscar gives her a small boost to help her through the window. Once she's inside, she leans through the window, kisses him quickly, and then is gone without saying anything else. No more good nights, no more I love yous. Oscar likes how she knows they've already said all the words they need to say tonight.

As he walks away and heads in the direction of the brothel, he cups his hand around his pocket, the pocket he'd stuffed the rock into. On one hand it seems like a childish thing to do, scavenging for a souvenir. Hell, two months ago he would have howled with laughter over the idea of doing such a mushy, pussified thing because of a girl. That was a long time ago though. Everything is different now.

There's music coming from the little house. It's the kind of music with screeching lyrics about violent things. It's Monty's music. Oscar isn't going to worry about running into the eldest Savage brother though. Chances are Monty is still balls deep inside that squirrel-faced snatch who'd followed him home. He'll probably pass out at some point. With any luck he already has.

Oscar lingers in the darkness, thinking about the promises he made to Ren, about how everything would be okay. It *will* be okay. Nothing on earth could make him let go of her as long as she wants him. Whenever Mina gets herself cleaned up and returns he'll have a talk with his flighty mother. She has her flaws and they are substantial but Mina Savage is nothing if not romantic. The idea of clandestine lovers will appeal to her. Mina will help them until he and Ren are old enough to be free from everyone else's temper tantrums. They can't stay in Atlantis of course but Oscar's had enough of the scorching desert anyway. He wants to show Ren what the rest of the world looks like. He wants to show her everything.

A pinprick of light catches his eye. It's a few yards to his left, very close to the old fake brothel. Oscar waits for a few seconds and it returns. A tiny orange light that flares and disappears, the light of a cigarette. He tenses, getting ready for a showdown with Monty.

But the owner of the cigarette shifts and Oscar can make out a female profile. "You're running around pretty late, young man."

Before he clearly sees her face he recognizes the voice, even though she hasn't spoken directly to him since the day Mina deposited him here. Annoyance pricks at him. What the hell is it with this family that they're always skulking around in the darkness waiting for someone to talk to? First there was Spencer accosting them in the cemetery and now Lita prowling around the sagging front porch of the brothel.

It creaks under her heels as walks across the rotting floorboards.

"It is late," he agrees. "Past my bedtime in fact so you have yourself a good night. I'm turning in."

Lita Savage chuckles. It's a gravelly, unpleasant sound, probably because her throat muscles aren't used to laughter. "Come here for a minute."

"Why?"

"Why not, Oscar?" She sounds too happy. Either she's high or she's fucking with him. He doesn't feel like talking to her. He just wants to get back to his bed and jerk off for a while to thoughts of Ren.

"Fine," she sighs when he still hesitates. "I'll come to you."

The closer she gets the more the air smells like decaying flowers. Oscar has to force himself to stand his ground. All he knows about Lita Savage is what Ren has told him. It would be enough to make anyone with some common sense a little wary, but Oscar detects something even worse than the gold-digging bitch that Ren has described. This woman is pure poison.

She takes a drag on her cigarette and looks him up and down. He can't quite read her expression in the dark but he's not sure he wants to.

"How have you been, Oscar?" she inquires sweetly. "I've been meaning to check in with you to see how things are going."

"Fine," he answers slowly. "No complaints. Hey, I never thanked you for opening your home to me. So, thank you."

"Hmm, yes. Wasn't my decision at all."

"I get it. Well, thanks anyway. Now, if you'll excuse me, I think I'll leave you to your night."

"Wait a minute," she murmurs, and suddenly she's right there, running a palm over his chest. It's a seductive gesture and Oscar recoils instinctively.

"Are you out of your mind?" he growls.

"No, not tonight."

"Don't fucking touch me again."

"You know, you really shouldn't address your aunt with such profanity."

"You're not my aunt."

"Technically I am."

"Lita, what in the hell do you want?"

"Isn't it obvious?"

She can't be serious. She just *can't* be fucking serious. She's not laughing though. He looks around to make sure they are alone. If anyone else is around, he doesn't see them. Telling her to piss off might not be effective. Oscar glares at her and decides to remind her of the way things are. "In case you don't realize it, what you're proposing is illegal."

"Illegal?" She tries out the word. "Illegal. Now why do you think so?"

"Because I know damn well that there are laws protecting kids here. And by American standards, I'm still a kid."

"No, you're not," she answers matter-of-factly.

That takes him back a step. She's goddamn crazy. Has to be.

"You look confused, Oscar. Let me explain. I called in a favor from an old friend of the family who happens to be a private investigator. Now, there wasn't much record of you, but there was enough to conclude you'd been in the New York State system for six years when Mina scooped you up."

He feels like he's missing a crucial deduction. "So?"

"So that was twelve years ago, Oscar. Twelve years. Remind me what six plus twelve is again?"

He doesn't answer. She nods. "That's right. You're eighteen. At least."

Though vaguely unsettled, he remembers something Ren told him. Something he believes completely. "You're a liar, Lita. You lie all the time. You don't know how to do anything else."

"Maybe," she shrugs. She drops her cigarette on the ground and grinds it beneath her heel. There's no warning when she grabs his shirt and rubs her body against his. She has the same willowy build as Ren but there's nothing soft about her. She's all hard edges and claws. He fingernails scrape the back of his neck as she pulls his mouth in. He tastes tobacco and something vaguely garlic as her tongue searches for his. Repulsed, he pushes her away.

"What the hell?" he snarls, wiping his mouth on the back of his hand to purge the taste of her.

Evidently unruffled, Lita straightens her skirt and lights another cigarette. "I might be lying," she purrs. "I might be searching for any reason to fuck that hot, hard body of yours, Oscar." She shrugs her bony shoulders. "Or I might not be. Either way, you'd better think twice before screwing any more slutty teenagers because that could get you in trouble. Especially since I'm letting you know that you've got a better option."

"You're fucking sick," he shouts at her back. She's already started walking away, strutting toward the big house as a handful of bats fly directly overhead. She keeps walking, giving no hint that she heard him.

Once she's out of sight the sordidness of the encounter catches up to Oscar and he sinks down on the brothel porch, feeling queasy. Even though the stink of her awful perfume still hangs in the air he can't quite believe what just happened. It's not the first time an older woman has taken a liking to him. Hell, two schools ago he had a brief and dirty thing going on with the headmaster's wife. This was different though. Even if Lita Savage wasn't the mother of the girl he's crazy about, he wouldn't touch her if someone paid him. She is lethal.

Oscar removes the rock from his pocket and all thoughts of Lita Savage fade away. She's either nuts or drunk and won't likely bother him again. As for all that nonsense about diving into his history, who cares? So what if he's eighteen and not seventeen? He doesn't care. His mother obviously doesn't care. Anyway, there's not much chance it's actually true. According to Ren, Lita can't tell her ass from her elbow.

Ren. Ren. Loren.

He pictured her stripped down to her underwear, cozy beneath her bedcovers, a smile on her face as she drifts off to sleep. She's thinking of him, he knows it. What she'll never know is how it nearly killed him to keep his hands off her for the longest time. It had to be the greatest testosterone restraint on record. And even after that first incomparable kiss under the moonlight he'd forced himself to go slow because he knew that's what she needed. Tonight though, that sealed everything between them. They did the deed and they said the words. It makes no difference how old they are or how many Lita-type monkey wrenches are thrown in the way.

She's his now. She always will be.

CHAPTER SIXTEEN

REN

I was always a miserable performer. Lita was forever scheduling screen tests during pilot season in Hollywood, that brief period when all the new shows are looking for their casts and would-be actors from across the nation camp out in seedy Boulevard motels hoping to catch a break. I never got any callbacks.

"Loren does not project."

"Loren is uniformly expressionless."

"Loren fails to occupy space with confidence."

It didn't take long for Lita to give up on me. Monty and Spencer wanted nothing to do with any of it, but Brigitte and Ava were willing so I guiltily thanked the greater powers for giving me some sisters my mother could exploit.

Speaking of sisters, Brigitte's been avoiding me ever since I *cough cough* 'assaulted' her in the kitchen. I can only guess what kind of sobbing show she's putting on for her private Blue Room interviews. I'm not going to ask. If I want to know I'll find out when the show airs, just like everyone else.

As far as Ava goes, she knows I'm rattled. She always waits until the crew is gone for the night before pulling me aside and asking if I 'want to talk about i..

I do not.

I do not want to talk about Oscar. No, not Oscar, *Oz*.

I do not want to talk about the contemptuous look in his eyes or the crass things that came out of his mouth or the way I had to bite the inside of my cheek to try to stop the trembling that threatened to devour me.

I do not want to talk about how every sexually deprived nerve ending in my body begged to be handled by him right there on the dirty floor of the barn.

I do not want to talk about how maybe if I fucked Oz – the man who was once Oscar - in the filthiest way possible I could get rid of it all. Maybe all it would take is ten minutes of animal humping to silence five years worth of grief for what we had, for what we lost. It must have killed some part of him too. I saw it in his face the night he walked away. Once I proved myself to be a coward I was nothing to him.

"Ren?"

A hesitant knock on the door, a soft voice. Ava.

"Ren?"

"Ren's not here," I mumble and pull the pillow over my face. I don't know what time it is. The sun is fairly high and the room grows hotter every minute. I'm sure I could find something more useful to do than lie in a bed of self-pity.

But I've made my own bed. Now I should be forced to lie in it.

I cackle to myself over the metaphorical non-humor of the situation. I think I'm losing my marbles, one marble at a time. By this time next month they will have all leaked out.

"Can I come in?"

I fling the covers off and unlock the door. Ava cracks it open slowly and pokes her head inside. She looks around with worried confusion, like she's crossed an unfriendly international border. She needs to do something about her roots. I can see the red peeking through.

"Hi," I wave.

"Hey."

She smiles. Ava has the most amazing smile. When Ava smiles you feel like the sun has just shined directly on you.

"What time is it?"

"Nearly ten."

"Shit. I forgot I told Spencer I'd help him with some chores. On second thought though, I'd probably just get in his way."

Ava chews her lip. "I saw Oz heading out with Spence pretty early."

"Oh. Oz." Defeat. Anger. Lust.

"Anyway," Ava continues as if an elephant hasn't just entered the room and stands there, swaying his bulbous trunk and blinking at us. "I was hoping you wouldn't mind watching Alden for a few hours. Bree asked if I would go with her to the Western Edge Stables. Apparently she's signed us up for a roping class."

"A groping class?"

"Shush, you heard me. The photo crew was here early in this morning. Even if Monty wasn't doing that ridiculous photo shoot today I couldn't ask him and I'd rather not drag the baby out when there's nothing for him to do there."

"Hold on, hold on." Jesus, a girl can't even sleep in for a few hours without all kinds of crazy news erupting. "Ava, you know I'll gladly look after Alden anytime so don't even worry about it. Now who is here? And Monty is doing what exactly?"

"I told you yesterday. Photographer from one of those celebrity rags is in town and got Monty to agree to some barely clothed on-location photo ops. They headed for the mountain trail a few hours ago. She wanted Spence too but of course he told her to fuck off."

"And Monty didn't? Monty tells everyone to fuck off."

"They must have caught him in an unusually good mood. Plus I saw him checking out the photographer's ass so he's probably expecting a tip."

"Naturally."

Since the girls need to leave in a half hour I hustle through a shower and don't bother about drying my hair. In this climate it dries quickly on its own anyway.

When I get to the kitchen, Ava is kneeling on the floor beside her son and Bree pretends like I haven't just entered the room. She's wearing a short swing dress with cowboy boots. If I had to guess I would say dresses probably aren't well suited to cattle roping lessons but since no one asked me I'll just keep my mouth shut.

"I'll wait in the car," Brigitte declares and shoots me a wounded look before flouncing out of the house.

I do feel slightly guilty because I don't know for sure if she was the one who aired all the dirty Oscar laundry at the feet of Vogel Productions but it doesn't matter anyway. Really, if it's anyone's fault it's mine. I should never have expected the private past to remain private. That's what you get when you open the door and let in the cameras.

"You and Auntie Ren are gonna have so much fun," Ava promises her boy with a smile and a kiss.

Alden looks at me with dubious blue eyes. I've never been the type to get all mushy about kids but this gorgeous little boy, my nephew, owns a piece of my heart without even trying. I hate that he's in the middle of all this garbage. Ava does the best she can, but I should make more of an effort to help her.

I grab a cup of coffee and sit down on the floor beside my sister's child. "You like chickens, Alden?"

Slowly, thoughtfully, the little boy nods his head.

"Well how about you help your tired old aunt feed all those chickens and clean out the coop?"

I know Spence probably already took care of that before the sun came up but I figure if it amuses the kid it wouldn't hurt to do it all again. Alden gives me a gap-toothed grin and Ava plants one more kiss on his little head before mouthing the words 'thank you' and heading out the door.

Alden is wary for few minutes after his mother's departure but then returns to his hyperactive little self. I'm laughing as I get his shoes tied and let him out into the yard. I forget to notice whether there's a camera following us but when I glance around I see Rash filming away at a discreet distance. I suppose I am becoming immune to being watched after all.

The day the chickens showed up, Spencer built a solid enclosure so they wouldn't become a coyote meal. It's positioned to take advantage of the shade provided by a sprawling mesquite tree that's probably been there for a hundred years. The enclosure is probably five times the size it needs to be for four lousy chickens. Maybe Spencer has plans to expand the flock after all.

After I hand over the bowl of feed to Alden, I sit down on a wide tree stump and laugh as my nephew throws the bowl's contents straight up into the air. It turns out little kids are good medicine. I haven't laughed as much in weeks as I have in the last twenty minutes. The chickens are going berserk, pecking at the food as fast as their skinny necks will let them.

I feel the shadow at my back before I hear his voice.

"You babysitting the kid or the poultry?"

That's how he always starts a conversation these days; some off-the-cuff remark that kicks my blood pressure into high gear. No matter what he says it sounds thickly sensual. Since our barn encounter I've managed to keep interactions to a minimum.

I don't fool myself though. I know I can only avoid him as long as he lets me. And sometimes I'm not even sure I want him to.

I don't turn around when I answer. "I'd heard you were gone for the day."

Oz opens the gate and strolls inside the chicken enclosure. He stands closer to me than he needs to but I don't even flinch.

"So is that why you decided to emerge from the cave? Because you thought I was gone?"

"No. I don't care where you are."

"I'm sorry I bother you so much, Ren." He sounds the opposite of sorry.

"You are not."

"I am. I always tell the truth."

"So do I."

"Do you now?" he says quietly, almost bemusedly. "That's interesting."

"I don't want you. I don't want you. I DON'T WANT YOU!"

I wonder if he's thinking of those words, if he can hear them plainly as if they are being hurled in live time. I know I can hear them. Their echoes are etched into this landscape. They are permanent.

"This is a stupid conversation." I have to tilt my head to see him. Somehow I manage to get hit in the eyes with the sharpest rays of the climbing sun. It hurts.

Oz shifts slightly. He's not standing as close to me anymore, but I can see more of him now. I wish I couldn't. He's filled out a lot in five years, all in exactly the places a woman would want a man to fill out. He crosses his tanned arms and whistles a few notes.

A bolt of desire slices across my lower belly and settles between my legs, throbbing. I don't know if it's a memory from my love-crazed teenage self or if it's something new. Either way it makes no difference. I just want him. Despite myself, I want him bad.

Oz stops whistling and gestures to my nephew. "So I never got the whole story. How did Ava wind up with a kid?"

"You're a sharp guy. Surely the biological basics aren't lost on you."

He lets out an exasperated sigh. "Tell me Ren, are you contractually obligated to challenge me every chance you get?"

"No. Care to answer your own question?"

"No." He's giving me one of his black-eyed glares. "No goddammit, I'm not."

"Lower your voice!" I jerk my head toward Alden even though the kid is obviously not listening to a thing. He's squealing and frolicking around after the chickens.

"I'm not the one screaming," Oz responds mildly.

I have to stop myself from staring at his lips. I have to stop myself from staring at his chest; his broad, absurdly muscled chest that provocatively stretches the fabric of his shirt from all the hard power that coils beneath it...

"Loren."

"Yes."

"Yes, what?"

"Huh? Where?"

He's giving me a funny look. It might be because I sound completely sun-addled. He pulls his hat off, rubs the sweat off his forehead and waits for me to make some sense.

My mouth is as dry as the ground. "I think I need some water."

Without pausing, Oz tosses over the bottle he'd been carrying. It's warm and half gone. I gulp it down anyway

Alden lets out a triumphant little yip as he clutches a fistful of chicken feathers. I'm watching him and then I reach into my bra, ripping out the microphone. Even though Ava's history is widely known, I don't feel like being the one to broadcast it. I look up at Oz but he just raises his eyebrows and shakes his head.

"No," he snorts. "I don't always wear a leash just because some fucker in a suit says so."

"Fine. So, about Ava. She can act like the simple-minded socialite. She's more like a walking heartbreak. I don't know if you heard about it wherever you were, but she had a role in a short-lived sitcom and started hitting the celeb party scene pretty hard. She got involved with a costar who happened to be one of earth's more colossal turds. Things went sour even before she got knocked up. The show was cancelled mid season and loverboy wasn't about to stick around and play daddy. He happens to be another like us, with a famous last name but without two dimes to rub together so there's no point chasing after him for child support. And that's just the way it is." I pause for a breath. "Ava's a good mom. She is."

"I believe you."

I shoot him a sharp glance because he sounds like he might be taunting me, but he's just watching the kid run around with a thoughtful gaze on his face.

Alden suddenly trots over to me, beaming. "You," he says and promptly drops the chicken feathers in my lap. I fuss over the bent, half-bald feathers and thank him profusely. Before returning to his chicken torture, Alden stops and stares at Oz. Oz stares back.

Once Alden is back at his games, I try to return Oz's water bottle. He ignores my outstretched hand.

"Tennessee," he finally says. "I've been there for a little while. Got a job, a nice place."

"And before that?"

"Before that I wandered."

"Wandered?"

"Yeah, wandered."

"You come across any other people in your so-called wanderings?"

A roughish smile crosses his face. "I *came* in a lot of other people."

"Jesus Christ," I hiss, standing stiffly.

"What?" he says innocently. "You don't want to hear about it? I'm trying to evoke some nostalgia here."

"You're disgusting, Oz."

"Probably. But you're a shell of what you were, Loren."

I can't breathe. If words could pack a punch, those particular ones are made of pure dynamite. Oz Acevedo, formerly Oscar Savage, just distilled my worst horror into one sentence. And he knows it. He waits for me to say something and I desperately want do want to say something. I want to cut him as deeply as he's just cut me. I want to hurt him. So I tell an enormous lie.

"I was just a stupid girl. In the long run you didn't mean a damn thing to me."

He doesn't even blink. "Ditto, sweetheart. You were just a ripe cherry to pop."

I'm shaking. I'm going to explode. "God, you've turned into such a foul-mouthed pig."

He answers me casually, like he doesn't care at all what I think. "And you've turned into a feeble-minded wreck."

He doesn't wait around for my response. He stalks away without glancing back and disappears around the corner of the barn.

Alden remains oblivious that there is anything more interesting going on than the sight of flustered chickens. Stoically I sit back down and try to banish Oz's final words from my mind. I don't know how much the cameras have captured. At this point I can't force myself to care.

For the rest of the day I focus on Alden. I feed him lunch, I tend to his scraped knee, I welcome him into my lap when he asks for a story. When Ava gets home she finds us on a back porch swing. Alden shouts with joy when he sees his mother and practically vaults out of my lap and into her arms. I stare at my sister and her child, at the pure, unsullied love between them. In a way I'm almost jealous.

Ava sits down beside me and sets the boy in her lap. She starts chattering about the disastrous cattle roping experience. Evidently Bree ignored all instructions and managed to get thrown from her horse, earning an ass full of sand and gravel.

"Well," I say with false cheer, "I suppose that's the end of the Savage cowgirl days. Perhaps we should try being farmers instead."

Ava's watching me. "Everything okay on the home front?"

No.

"Yup. Everything is fine. If you guys will excuse me, I think I'll head to the kitchen and bake a cake."

"I thought you never cooked anymore."

"I don't."

"You used to cook all the time. Back in the bad old days when we lived here. If not for you, we would have been eating cheese sandwiches every night."

"Just trying to contribute."

"Ren?"

"What?"

Ava sighs and heaves herself up with Alden in her arms. "I'd better put this kid in for a nap or he'll be the devil later on."

Someone has been keeping the fridge and pantry well stocked. I have no difficulty finding enough necessary ingredients to bake a yellow cake with buttercream icing. Once I'm in the rhythm of kitchen activity I decide to cobble together a dinner of roast chicken, pasta salad and baking soda biscuits. The oven is something of an antique but it still works when it needs to.

As soon as I start setting food on the table, my siblings seem to magically materialize. It's all too familiar. Lita floated far above kitchen tasks and we couldn't exactly eat out every night all the way out here, even if we'd been able to afford it. If there was any cooking to be done so people could eat, then I was the one to do it.

I wash dishes in the background as Ava happily feeds her son, while Bree grudgingly takes a few bits of salad and then limps elsewhere, when Spence wanders inside looking as rough as if he'd just spent a few hours running with the bulls, which might very well be accurate.

There are cameras.

There is no Monty.

There is no Oz.

The sun is sinking below the horizon by the time I finish putting the kitchen back together. Cate Camp knocks on the door. She wants me to know that I seem to have misplaced my body mic. I don't answer her. I'll play the game again tomorrow. Tonight I don't feel like being wired. In a few hours the crew will drive back to town. Of course, cameras are installed all over the property but they seem more innocent when they aren't attached to people.

I invent work for myself by cleaning up the house. It's mindless and nearly pleasant. Anything to avoid thinking about Oz. Every strange sound makes me recoil though. I'm always afraid it's him. And in a sick way I hope it is him.

Finally the crew departs. I linger on the front porch with the lights off, listening to the fading sound of the two trucks heading toward Consequences.

Montgomery lumbers up to the house with a cigarette in one hand and a bottle in the other. He pauses and takes a drag on the cigarette while squinting at the fading light in the western sky. It looks like he's already made some progress on the bottle.

"Where's your fan club?"

He shrugs. "Gone hours ago. That bitchy photographer had some ideas but I couldn't get excited about the idea of more of my dick pics floating around the world wide web so I passed on that."

"Charming," I mutter.

"You asked," he yawns.

"I guess I did. Anyway, there's food in the fridge if you're hungry."

Monty doesn't answer. He doesn't move either. He just stands there puffing on his cigarette while staring into the distance. After a full minute of silence he tilts his bottle in my direction. At first I shake my head but then I take it and cough back a mouthful of liquid fire. Whiskey.

When I can see straight again I realize Monty is watching me. "I thought he was an asshole then," he says. "I still think so."

"Oscar?"

"Oscar. Oz. Whatever."

"Well, I guess score one for you being right then."

"I don't give a shit about being right. But maybe just because he's an asshole doesn't mean he's a dickhead."

"Monty Savage Reasoning at its finest."

"Just saying, if he wanted to really fuck up your life he had his chance."

"Cameras are still around," I grumble. "He'll get more chances."

"No he won't."

I'm curious now. "Why?"

"Because he's leaving, Ren."

CHAPTER SEVENTEEN

OZ

Fuck it all. I'm done.

The way we are with each other, it's nothing but toxic.

In the afternoon I take a long hike and it's while I'm among the lizards and the snakes that I think about every word Ren and I have exchanged since I got here. However hostile she is to me, I manage to one up her every time. I can't seem to help it.

Every day I'm becoming a worse version of myself.

Did I come here to mess with her head? Or did I come here because despite the pain of the past and the silence of five years I still had some hope? That maybe with one look we would find our way back to those two kids who connected so strongly, loved so hard.

I don't know the answer. I never did. This has been one massive fool's errand. The whim is over now. Loren Savage and I are strangers. Oscar Savage never existed. It's time for me to duck out of this fantasy and return to the world of Oz Acevedo.

Evening is well underway by the time I get back. The minute I see Atlantis again I know what I need to do. Once I'm in my room I'm practically kicking shit around from one side of the floor to the other in my haste to pack. It doesn't seem important that I've left the door open until Monty regards it an invitation to park himself in the frame and blow cigarette smoke into the room.

"Why don't you take your temper tantrum somewhere that doesn't share a wall with me?"

"Fuck you, Monty."

"Fuck me," he chuckles and inwardly I groan because I can tell where this is headed and at the moment I don't feel like being locked in mortal combat with this jackass.

I drop a duffel bag on the floor and meet his eye. "You want to do this in here or outside?"

"Don't look so terrified, Mr. Oz. At the moment I'm not excited about cutting up my knuckles on your face."

"Lucky me," I mutter, picking up the duffel bag and zipping it shut.

Monty continues to smoke. He leans against the doorjamb, all puffed up with big ideas about his cocky ass. He's insane if he thinks he could take me down, especially right now. Right now I feel like I could punch my way through six feet of cinderblock before it would sting. I hate the smell of cigarettes.

"You know, Oz, I keep trying and I just can't figure out what the hell your end game is."

"Well, you keep on figuring. You can even send me a postcard when you reach a conclusion."

His tone gets darker. "I think you're actually just biding your time, waiting for the right moment when you can hurt her the most."

"God, you're smart, Monty. That's exactly what I'm fucking doing. That's why I'm packing up all my shit and getting myself hell and gone from you people and your sick reality."

Monty has no answer for that. He doesn't leave right away either though, so I just keep packing, breathing out of my mouth so I don't have to smell his disgusting smoke. After I zip the duffel bag closed I notice he's finally gone. A second later I hear the front door. Good. With any luck I can get out of here without running into him again. Him, or any of the other Savages. If Vogel Productions wants to chase after me for breach of contract or whatever those people call it, best of luck to them.

I throw two hastily packed bags over my shoulder and head for my truck. It's parked about twenty yards away, all by itself. I toss the bags into the back bed and slam the door. I think I heard the crew truck taking off a little while ago, which is a good thing because I'm not too excited about explaining myself to anyone right now. There's an acrid, smoky taste in the air. A fire burns somewhere up north, sparked in the dense forests surrounding Flagstaff. I hear that the season has been dry, meaning any fire will spread quickly. Not down here though. There's not much in the way of brush so when fires start they don't burn for long.

There are just a few more things I need to grab and then I'll be out of here. It's quiet, no one in sight, so I should be able to make a clean exit. Now that I'm thinking about it, instead of heading back home straight away I'd rather take a detour for a week or two. Someplace cold. Someplace that looks nothing like the barren wastelands of the Sonoran desert. Montana sounds good. I've always been meaning to go see Glacier National Park. This is a perfect time for a fresh odyssey.

So why is there a gnawing hole in my chest right now? Tomorrow morning I'll wake up somewhere else. I've spent five years troubled by the idea of what would happen if I ever saw Ren again. Now I know. And the answer is nothing. Nothing good, anyway.

Yes. At least now I know.

Once I'm back in the house I spend a few minutes snatching up the rest of my crap. There wasn't much to begin with. And if there's anything I'm forgetting it's either replaceable or not worth having in the first place.

After some quick searches on my phone I calculate that I can be in Montana the day after tomorrow, especially if I push through and drive until morning. I'm so keyed up, I bet I'll end up doing exactly that.

When I return to the truck I stop in my tracks for a second because something that looks just like Loren Savage is sitting in the passenger seat. She doesn't turn her head even though with the window open she must realize I'm ten feet away. She just sits there all statue-like, not even blinking. Her long dark hair falls over her shoulders, grazing the swell of her breasts.

I open the driver's side door and climb inside even though I almost can't stand being this close to her. "Hey, you lost?"

"Yes." Her voice is a husky whisper. "I'm lost."

I toss the rest of my crap into the back and lean against the side of the truck. "I don't think I can help you with that, Ren."

"I know you can't."

She's too beautiful. I don't want to look at her anymore. Instead I look at the last wisps of light in the western sky. "What the hell do you want from me then?"

"I want you to drive into the desert."

"What for?"

She looks straight at me. "Just drive," she whispers.

"Just drive," I mutter, but I jump behind the wheel.

At this point I know the surrounding land pretty well. The terrain isn't that rough until you get real close to the mountains. I drove slowly, using the brights to guide my way around towering saguaros and spectral Joshua trees. After coasting for over a mile I stop and switch off the engine, waiting.

She's watching me. My eyes are pretty sharp in the dark, probably on account of spending so much time exploring the underground.

Damn, the beauty of her can still catch me off guard. Her full lips are parted slightly and I think about tasting them, sucking them. She stares at me for a moment and then glances around the dashboard.

"You got a camera in here?"

"Fuck no."

With no warning she grabs my hand off the steering wheel and presses it firmly to her tits. The hot flesh beneath her flimsy shirt arches against my palm. All the blood in my body roars straight into my cock. Whatever she's doing, I'm not about to put a stop to it. I flex my hand, lightly squeezing.

"Harder," she whispers.

I get both my hands on her, one palm on each pleading tit, and start kneading them roughly. Ren gasps once, then melts right into the seat, letting out a soft moan and covering my hands with hers. The more I work her the more she gets off on it. She wants me to be rough.

Fine. I'll give it to her rough. But it will be *my* version.

With a grunt I ball up the front of her shirt in one fist and haul her toward me. I feel the snap of her bra breaking as I get her straddled across my lap. Her hair has fallen in her face so I seize two handfuls of it and yank hard until she winces and finally looks me in the eye.

"I know what you're doing," I growl at her.

She cocks her head to the side. "Do you now?"

"You think if we go at it this way, all filthy and empty, that you can kill every bit of unfinished business there is between us."

She just stares, stubborn and silent. But the flash in her eyes tells me I'm right.

I push open the door and drag her outside with me. I slam the door shut and press her against it, pulling her skirt up and parting her legs with my knee.

"You know what? I need you gone for good too and maybe this is what it'll take." When I push my hands between her legs she shudders and grips my shoulders as her body rocks against the rhythm of my crude stroking. She's ready all right. This is what she's here for. My cock is so hard I'm about to bust out.

"Tell me that's what you're after."

"Yes, Oz," she pants through gritted teeth. "This is what it'll take."

"And you know that once I'm done with you tonight you'll just be another dumb snatch I've greased."

She flinches but doesn't back down. "And you'll just be another disposable dick. Like you always were."

I take a step back and yank my shirt over my head. "I'm not kissing you. I'll never kiss you again, you cold-hearted bitch. Kissing means something and this don't mean shit."

"No, it doesn't mean shit."

I drop my pants and close her hand around my cock. She gasps slightly and squeezes her way along the hard flesh. This is what I've fantasized about. But there's a crude, angry quality to it now. I let her stroke me for a few more beats before I swat her away and start pumping my junk myself.

"Get it all off."

Her hands grasp the hem of her shirt but then she hesitates.

"*Now*, Ren. You wanted nasty and I'm going to give it to you nasty as all fuck, but that means I'm sure as hell not undressing you all gentle and sweet."

"Fuck you," she sneers, "if I wanted gentle and sweet I wouldn't be here."

"Glad we finally understand each other. So get all your shit off and get spread out."

Her chest heaves as she gets rid of her shirt and her torn bra. "You're despicable now. I really hate you."

"You don't hate me at all. But you will by the time I'm done tonight."

I know there are some condoms in my bag but it takes me a minute of hunting around in the dark to find them. Ren still has her skirt on and she's slow about sliding her underwear off. She hasn't moved from the side of the truck. The tailgate creaks in protest when I tug it down.

For a second the insanity of the situation hits me and I'm almost ashamed. If I still had some shreds of decency to rub together I would drive her back to Atlantis, bid her a cordial farewell and then drive off forever. What's about to happen isn't going to do either of us any good but somehow I can't stop it.

I don't want to stop it.

I snap my fingers at her face. "Now get your spoiled little ass over here if you want to do this."

Ren slides slowly around to the back and faces me with her tits bared and her skirt bunched up in her fists. My cock is pointed straight as a thick arrow and with my teeth I tear open the condom wrapper.

She's staring at my cock and she's still clutching the sides of her skirt around her thighs like she's about to go wading in shallow water. That drives me slightly crazy and I grab the fabric, crudely yanking it over her hips until she's forced to let it go and puddle on the ground.

Goddammit, why does she have to be so beautiful?

Her high gasp makes me think she might just be all talk here so I shove my hand between her legs to find out.

"Fuuuck," I groan because she's so open and ready I lose two fingers inside her without even trying.

"No!" She pushes my hand right out of her and spins around, bracing her hands on the flattened tailgate and rubbing her lush little ass against my extended cock. She knows what she's doing, teasing with that ripe little cleft until I almost forget where I am and who I am because above all else there's the big fat fucking need to get my shit buried in a tight spot.

"We're doing it like this," she whispers.

Ren's long dark hair cascades over her bare back and there's never been anything that screams SEX as loud as this goddamn woman bent naked over the truck and trying to swallow my cock with her ripe ass. She jerks her head suddenly, swinging her hair aside and looking back at me to bark out a terse order. "And Oz, you damn well better make it hurt!"

I could. I could bore straight into that sweet center like a fucking jackhammer and *pound pound pound* without mercy until she cries. Instead I get my hands around her hips, arch her body slightly and slide carefully into the tight, slippery entrance I had once been the first man to find a way into.

"Oz!" she gasps, then groans as I get into the rhythm.

Damn you. Damn you. Damn you. I loved you. Damn you.

She's clenching, arching, doing everything she can to push back and work her body so that I'm reaching the sweet spot. I'm not gentle. I squeeze her tits, suck her skin and keep pumping until she's so far gone into her moaning ecstasy she probably doesn't remember her own name. That's when I slide a hand underneath where we're joined, find her swollen clit and press down with two fingers until I feel the shudder of a powerful orgasm start to claim her.

Then I abruptly stop. It's kind of cruel but that's the idea. I take my hand away, pull my cock out and grab a fistful of her thick hair, clawing my fingers close to her scalp and then tugging hard enough to make her yelp.

"You still want me to make it hurt, Ren?"

"Oh god, yes!" She grinds her lower body against the hard shell of the tailgate, desperate for release, bringing a perverse smile to my face. If I so much as fucking breathe on that needy little pussy right now she'll come so hard she won't be able to stand up afterwards.

But I'm not giving that to her.

She told me to make it hurt and I'm damn well going to make it hurt, just not the way she had in mind.

She's light enough so that I can flip her over with ease. The moonlight pours over her tits and her belly and every cursed perfect inch of her. All I want to do is bend my head and use my mouth, my tongue, to worship all of her until the sun reclaims the sky. Instead I spread her legs wider, grip her hips and plunge inside, barely hanging on to my own reason when she arches her back, bends those pretty tits toward my face and lets out a low, throaty moan that I'm dead sure will give me mental jerkoff material until the day my cock stops working. She's so close to the edge she's shaking and I'm about ready to bust my load wide open but I pull out again anyway.

"Please," she moans, shaking her head from side to side, "I need…"

I climb on top of her. "Look at me."

She's drunk with passion, can hardly hear me. "Wha-"

With a roar I grab her face in my palm, my fingers digging into her soft cheeks until she winces.

"Look at me, Loren Savage! You better open up and fucking see me!"

She opens her eyes and there must be something terrible about the look on my face because they widen with alarm. That's when I plunge into her again. Hard. Deliberate. She responds with a wild buck of her hips and a scream of pleasure that's swiftly drowned with my mouth.

I'd told her I wouldn't kiss her and true to my word, this is no kiss. This is a ruthless invasion of tongue and force that doesn't let up until we are both trembling from the spasms of our violent climax.

"Oscar," she sighs softly when I finally let go of her.

"I love you."

"I love you too."

No, that's not this night. That was another night, a long time ago. It happened to two utterly different people who are long gone. They won't be coming back.

I don't watch her as she pulls her clothes back on. I sit there on the edge of the tailgate, naked and hollow, saying nothing. Every ten seconds or so a flash of lightning burns the sky and shows the mountains hiding in the dark. The wind kicks up slightly, rustling the dry mesquite leaves and stirring the dust on the desert floor.

Ren is beside me now, waiting. Waiting for me to say a word, waiting for me to hop back in my truck and leave her out here to find her way back alone. Without acknowledging her at all I manage to locate my clothes in the dust.

The used condom has already been tossed somewhere into the darkness. Usually I'm scrupulous about such things but fuck it. The desert can keep that one little sordid piece of us.

Once I'm behind the wheel again, Ren climbs into the passenger seat beside me and folds her hands primly in her lap as I steer the truck back to Atlantis. There are lights on in the big house, not surprising since it isn't really that late. It's not even nine o'clock.

I brake to a stop about fifty yards away from the house, close to the sadly overgrown plot of what was once a fake cemetery in a dozen old west movies. On one side, the caretaker's house squats behind the dark, silent brothel. On the other the white clapboard church stands sentinel. Last week when I ducked inside there I noticed weeds poking through the floorboards and thought it was possible no one had walked the floor in years. I suppose that for Spencer the old church is simply not a caretaking priority. It'll probably just fall over one of these days. In the distance, the faded letters on the broad Mercantile are visible if I squint. I allow myself to have a few seconds to take in what I can see of the place in the dark because I've already made up my mind.

This will be the last time I ever see Atlantis Star. This will be the last time I see Ren.

She already has her hand on the door but she pauses without opening it. If she's waiting for some poignant last words she's not going to get them. Even though my heart is full of chaos, confusion, even sorrow, it has to be this way. If I ever had any doubts that we're an unhealthy mix, that frenzied fuck fest in the desert just answered everything.

I never really did want to hurt her. Not years ago when she kicked me out of her life, not when I landed back in Atlantis amid all the surreal camera craziness and not even tonight when she opened her legs and begged me to.

She was, and is, the owner of my heart.

She whispers my name. "Oz."

I have to pretend I just don't hear it because I'm aching to pull her against my chest and stubbornly keep her no matter what it might do to my sanity.

I just turn my head and face the open window. It's as definite a refusal as I can muster without saying the words. If I try to say anything right now I know I won't end up leaving. And at this point I'm leaving as much for her sake as for mine. Thanks to this circus the world would sniff out a 'cousin fucks cousin' scandal without a care about whether there's any actual biology involved. They would harass her to the end of time. Funny how after everything I still care about how she feels.

So I wait in silence until she gives up and slowly opens the door. She's probably combing her brain to figure out how to bid a final farewell to a hated ex-lover. I guess she can't come up with anything because after a moment I hear her footsteps heading in the opposite direction, toward the big house. Only then do I look at her, just to catch one final glimpse of the swing of her hair and the straight line of her back before she melts into the darkness.

There's nothing to do now but start the engine and head for the road. In two minutes I'm outside of Atlantis and I don't look back.

Now that I'm out of there can I start to think straight again.

Really, I lost my grudge against the Savages a long time ago. Maybe it never existed in the first place. I was angry and hurting for a long time so whatever reasons there were for my exile seemed unimportant.

I do know one thing. No matter what she says these days, that girl loved me once. She loved me as much as I loved her. But the world is filled with a million sad stories, stories of what's been lost and who has suffered. Ren and I, we're just another of those stories.

And now I can finally say that the story has ended. Not happily, but ended just the same.

CHAPTER EIGHTEEN

REN

Nothing seems real tonight.　Not the ache between my legs or bruised sensation still on my lips or the fresh smell of the approaching rain.　My steps are leaden as I leave Oscar and I don't take a breath until I hear his truck roaring away into the night.

Spencer happens to be coming around the side of the house with a thick coil of rope around one shoulder when I reach the porch.　I try to avoid being bathed in the yellow porch light, but it's not enough to escape my brother's scrutiny.　He stops, staring.　"What the hell happened to you?"

"Nothing. "　My voice sounds froggy so I clear it and try again.　"I was just out for a walk."

"You look pretty messed up for a walk."

"Yeah, well. It got windy, okay?"

Spence glances in the direction where Oz's truck disappeared.　The sound of the engine lingers but the taillights are no longer visible.　He must have already gone around the bend of the road that leads out of Atlantis.　He's gone.　There will be no answer to the misery in my soul.

Could I have stopped him from leaving? No, there's no use running after a man who finds you contemptible. Twice now I've watched him leave. At the moment I couldn't say which occasion was more devastating. I'm not as raw as I was five years ago though.

Perhaps my transition is complete. I'm a *'cold-hearted bitch'* who has finally turned to stone.

Spence shifts his weight around and seems like he wants to say something but Monty interrupts, flinging open the screen door like a cocksure king busting out of his castle. He steps onto the porch, still holding the same bottle as earlier, but in the glint of the moonlight I can see it's not as full. Nonetheless, the look he gives me is sharp-eyed and suspicious, not dull and drunk. Montgomery could always hold his liquor. He crosses his arms and looks from side to side as if he's searching for a hidden predator. He gives me a nod. "What's going on, Ren?"

For a second I try to pat my wild hair down, then give up. I realize that the shoulder of my shirt is torn but there's nothing I can do about that right now. I can't make myself care much about appearances at the moment anyway. "Jesus, you guys," I snap. "Nothing happened."

"She went for a *walk*," Spence pipes up with helpful sarcasm.

Monty leans against the knotty wood porch beam and looks me over. He evidently doesn't like what he sees. "You fall down the side of a fucking mountain on your walk?"

God, I'm tired. I could sleep for a week. Perhaps when I wake up the dull pain will be gone. "I fell down something."

"Did that something have a pickup truck and a shitty attitude?"

I lower my head. My hair falls across my vision like a dark veil. "So what if it did?"

Monty spits into the dirt. "Fuck him. I'm glad he's gone."

"Oz is gone?" asks Spence.

"He'd better be."

Spence is looking at me. "I never really understood what he was doing here anyway. Doesn't seem like the Hollywood type who would fit into all of this."

Monty laughs. "What about you, fantasy cowboy? You're not exactly the type either."

"Shut up, you jailbird piece of shit."

Monty lights another cigarette. He's becoming a goddamn chain smoker. "Hey Ren, you let me know the minute that prick shows up here again and I'll drop kick him to fucking Flagstaff."

I raise my head and glare at him. "Really, Monty? I have my doubts that assault is encouraged during your parole."

Monty grunts in response and takes a drag.

Spencer comes closer, really takes stock of my messy appearance and adopts an expression of supreme concern. For Spencer, that means his eyebrows are slightly furrowed. "Hey. He didn't rough you up or nothing, did he?"

"Oz? Rough me up?" I throw my head back and laugh crazily. I'm laughing because the concept so far from the truth and yet so completely true. Yes, he roughed me up. He told me the truth about myself and treated me how I deserve to be treated.

While I keep cackling, my brothers assume identical macho glowers. They glower at me. The glower at each other. They glower at the darkness and the sky. I'm sick of both of them and their stupid fucking glowering maleness at this point. I stop laughing like a wild hyena.

"Whatever happened out there tonight is my business so let's knock off the inquisition. Ninety nine percent of the time you don't seem to give a damn about what I'm doing anyway. So let's save the show of brotherly concern for the daylight hours when the production crew can get some useful footage out of it."

 On that tender note I slam my way into the house. Brigitte's startled face is the first thing I see because she's scooted a chair right next to the door, pretending to be immersed in her phone while discreetly listening to the conversation on the front porch.

She calls my name but I ignore her and head for the kitchen. My mouth feels like it's layered with mesquite bark. I fill a glass with water from the sink even though the tap water tastes like warm sulfur out here. When I'm gulping it back, ignoring the awful taste, I catch sight of a camera that had been installed just above the sink. I'd stopped noticing it days ago but now the empty stare of the black lens infuriates me so I rip it right out of the wall. A few errant wires trail from its guts so I stuff the whole thing into the very back of the freezer, slamming the stainless steel door shut.

"Like that'll do anything," Brigitte snorts from the doorway. She wafts into the room, grabs an apple from a bowl in the center of the table and flashes me a bemused glance. "They'll just put it back tomorrow. Besides, there are about a hundred and seventy five more of them sewn into the walls of the house. I'll bet someone will still be picking hidden cameras out of the eaves fifty years after we're dead.

By the way, big sister, you look like the proverbial cat who ate the canary."

I empty the glass and set it down in the sink. "So I guess you're speaking to me again?"

She takes a bite of the apple, chews and looks thoughtfully wounded before opting to answer. "I'm choosing to overlook your occasionally aggressive nature. After all, I know this is a stressful environment. I also know that I have the capacity to be a terrible bitch."

I sink down in one of the hardback chairs. "Cut out the theatrics. You know Bree, I have to wonder if you have to ability to stop acting even if you try."

Another bite of the apple. "I'm not acting right now. I'm just being your sister."

"Then just be my sister and stop trying to direct a script."

She sighs, touches her left palm to her forehead. Bree suffers from frequent migraines, one of the few things we have in common.

"Loren," she says quietly, "why are you in the habit of forgetting that I'm on your side?"

"Why are you in that habit of behaving as if you are starring in a vivid mini-series about your own life?"

"I don't even know what that means."

"Yes you do. It means I have to watch my back lest I get broadsided by your ambitions."

The hand holding the apple wilts at her side and the flash of genuine confusion in her eyes makes me wish I could take my own words back. I've been wishing that a lot lately. Someone really ought to muzzle me.

We're turning on each other. Or maybe it's all me, turning on everyone.

She shakes her head, catching onto my meaning. "Ren, I didn't tell them anything they didn't already know."

I close my eyes. "Really?"

"No, I really didn't! If you want to know how it went down, well, okay. Gary asked. Repeatedly. Like he already knew everything about you and Oscar but was looking for someone to go on record with it. But that someone wasn't me."

"You could have warned me, Brigitte. You could have warned me that his name had come up."

"Ren, why did you ever fool yourself into thinking it wouldn't?" She sighs. "You're right though. I should have said something. But I thought if I did-"

"You thought I'd back out of the show."

She lowers her head. "Yes." After a long exhale she swallows and meets my eyes. "I'm sorry, okay? But I swear, the day he showed up I was as shocked to see him as you were."

"Oh, I doubt anyone was as shocked to see him as I was."

Bree scrunches up her nose and starts to say something before changing her mind and shutting her mouth.

"What do you want to say?"

Brigitte slides her lithe body into the chair across from me. "I never even knew exactly what happened between you guys. None of us really did. I mean, we all knew you were together. We knew Lita was simmering to a slow boil over it. But the things she said about him, they couldn't all have been true, right?"

The flashback to that night is visceral. The smell of smoke, the feel of Oscar inside of me, my mother's hand slapping my face hard enough to bring a trickle of blood to my nose. Threats, promises, screaming, desolation. And finally, emptiness.

"No, Bree," I assure my sister. "They weren't all true."

But it didn't matter. Not then, and certainly not now. Lita was pathological about her lies but her promises were another story. She'd left me with the cruelest choice she could think of. But then, that was the idea.

"I figured as much," says Brigitte with a wise nod. Funny how I always think of my sisters as very young, even though I'm only a year older than Ava and barely two years older than Brigitte.

My sister winds the end of her brilliant red hair around a forefinger with a troubled expression. It's eerie how much she resembles Margaret O'Leary, film goddess from the last century. She has the kind of face loved by the camera. Suddenly her eyebrows knit together. "I should probably tell you something. The other day, that parasite Cate Camp let her guard down and said something about the show having some contact with Lita. She realized right away she'd made a mistake mentioning her and started falling all over herself to cover it up, telling some spontaneous lie about how Lita was demanding that her name be kept out of the show altogether."

The sound of my mother's name is a sour one and I feel my face scrunching up. "I thought that was always the idea. But escaping publicity doesn't really sound like Lita."

"I didn't think so either but who knows? I haven't heard from her in over two years, not since I turned eighteen. She didn't even want to know about it when Ava had her baby. Supposedly she's holed up in her mansion in Beverly Hills, waiting for her meal ticket to stop breathing so she can enjoy the fruits of California's community property laws. God, she's a bitch."

I find it hard to picture my mother. The last time I saw her was the morning of my father's funeral three years ago. We didn't even speak that day. "Gary and his minions swore from the beginning that there wouldn't be any Lita. It's the one condition I had, although now I realize I should have added a few more."

"Hmmph," grunts Brigitte.

"What's that mean?"

She wets her lips and leans across the table. "Did you get an attorney, Ren? One who wasn't on Gary's payroll to look over the show contract?"

I hadn't. I couldn't exactly afford to retain an entertainment lawyer so when Gary offered to have his legal team broker the arrangement I didn't come up with a reason to turn it down. "No," I admit slowly.

Brigitte slumps down with a grimace. "Me either."

"So what are you worried about exactly?"

"I don't know. But I also don't really know what the hell it is I signed."

I can't really make myself care about the show or the contract or whoever might be listening to us at this point. Once upon a time I used to flatter myself that I was the sensible sister. In reality, I'm just a scabbed wound, so closed off that simple honesty is a foreign language.

Bree seems to sense my thoughts. "He could have been colluding with Gary from the beginning. Who knows, maybe it was even Oscar who started feeling around to see if there was any tabloid interest in the half-forgotten Savage family. I imagine there must have been something there, a desire for revenge or whatever. I know it's been a long time and you guys were just kids but time does funny things to people."

Of course I'd thought of that the minute he showed up. Oscar hadn't exactly been forthcoming about the circumstances surrounding his sudden arrival. He danced around difficult questions with course teasing and watched me with those dark, inscrutable eyes. And then tonight…

No, it's too fresh. I can't stand thinking about the feel of him all over me. I can't even bear to examine what led me to stubbornly climb into his truck as soon as I heard he would be leaving.

Sooner or later I'll have to come to terms with how Oscar and I crashed together, fucked like enemies and ultimately resolved nothing. We just used each other as a way to forever kill what we once had.

Yet whoever Oscar's become, there was once a sense of honor in him. I won't let myself believe that's a quality that just disappears completely. He was right. I don't despise him at all. I don't even know why I said otherwise.

"No," I finally say. "If he was out to humiliate me and make a few dollars in the process, he had his chance and he threw it away."

"So Monty wasn't just talking out of his ass? Oscar really left?"

"He did."

"Oh," Bree frowns. "Better that way I guess, although I'm going to predict Gary and company will be shitting bricks tomorrow."

"Gary can suck it."

Brigitte smiles. "He doesn't have to. I hear Cate Camp does it for him." She raises her voice, yelling at the air. "Did you catch that? Did you?" She winks at me. "Not wearing my mic."

I look at my sister. She isn't perfect. But I love her and she loves me. We both need as much of that in our lives right now as we can get. "I shouldn't have lashed out at you. I'm sorry."

She gives me a faint smile. "I suppose I've done a few things to deserve it." She loses her smile. "Look, I know all of this isn't your idea of success. I know you're here because we asked you to be. And I'm not sure I ever thanked you for that. Or for the fact that you've always been more of a mother to all of us than Lita ever was."

I swallow. There's a bitter taste in the back of my throat that won't disappear. "I'm not going to pretend like anyone's twisting my arm. It's my choice to be here, Bree."

"Fair enough. But I'll only forgive your worst assumptions about me if you quit using that wretched nickname. It reminds me of childhood."

A small, rueful grin creeps across my face. "Not a chance. Habits die hard, or in my case, never. It's my chief flaw."

"Oh, Ren. We're all flawed." Brigitte rises from the table, heads toward the door and then spins suddenly, dropping a graceful curtsy. "Terribly, *savagely* flawed."

CHAPTER NINETEEN

Five Years Ago: The End

Mina Savage is dead.

A week ago Ren stood right beside Oscar as they learned the news together. Her father was the one to say the words. August had summoned her to the house along with Oscar and for a defiant moment Ren was sure it was because August planned on confronting them about being together.

She was ready.

With Oscar next to her she could be brave enough to face the censure of her parents, even if it meant she lost them. She didn't care a bit how it would look to the world, or that they were only seventeen or that her family would have hysterics. No one would take Oscar away from her.

But when they reached the paneled study where her father spent most of his days he sat there alone, looking far older than he had just that morning when she'd caught a fleeting glimpse of him. Then, in a halting, sorrowful voice he told them what he'd learned an hour earlier over the phone.

"Her heart was weak. So many years, so many pills. I don't have the whole story but she'd apparently been stealing another patient's meds and she took them all at once. It was a full cardiac arrest. Very quick. There will be no funeral. She'd arranged to be cremated immediately upon death. Oscar, you hear what I'm telling you? Do you hear me?"

"Yes. I hear you, sir."

Oscar hadn't cried at all until much later. And then he cried only to her.

Life stayed quiet for a few days. The girls were unusually somber, Spencer kept on being Spencer, August closed himself in his study and even Monty stopped hassling Oscar, giving him space to mourn.

Ren spent every moment with Oscar, even climbing through his window to lie in his arms for a few hours while the rest of Atlantis slept. She worried about the watchful glare of her mother. Sometimes it seemed Lita was everywhere – haunting the front porch of the big house, lingering by the staircase of the brothel. Always with the same impassive mask and never saying a word. The fact that her mother had stopped speaking to her was no great loss to Ren, but she'd spent seventeen years learning to mistrust the woman. The flat, dead-eyed look in her mother's eyes chilled her more than she could admit.

Now, every day she wakes up to a growing fear of a threat she can't name but is sure draws closer to her with each stolen moment.

Oscar just kisses her worries away and promises that soon they will leave Atlantis behind. He pointedly ignores the ominous Lita menace. Whenever and wherever she appears, he just stares right through her.

This morning a sleek BMW coasted through the rusty gates of Atlantis and parked in front of the big house. The grey-suited man who exited the vehicle was expected by her father. August shook the man's hand and led him into the house while Lita trailed after them. Ren had watched it all from the shadows of the brothel where she was sprawled with Oscar, smoking some of Monty's cigarettes.

"He's a lawyer," Brigitte is now saying with snotty authority when Ren enters the bedroom where her sisters are trying on clothes and admiring their bodies in the closet mirror. Bree smiles at her reflection and twists sideways. "He's here because Mina made such a shit show out of her life and now there's some housekeeping to be done."

Of course a man like that would have to be a lawyer but it annoys Ren that Brigitte seems to have all the information already.

"How would you know?" Ren grumbles, flopping on her own unmade bed.

"If you climb over all the antique crap in the den and stand underneath the air vent you can hear every word that's said in Daddy's study."

"And I suppose that's what you did." Ren rolls over on her stomach and despite herself, hopes Bree will share whatever else she learned, especially if it involves Oscar's mother.

"Naturally. It's not like August and Lita ever tell us anything."

Ren sits up. "So?"

"So what?"

"So what's this garbage about Aunt Mina?"

Brigitte preens and rolls the side of her shirt down, exposing a shoulder. She sucks her cheeks in and offers the mirror her most provocative pose. "You're always yelling at me for gossiping, Loren. I should probably try to turn over a new leaf for your sake. Starting now. So I don't think I should say a word about Aunt Mina and the disaster she made."

Ren jumps to her feet and gets between her sister and the mirror. "Bree! You better tell me whatever you know right now."

"You shouldn't threaten people, Ren. You sound preposterous."

"What threat? That was a threat?"

Brigitte pouts. "Your tone was negative. It startled me."

Ava finishes smearing a thick layer of lipstick on herself and joins the conversation. "Come on, spill it. I want to know too. Do we have another hot blooded cousin stashed somewhere?"

"Nope," Bree smiles. "In fact we don't even really have one."

Ren shakes her head. "Quit speaking in riddles."

"I'm not. Mina never went through with Oscar's adoption. She paid off a stack of important people for that kid and then didn't even bother to finish the basic paperwork. So Oscar Anonymous is no Savage."

Ren mulls this over. It sounds just like everything she's ever heard about the chronically irresponsible Mina. It might be a pain in the ass for Oscar, but not the end of the world. "Is that all?"

"Hmmm," Bree taps a fuchsia fingernail against her teeth. "Almost. Apparently the great globetrotting basket case didn't leave a will either so Oscar doesn't get anything, which actually doesn't matter since she didn't own shit except a pile of debt and eight trunks full of the tackiest designer labels her bad credit would buy her."

Ava stops examining a turquoise necklace and looks at Ren. "What does all that mean exactly? What does it mean for Oscar?"

It means he's nameless and penniless.

Brigitte is staring at her and looks slightly mournful. "It means Lita is already making the case to toss him out on his ass."

Hearing it out loud is unsettling but Ren and Oscar have already talked about what they would do, where they would go. Of course they were counting on having a few more resources at their disposal but Ren isn't bothered by the idea of working hard, doing without. As long as she gets to keep Oscar nothing else matters.

"Well," she says lightly. "Lita never did waste an opportunity to be a bitch."

Ava's eyes are wide. "You'd better watch out for her, Ren. There's something off between her and Oscar. It's like she hates him or something."

"The feeling is likely mutual."

Ava swallows and sinks down on the edge of her bed. "Sometimes I think she hates you too."

"Again, mutual."

Bree pulls her shirt over her head and cups her breasts, pushing them together. "Did you guys do it?"

"Who? Do what?"

She grins sweetly. "You're such a shitty liar. You fucked him, didn't you?"

"Brigitte!" Ava squeals.

"What? She can do it but I can't even say it? I am surprised, Loren. I kind of thought you'd die a knee-locked virgin."

Ren doesn't react. Bree's just fishing like she always does. She knows nothing.

"We haven't done anything. We're friends. And to hell with you and your filthy mind, Brigitte."

"Don't be pissed at me. I just repeat what I hear. Although it would be better if it wasn't true, especially given all the circumstances."

"All what circumstances? So he's not rolling in cash and his last name is a question mark. So what?"

"I meant in light of who else he might have fucked since he got here. Although if that's true, his standards are disgustingly low. Oh my god, would you stop with the face of shock every time I drop the F bomb? Let's all say it! Fuck fuck fuck fuck FUCK!"

"Fuck," says Ava with a weak smile.

Ren feels slightly dizzy. "Brigitte, you're not making any sense. You have *not* messed around with Oscar."

"God no. Not me. And you can't point the finger at Ava either."

"Then what in the hell are you babbling about?"

Bree starts to talk, then seems to change her mind. She glances out the window and sighs. "Nothing. It's nothing."

Ren's had enough. If she hangs out in here for much longer trying to dodge Brigitte's outlandish crap there might be blood. She rushes out of the room and ignores Ava when she tries to call her back.

When she reaches the hallway where her father's study is, she hears voices and the sound of a slowly opening door. She feels slightly idiotic ducking into the den and flattening herself against the wall but further family communication isn't appealing right now.

The den is densely packed with the possessions of the dead. Every once in a while August mentions clearing it out and letting Ren have it as a bedroom but that day will likely never come. Ren finds herself wedged between an empty curio cabinet and the mounted head of an antlered creature that was probably felled by Rex Savage.

There are footsteps in the hallway and the murmuring of men. And one woman.

Murmur murmur "of course" *murmur murmur* "rotten publicity" *murmur murmur* "good thing he isn't a child" *murmur murmur*. Then, nothing.

Once the men's voices recede, Ren peeks out from behind the bristly animal head and sees Lita there alone, standing in the hallway, examining her reflection before a giant round mirror in a manner reminiscent of a gothic evil fairy tale queen.

But Ren's stomach grows queasy when she sees the wide smile on Lita's face. On Lita, a smile is as natural as blue jeans on a cat. She waits for Lita to quit admiring herself and move on before stealthily heading for the back door. She wants out of this house. She wants away from these people. She just wants Oscar.

She finds him with Spence. They are spaced about twenty yards apart, clutching shotguns and scanning the desert brush beyond the fake church. Oscar has his shirt off and in Ren's utterly unbiased opinion he is the hottest guy in the solar system. He glances up as her shadow approaches and immediately breaks into a grin. She's so lucky. What girl doesn't pray to be smiled at like this? Lita can issue threats until her face melts off. Every lawyer in the country can drive their suits and phony concern to hell and back. Nothing is going to pull them apart.

"Hunting rattlers?" she asks, turning her face up for a quick kiss and not bothering to check whether Spence is watching. Spence continues combing the ground. Spence doesn't care who is kissing who.

"Yep." Oscar shoulders the shotgun and circles his arms around her waist.

She loves being close to him whenever she can, every way she can. She understands now what happens to people, how they lose all sense and reason when they fall as hard as this.

Oscar squints into the sun. "Too many of them around here lately. Someone's going to take a bad step and wind up with a leg full of venom."

"We have to talk," Ren whispers.

Oscar doesn't ask her what it's about. He just nods and calls to Spence that he's talking off for a while. He leaves Spence his shotgun and holds Ren's hand as they head for the barn where it will be stifling hot but quiet.

There's a place in the narrow loft they like to go when they need to be alone and can't find anywhere else. Spence's tired old mare, Pet, chews lazily and seems to be listening as Ren tells Oscar everything about the lawyer and about Mina.

He seems rather unsurprised, or else he's putting on a brave face for her benefit. He tells her to stop talking and then sets her gently on her back for a long kiss. She says nothing about Brigitte's strange claim that Oscar has been with someone other than her since arriving at Atlantis. It's impossible. He tells her every day that there will never be anyone else, never again. She feels him pressing into her and wants to give him everything he needs. She needs it just as much. His strong hand moves over her skin, underneath her shirt and she arches her body, pushing him higher.

"You sick motherfucker!"

Oscar jerks and springs upright as sharply as if he's been shot. Ren furiously rolls her shirt down and dares to glance down into Monty's raging face. He's not looking at her though. Every ounce of his fury is directed at Oscar. "Yeah, you better get your ass down here!"

Oscar jumps down and circles warily. "Stay up there, Ren."

"You think you need to protect my sister from me? Is that what you think you shitty little punk?"

"Right now? Yes."

Monty swings. He's got a hard right hook but Oscar's quick. He manages to dodge sideways.

"Montgomery!" Ren shouts. "You stop this right now!"

He flashes her a look that seems almost hurt, probably because in his mind he's doing his lousy best to protect her honor or whatever from the predatory Oscar.

"I don't want to get into this with you," Oscar growls. "Not right now." Then he sighs tiredly. "Goddammit, Monty, haven't we knocked each other around enough this summer?"

Monty thinks. Then he smiles, a cold smile. "No," he says and his next swing is abrupt enough to connect with Oscar's jaw. Another guy would probably have been knocked over but Oscar just reels backwards momentarily and then rights himself, spitting out a quarter-sized bullet of blood. Without pausing to blink he knocks his right hook against Monty's jaw. Monty curses, stumbling, and the two of them stand off, each ready to charge ahead and send the other straight to the next county.

Ren jumps down from the loft and gets between them. Monty is startled, dropping his stance and staring down at her with vague puzzlement. "This is between me and him, Ren."

"No, it isn't. You knock it the hell off or so help me I'll never consider you a brother again."

He's dumbfounded. "Holy shit, don't tell me you've bought into his act. He's a horny little con artist."

"Monty," she warns, falling back to stand beside Oscar. "I mean it. Whatever battle you think you're fighting doesn't exist."

Ren watches her brother shake his head in disgust. He spits on the ground and addresses Oscar. "This sure as shit isn't over. You stay the fuck away from my sister or I swear one of these days I'll kill you."

Oscar just snorts. "Drop dead you mouth-breathing prick."

With one more ominous glare at Ren, Monty takes off, stalks over to the pickup truck and peels out of Atlantis.

"Asshole," Oscar says.

"Sometimes," Ren sighs. She touches Oscar's swelling jaw. "Does it hurt?"

"It's nothing."

Ren runs her fingers across his cheek, feeling a hint of rough stubble. It excites her. He always excites her. "You know, I bet he'll be gone all day. Monty's fits are usually good for about twelve hours of Monty-free living."

Oscar grins. "Well worth the pain then."

The little caretaker's house is messy but blissfully empty. Ren prepares a gourmet lunch of grilled cheese and for the afternoon they pretend there is no Monty, no Lita, no such thing as a Savage. They spend hours in Oscar's bed, making love tenderly, then playfully rough, then tender once again as the sun fades and an electrical storm rolls through.

"You smell that?" Ren asks as she straddles Oscar and listens to the wind outside.

Oscar props himself on his elbows, leans over and pushes the window open. "Fire," he confirms. "Probably sparked by a bolt of lightning, likely in the mountain foothills."

Ren shudders. The wind must be blowing the smoke right in their direction. The acrid stench fills the room. "It won't reach here, will it?"

Oscar thinks about it. "Nah. There's not enough on the desert floor to burn. Besides there's probably rain coming right up. That'll take care of things."

"Oscar." She rests her cheek against his hard chest. "We need to leave. We need to get out of here."

He strokes her hair. "I know, baby. I know. Just need a few days to get a plan sorted out. Trust me, Ren. We'll make it. As long as there's us, there's everything."

"I love you, Oscar. I want to keep saying it in case I don't say it enough."

"You say it plenty. And you're the only one I ever want to hear it from. I love you too."

She shivers and tries to burrow closer to him. She can't. She just can't get close enough. "Show me," she whispers.

It's ecstasy, as always. He grips her hips and helps her move with deliberate care as they connect yet again. Ren keeps her eyes closed, letting herself go completely, and in that moment she glimpses her future, a future full of Oscar and of bliss, and she knows it will be hers.

It only takes an instant for the vision to shatter.

"What's wrong?" Oscar asks. He sits up and tips her chin toward him. "Ren. You look terrified. What is it?"

She tries to smile but realizes her right hand is still clapped firmly over her mouth so a smile would make no difference. Slowly, she removes the hand that had flown to her face in horror the moment she'd opened her eyes and looked at the dark open window. Horror, because someone was right there, looking back at her. Someone whose features were twisted into an expression of hatred in its most unfiltered form. And then it was gone.

"Let's go away," she begs, clutching him. "Let's go away tonight. I have a little bit of money from when I did some catalog modeling before we moved out here. Let's just go. We don't even have to tell anyone."

"We will," he whispers, kissing her lips. "Not tonight but we will."

"Why not tonight?"

"You're not eighteen."

"Neither are you."

He grimaces. "Maybe," he mutters. "In any case no one would be looking for me. You're a different story. This isn't a movie, Loren. We need a plan. We can't just slide into the night like a pair of criminals and expect there will be no consequences, that it will all turn out happily ever after."

He's right. Of course he's right. She would be reported, the news would hit the tabloids.

"Teenager Loren Savage, daughter and granddaughter of Hollywood legends, runs away from home with a man rumored to be her cousin. The two are thought to be at large somewhere in western Arizona."

"I know that," she says with some bitterness as she slowly pulls her clothes back on. "Believe me, I understand exactly how it is."

Oscar watches her. "Where are you going?"

"The big house. I have a feeling someone's waiting for me there."

His dark eyes are troubled and he starts to rise. "I'll go with you."

"No." She kisses him. "No. I'll be back soon."

The smoke smell is stronger outside. Ren walks slowly, pausing on the porch of the brothel. The wind plays havoc with her hair and darkens her vision with dust. But in the west, toward the mountains, she thinks she sees a faint orange glow. It could be a brush fire or it could be the last gasp of the vanishing sun. It's impossible to tell.

Why does she feel like she is being slowly choked from the inside? Every step toward the house is more difficult to take than the last one. She tells herself there is no reason to feel this way. Yes, it was her mother's face at the window, her mother's cold eyes of loathing, but there is nothing Lita can do to her. If she tries, Ren will convince Oscar that they have no choice but to leave, authorities and tabloids be damned.

The porch light is dark and she fumbles for the doorknob. The pickup truck is still gone, meaning Monty has not returned. For all their differences, Ren would rather have Monty around right now. No matter how much he despises Oscar, he would never stand still and allow Lita to hurt her. Ren has no such faith in her father.

At first the house is silent and Ren breathes with relief. She tiptoes past the front room and takes a right turn down the hall towards the bedroom she shares with her sisters. Suddenly she wants very much to be where they are.

A door opens at her back and light splashes the dark corridor. "Loren," says her father. "Come here please."

Ren tries to calm her quickening pulse as she turns around and cautiously enters her father's study. She has never been frightened of her father in her life and she isn't afraid of him now. But when she sees Lita sitting in a leather armchair with her legs crossed, a triumphant smile on her lips, Ren can hardly breathe.

She can't do anything to me. She can't do anything if I don't let her.

Ren crosses her arms and stares straight ahead as August closes the heavy door at her back. That's when Lita unexpectedly rises, crosses the room, and with the strength of a man strikes Ren across the face so hard her ears ring with the echo.

"You fucking whore," Lita spits.

Ren barely notices the pain. There is just the shock of being hit. Her nose feels funny and when she touches it with her fingers they come away bloody. She inhales hard, levels a loathing stare at the woman who gave her life and says with stark clarity, "You goddamn bitch."

"Stop it," August demands but there's no authority in his voice. Only exhaustion. "Goddamn it, both of you. Stop."

"Gladly," Ren says and turns to leave the room. Whatever these people need to talk about, they can do it without her. She needs to find Oscar. She needs to let him know that remaining in Atlantis is no longer an option.

Lita tears past August and blocks Ren's exit. "You're going nowhere. Not tonight. Not ever." She shakes her head as her silver earrings catch the soft light of the Tiffany lamp on August's desk. "I knew you were a loser, Loren. I knew it from the moment I laid eyes on you."

"Enough!" August actually raises his voice this time. "Lita, you've crossed the line."

Lita throws him a withering look. "Oh, be quiet, old man. You might strain a vocal chord pretending you care."

Ren clenches her fists. If Lita wants a fight she can have one. "Get the hell out of my way you poisonous cunt."

Her mother seems merely amused. "Trashy little words from a trashy little girl. My god, I always figured you for a pathetic fool but assumed you would know enough not to slut it around with the gutter rat your crazy aunt kept for a pet."

Ren closes her eyes, wishes to be somewhere else, anywhere else. "What is it that bothers you, Lita? That I'm with someone you consider inappropriate? Or that I've found something you've never had?"

"Oh," Lita says softly as her smile returns. "I guess it's time you heard. Loren my dear, sweet, supremely idiotic child, I've had *everything* you've had. Only I had it first."

That's what Brigitte meant. It's not true. It's not even in the same hemisphere as the truth.

"If you think I'll believe that you're more vile and crazy than I ever gave you credit for."

Ren recoils when Lita suddenly reaches out to brush a few fallen strands of dark hair from her forehead. She doesn't retreat soon enough to avoid being lightly scratched with her mother's fingernails.

"You fucking little moron," Lita sighs. "You actually believe he cares. No Ren, he's the sort of trash who's only looking for the next hole to satisfy himself."

Ren glances at her father, silently begging him to put a stop to this nightmare. She doesn't believe it. Not even for a blink of an eye does she believe Oscar would have a thing to do with Lita. August believes it though. Either he believes it or he can't be bothered with a contradiction. He breathes heavily and sinks down into a chair.

Lita laughs. "Oh, don't look at your father as if he'll object. Oscar's not the first one I've had fun with and he won't be the last. I suppose you're old enough to hear that your father and I have had an arrangement since Brigitte was born. I'm free to do as I please. And in this case, like so many others, that's exactly what I did."

Ren runs the back of her hand beneath her nose. It has stopped bleeding. "Sorry. It turns out you've wasted a round of theatrics, *Mom.* I know exactly what you are. You don't know how to do anything but lie and inflict pain. But I won't be your problem anymore. And neither will Oscar."

Lita is amused. "Is that because you believe you two will just ride off into the fabled sunset like the dreadful films once set here? No." She shakes her head with a private smile. "That won't be happening, Ren."

"Empty threats," Ren whispers. That's all you are. You can't stop us."

Lita clucks her tongue. "Well now, that's not exactly true. Do I really have to remind you that you are a minor?"

"Fine, I'll get emancipated. I have less than eight months until my eighteenth birthday."

"Yes, a lot can happen in eight months. Scandal and disgrace. And of course a trial."

"A trial?" Ren is startled. "What *crime* has been committed for god's sake?"

"Do you really think we would allow Mina's stray to camp out here without performing a few background checks? Among the more interesting nuggets of information we uncovered is the fact that Oscar is over eighteen and of course, as I just pointed out, you are not."

"Oh god, Lita, you think anyone will care? No one in their right mind would bother with a case like that."

"They will if I make sure of it. And just imagine all the lovely publicity that will surround you for the rest of your life. I'm aware of how much you adore the spotlight, dear daughter. Loren Savage will go from being Failed Actress to The Girl Who Fucked Her Cousin."

"This is insane. You are insane. You think no one will realize there's no biological connection between us? And by the way, I know that Mina never actually adopted him so that means his last name is not even legally Savage."

Lita sighs. "It saddens me that you've learned absolutely nothing. Truth is merely incidental. The story is whatever will sell. Always. The world will see you as cousins because I will make sure of it. And as far as legal trouble goes, if one charge doesn't stick we can just try again with another. For instance, I believe we will discover that there are some valuable things missing around here. Do not underestimate my resources, girl. What do you think his chances will be by the time I'm finished with him?"

Ren won't believe that. Even though she's seen the evidence her entire life she doesn't want to be part of a world where Lita is right. She holds her head up. "No. You're just so pathetically twisted that you don't understand that the truth actually matters to people."

"Well, by the time you get all that sorted out you won't be able to set foot outside the door without a camera in your face and your lover will be passing time somewhere in the Arizona penal system. You called me a liar, Ren, and sometimes that's true. But believe me when I tell you that I will not sleep until that boy is gone, one way or another."

Ren stares at her mother, true horror settling in. Lita believes in a scorched earth policy. She will set the world on fire to get her way.

"What do you want from me?" Ren whispers. "You just want me to be as miserable as you are?"

Lita's lips quiver and anyone else might believe she's trying not to cry. Ren knows otherwise. Her mother is stifling a smile, barely holding in laughter.

Ren turns beseechingly to her weary father. "Daddy. Do something."

But August Savage's tired eyes ask her to understand that he simply doesn't have it in him to stop his wife this time. He doesn't even want to try. He just wants to remain buried here in the peaceful desert and let all the noise disappear.

"I'm sorry, honey. He's a grown man and he's not even a member of the family. There's nothing I can do for him."

Ren backs away toward the door. She opens it and flees the room. The two people who are responsible for her life are repulsive. She needs to get free of them. She needs to find Oscar. But she needs a few minutes first. Just a few minutes to think.

Her bedroom is hardly a refuge, especially with Brigitte and Ava in there, heads together, watching some inane reality television show on a tablet.

"Oh my god," Bree exclaims. "What a fucking tool if he did it. You think that's what happened?"

"Of course it's what happened," Ava says with confidence, swinging her long, artificially blonde hair. "It's on camera." She glances up when Ren enters the room and shuts the door, giving Bree a little poke in the side.

Brigitte props herself up on her elbows and looks curiously at Ren. "You look like you're about to hurl."

"I might," Ren says, crossing the room and heaving her mattress off the box spring. She picks up a small velvet pouch and removes the contents. Six hundred and seventeen dollars. Not enough. Not nearly enough.

Ren holds the wilted bills in her hand and drops to the floor. She needs more time to think and there is no time. After everything that's been said, a critical stage has been reached. Whatever is going to happen is going to happen tonight. There will be time for doubt and regret later. That's something she knows with utter clarity; later on there will be too much time.

Her sisters are watching her, their solemn faces excessively painted with makeup.

Ren clears her throat. "You guys. If I ask to borrow whatever money you have, would you give it to me? I don't know when I'll be able to pay it back."

The girls do not say a word. They search briefly through their belongings and deliver every bit of cash they find. The gesture, just a small favor between sisters, means the world right now.

"Thank you," she whispers and leaves them, praying for a few minutes of quiet so she can find Oscar, so she can make him understand what needs to happen now.

But there is no such thing as quiet. There is her mother charging from August's study, her father's tired protests, her sisters' confused whispers.

Ren flings open the front door and her first deep breath is full of smoke and dust. The rumbling approach of thunder, the crack of nearby lightning, and the sight of Oscar Savage all collide. Every nerve in Ren's body begs her not to descend those stairs and face them. Not because there is anything terrible waiting. But because she will make it all terrible herself.

"Hey," Oscar calls above the wind, waving from where he'd been lingering by the old hitching post, likely waiting for her. Ren stops and merely watches as he hurries over. She forces her body to be rigid when he tries to take her hand.

Oscar frowns. "What is it?"

I can't. I can't. I can't.

"Don't touch me."

"Ren, what the hell is wrong?"

"You are."

"Baby, what are you talking about?"

She feels a slow tremor as it begins in her heart and spreads everywhere. She clenches her fists at her side. It's the only way she can avoid throwing her arms around his neck.

"I know," she says quietly.

"You know what?"

Ren forces herself to look into his face. He's full of confusion, concern. She'll break his heart. She'll break hers too. "I know all about you, Oscar. All about you and Lita."

Immediately he lets out a snort of laughter. Of course. Because it's absurd. He won't believe she's serious. She has to make him believe. She takes a step back and looks at him with loathing.

"I know you fucked my mother and then moved on to me. It's disgusting. You're disgusting!"

"Are you crazy? If this is a sick joke it isn't funny, Ren."

She remembers Lita's words, hears her cold voice repeating terrible things that are a lie. "You are the sort of trash who's only looking for the next hole to satisfy yourself."

"Loren."

"You got what you wanted. Now you need to go."

"This is bullshit! I don't know what the hell this is really about but I'm not going anywhere."

"Yes, you will. You have to." She pushes the wad of bills against his chest. "Here."

He stares down at the money. "What the fuck is this?"

"It's not much, but I'm sure my father will give you more if that's what it takes."

Oscar grabs her by both wrists just as a cannon of thunder explodes overhead. "You don't fool me," he whispers, his breath hot on her neck. "I know this is not you talking."

She almost wavers. She closes her eyes and nearly tips forward right into his arms, knowing if she does she won't have the will to ever leave them again. Rain begins to fall; slow, fat drops. When she opens her eyes the scene is full of people. It's no longer just her and Oscar.

As of right now there can't be any more Loren and Oscar.

Monty has chosen this moment to return. He parks the truck less than ten yards off and doesn't cut the headlights, perhaps just stunned and perplexed by the sight of everyone hanging around in the muddy yard. The harsh yellow light of the beams let Ren see everything, more than she wants to see. Spencer stands about ten feet away, two shotguns slung over his shoulder. Brigitte and Ava have emerged from the house, wide-eyed with bewilderment, sharing the shelter of a pashmina scarf to keep the rain from their carefully teased hair. Lita and August are not far behind, Lita trying to elbow her way closer to enjoy the chaos she has caused.

And Oscar...

Oscar who she loves more than she loves herself is wearing a mask of betrayal and anger. She steps away from him, knowing there won't be any forgiveness for what comes next.

"Go," she whispers.

He shakes his head. "No."

"Go, Oscar!"

"You don't mean it."

"Yes I do. We are finished. We are nothing. And you just...you need to leave me alone now!"

He doesn't touch her again. He leans in close and speaks in a low voice that only she can hear over the wind and thunder. "Then you better goddamn well say it. Tell me you don't want me. Ren, you tell me that and I swear to god you'll never fucking see me again."

She pulls back. "I don't want you, Oscar. I don't want you. I DON'T WANT YOU!"

A bolt of lightning. A sonic boom of thunder. One final glimpse of his devastated face before she turns and walks deliberately away.

The first person in her path is Spencer. She gives her brother a beseeching look and silently begs him to understand when she whispers, "Help him."

Walking is difficult. Almost as difficult as breathing. Her mother, a malevolent wraith, and her father, a weary loser, say nothing as she passes them.

But then suddenly her sisters are there, on either side, supporting her. She's never leaned on them before in her life but now she's so very grateful that they exist. They bring her indoors, to the sanctuary of their shared bedroom and they fall in a pile on the nearest mattress. Ren doesn't even know whose bed it is. All she knows are the soundless wails of anguish that shake her soul as she curls into a ball and shivers while her sisters hover, silently stroking her hair. She hopes it's not the same for Oscar, that he feels more anger than grief.

It's the grief that's unbearable. Anger is easier. Withdrawal is easier. If anyone dares to ask her for an explanation she will never tell them. At this point there is nothing to tell. There is no repairing this. The only way to endure, to survive, is to forget.

She closes her eyes, sees Oscar's face, and then willfully banishes it. As her chest heaves and her body is wracked with sobs, only one thought rolls through her mind, over and over.

A plea.   To herself, to Oscar, to an infinite and unsympathetic universe.

Forget me. I'm sorry. Forget me.

CHAPTER TWENTY

OZ

I can't seem to follow my own plans so I keep inventing new ones. Two nights ago when I drove out of Atlantis, my agenda involved several days of wide open roads before landing in Glacier National Park. I could picture myself hiking through the stunning scenery as clearly as if I was already there. It would be clean, the air crisp. It would look nothing like the desert. There, in the Big Sky Country, I could salvage the peace of mind I'd lost the minute an oily California opportunist called for a man named Oscar Savage.

Somehow though I wind up in Flagstaff and decide the world might look a little more cheerful after some sleep. My phone remains in my glove compartment and I haven't touched it. It makes my head hurt a little bit to think of how much it'll be blowing the fuck up if I actually dare to turn it on.

There's no reason for me to hang around in Flagstaff for an entire day but that's exactly what I do. Four hours get swallowed up in a black hole at a greasy café that serves good coffee and buzzes with the chatter of tourists en route to the Grand Canyon. Even though I've seen the Grand Canyon before, there isn't anything on earth quite like it so I abruptly decide that I ought to see it again.

On my way out of Flagstaff I stop to pick up some supplies. It's enough to camp out comfortably for at least a week although I don't really have any sort of a timeline in mind right now. No one on earth knows where I am. As I follow a line of cars on US Route 180 I wonder if I should examine why I can't seem to find my way out of the state of Arizona.

If I say I'm not thinking about her I'd be lying. If I insist that my own actions deserve an ounce of pride I'd be lying about that too. I can't shake the feeling that I've royally screwed up.

Since it's summer, the park is pretty crowded. It's mostly families of all shapes and sizes posing by the rim, grinning ear to ear before a backdrop of one of earth's most stupendous wonders. Snaking down the Bright Angel Trail behind slow-moving crowds and tourist-laden pack mules isn't appealing at the moment so I decide to go hunt down a place to settle. I grab a spot in the middle of a crowded campground and pitch the cheap tent I'd impulsively purchased in town.

It doesn't take long to get set up. The faint breeze blowing through the tall evergreens is a welcome change from the bleak blaze that scorches the central part of the state. But once I get a look around I realize this is bound to be pretty far from the journey of serenity I had in mind. There are kids tearing pell-mell every which way, music blaring, couples bickering, grills smoking and dogs barking. The campsites are so close together I can almost reach one-handed into my neighbor's site and spear a brat from the hibachi.

On my other side, a family rolls into camp in a stuffed minivan that spits out two restless little boys as soon as the wheels stop moving. A man who probably spends as much time outdoors as I spend dressed in a kilt spills out of the driver's side and I expect to hear him start bellowing at the kids. But he just smiles at them indulgently and leans against the van as his boys start fencing with long sticks. After wiping his sweaty red face with the hem of his shirt he starts unloading a ton of crap from the back. His tent is one of those monsters that's large enough to be a small house and I can tell he's gong to have a hell of a time getting it to stand. He seems to realize that too. Dismay is written all over his face when he gets a load of the size of the thing and all the poles and stakes involved. Meanwhile, a woman exits the van, checks the kids and walks over to him. She's pretty. Petite and dark-haired, with a gracefulness about her, she takes the man's arm and rests her head on his shoulder in a way that any red-blooded guy would envy.

He kisses her on the forehead and says something, pointing to the two boys. I shouldn't be staring and listening but I can't hear anything anyway because someone nearby has decided everyone within a one-mile radius needs Taylor Swift telling them to shake it.

The woman nods, kisses his lips, and calls to the boys, who apparently have rhyming names ending in 'aden'. The three of them wave at the man and start walking cheerfully away as he begins surveying the tent pieces at his feet. He probably sent them on a hike so he can figure out how in the hell he's going to get this thing upright without losing his man card in the eyes of his wife and kids. He pulls his phone out, squinting and scratching his head. When I catch a few words and realize he's watching some 'How To Put Up A Tent' video that he probably found on YouTube, I've had enough. I hop off the flat rock I've been sitting on and decide to be useful.

He looks up expectantly when he sees me closing in. "You staying right next door?"

"Yeah. Look, I've got time to kill. Don't mind helping you get your camp sorted out if you want."

He stares at me a moment, apparently decides I'm non-threatening and then extends his hand. "Appreciate it. Name's Steve."

"Oz."

"As in wizard?"

"As in short for Oscar."

Steve turns out to be chatty. He's a financial adviser from the Phoenix area and this is his first family vacation in two years. The people who look like his wife and kids are in fact his wife and kids. The way he talks about them, with a kind of shining pride, marks him as one of the good guys even if he can't pound a stake into the ground to save his life.

After I get the stakes in and the tent upright there doesn't seem to be much point in hanging around. Steve's family is bound to return sooner or later and it would be better if I wasn't here saving the day. Anyway, there's got to be a less traveled trail I can explore for the remainder of the afternoon. As I'm grabbing some water from the truck and getting ready to head out, Steve calls me back.

"Thanks for the hand, Oz. Listen, I may not be winning any prizes for outdoor survival anytime soon, but I can cook up a mean rib eye on the grill. Why don't you drop by later and take advantage?"

I have to grin over his earnestness. "I may just do that, Steve. Thanks for the offer."

When I'm out of the carnival-like camp atmosphere, I pause, check the position of the sun and start heading due east. I've got a bit of time before dark sets in and I plan on using it to clear my head. The other night when I drove out of Atlantis, I was just fine for the first hour as I rehashed current events.

I thought I'd climbed out of the shadows and jumped back into Ren's life just because I needed to see if there was anything left between us. But now I think maybe I wanted to torment her a little in the process. That's tough for me to admit to myself but it's true. A good guy, a guy like Steve for example, would have chosen to do it somewhere that didn't have cameras. I could have done that. I *should* have done that. Maybe that old grudge was never as distant as I'd thought.

There haven't been any other hikers in sight for the last half hour. I'm probably several miles from the rim of the canyon but that's okay. The woods have a special brand of peace all their own. The colors here are faintly pastel, punctuated with thick greenery. I hear a rustling in the leaves to my right and for a split second I'm looking straight into a pair of startled brown eyebrows before the creature – no antlers, a female – bounds off elsewhere.

A few steps later I hear the rolling sound of nearby water and turn towards it. The brook is narrow but moves along at a good clip. The deer had probably paused here for a drink before I scared her off.

Now that Ren is back in my head I can't get her to leave. What's more, I keep flashing back to that sex show in the back of my truck. If the idea of using her that way was to get my fill and move on then it doesn't seem to have worked. At least for me. Maybe it did for her.

All it takes is a quick memory jump, featuring her perky rosebud nipples and her sleek body opening underneath me, and I'm hard as fuck once more, wondering when it's going to stop. Is this how it's going to be forever? Is it what's going to happen next time I'm getting it on with some other girl? Instead of being all pumped up about what's in front of me I'll just be comparing her to Ren Savage.

I've got to get past this. I've got to replace her with something else, anything else.

Yup, I'll get right on that as soon as I finish kneeling here on the creek bank and punching the clown with my hand while I fantasize about fucking her.

I had her down. I had her conquered. I had her begging for sweet release and willing to get busy in seventeen filthy ways. And even as it stings the edges of my heart a little I can't stop thinking about it.

When I'm done, I rinse off in the creek and zip my pants up, feeling guilty as a fourteen year old kid who's dicking around with himself in the bathroom while his mother screeches from down the hall that dinner is ready. For a while I just sit on a wide rock, listening to the water and trying to remember details about one single other girl that I've dated or fucked or just had a cup of goddamn coffee with.

And that's the problem with trying to replace Ren. That's always been the problem.

In spite of everything, I don't want to replace her. I can't.

When I get back to the campground it sounds like a street festival and smells like burnt hot dogs. Sleep may not be on the table tonight. I figure I'll just make do with the granola I'd picked up at the store and keep to myself. If the spirit of masochism takes over I can check my phone and see what kind of damage I missed over the last few days. I haven't touched base with Brock in over a week. It might not be a bad idea to let someone know where the hell I am. It's a pretty safe bet I have about sixty-eight voicemails from Gary and friends reminding me of contracts and other failures. Sooner or later I'll call him back. Maybe tomorrow. I'll tell him I'm done answering questions and that I'm not going to interfere with whatever they decide to do with the footage.

I'd forgotten all about Steve and his promise of steak until he yells good-naturedly that I ought to come on over.

Steve blinks the smoke away and offers me a plate. "I took a guess that you're a man who likes his dinner well done."

"You guessed right," I say and confess that once I've got the juicy rib eye under my nose I'm suddenly hungry as a bear.

Steve's wife, Michele, perches on a footstool and eats daintily while asking me polite questions. The boys, who I have started thinking of as Aden 1 and Aden 2, toast marshmallows and make charming messes of their faces until Michele sighs and escorts them to the campground bathroom to get cleaned up.

"You're not here with any friends?" Steve asks, blotting his dripping chin with a paper napkin.

"Nope. I tend to travel alone."

Steve doesn't say anything and I wonder if he's having second thoughts about inviting some sketchy loner to hang out with his family. He doesn't let on if anything's bothering him though. He just starts gathering trash in a plastic bag while I chew my steak.

"First time at the Canyon?" he asks.

"No. You?"

"Drove up here once before, years ago. Day trip. Asked a girl to marry me that day." He pauses and smiles wistfully at the memory.

"I hope she said yes."

"She did. I've got the boxy minivan to prove it."

"We should all be so lucky. I just lost my girl."

What in the god almighty hell made me say that??

Steve is looking at me now. I wonder if he drugged my steak with some sort of suburban truth serum. That doesn't make any sense though. Especially because what I said isn't even the truth. Ren hasn't been 'my girl' for a long time. The shit that happened between us during my brief Atlantis intrusion sure can't count as a relationship. I'm just dehydrated or something.

Michele returns with the two boys, who are now dragging their feet like they are in the throes of a sugar crash. She stands behind Steve's chair, rests her soft hands on his shoulders and gives him a quick kiss on the cheek. "I'd better get these two rascals off to bed."

"I'll be inside in a little while," he tells her and she blows him a kiss before disappearing behind the tent flaps with the kids.

Steve leans over, opens a red cooler and withdraws two dripping cans of beer. He tosses one to me and I'm happy to catch it. It only takes me a few seconds to drain the whole thing. Steve, on the other hand, takes one careful sip and lets the can rest on his knee.

"Sorry," he says, "about your girl."

I feel like I ought to correct my earlier statement, about how I didn't really lose a girl because she wasn't mine in the first place. But I don't. I just sigh and lower my head. "Eh, it was my fault. This time anyway. Just couldn't get out of my own way."

"That sounds like a bad case of regret."

I think about the look on Ren's face when she first saw me pull up to Atlantis. I think about how I played it like a cocky fucker right up until the end even though all I wanted to do was talk to her. It's never made any sense to me, the way she turned away from everything we had. I have no doubt her parents made some threats but that wouldn't have stopped the girl I thought I knew. Yet when I finally sought out the chance to get a real answer I couldn't seem to say one single honest thing. So of course neither did she.

"Yeah," I admit slowly. "I've got a few regrets. She might have some too. But I guess there just comes a time in every doomed relationship when you've got to cut the ties for good, you know? Move on."

Steve doesn't respond right away. He takes a long gulp from his can of beer and glances at the tent when the sound of a giggling child filters out. A vague smile crosses his face and then disappears. He looks at the ground and keeps his voice low. "I'll tell you something. We've had our moments, Michele and I. We were young when we met, about your age. My frat boys were giving me a time about being pussy whipped. Said there'd be plenty of more chances to find something just as good or better."

"Obviously you knew they were full of shit."

Steve nods. "I know that now. Back then it took me a little while to locate my brain. We were apart for a year." Steve frowns, perhaps remembering what it was like to nurse a huge hole in the heart for a while. "I wish I could say that I came to my senses overnight but in truth it was a slow process. Had a lot of growing up to do. I don't know why she took me back. God knows she could have done a thousand times better."

"Well," I say because there's no non-corny way to respond when some dude spills his guts over a campfire. "Looks like it all worked out pretty smoothly. You guys seem like you've got the dream."

He leans back in his chair and sighs. "Oz, you'll probably never meet a happier man but that doesn't mean we don't have to work at it. Even if it's the best kind of work it'll still twist your heart into knots sometimes. All I can do is try to be worthy. And let me tell you, I'll try every day until I run out of days."

While I mull over Steve's words he finishes his beer and carefully places the can in the garbage bag. Suddenly he lets out a small chuckle.

"Forgive me if things took a turn for the heavy handed. I'm not really in the habit of dispensing random advice like the wise old man cliché at the end of every story. Just hate to see a young guy like you all lonely and defeated if you've got someone worth fighting for."

Lonely.

The word tugs at me. Am I lonely? Seems like a weak question, a question for guys who wax their forearms and shiver when it's seventy degrees out. I've always thought of myself in solitary terms. Never as part of anything. Well, never except for those few ancient months I was with Ren. And however that turned out, it was special at the time. Maybe if the world had just tilted a little bit differently it could have been something that lasted. Maybe I could have been like this guy, a vital piece of a bigger picture.

"Not sure if there's enough left to fight for," I tell him. "At this point we've done things to each other. Hell, we might both be tired of fighting anyway."

Steve tilts his head back and peers at me shrewdly. "Are you? Are you tired of fighting?"

I think about the question for a long time. "I thought I was. But maybe not. Maybe it's a little closer to the truth that I haven't even started fighting yet."

Steve seems pleased with my answer. "That's how you know it's not over, buddy. That's how you know."

I sit there grappling with the idea while Steve ties the corners of the trash bag together. The sounds of the campground are softening as the night settles. There are low voices and the faintest wisps of music.

The flap of the big tent opens and Michele pokes her head out. "Babe, can you bring me some water when you come inside?"

Steve winks and reaches over to dig around in the red cooler. "I'll do better than that," he says and triumphantly produces a bottle of wine. His knees pop when he stands and he turns to me with a raised eyebrow. "You planning on sticking around tomorrow, Oz?"

I *was* planning on it, but now I'm not. "Actually I think I'll be heading out before dawn."

"Ah, hitting the road early."

"Yep. Want to be well on my way before the crowds get moving."

He stretches his torso, twisting first one way and then the other before extending the hand not holding the wine bottle. "Well buddy, best of luck to you in your travels."

I shake his hand gladly. As he disappears behind the tent flaps I have to wonder what it's like to be him, to be a man who the world would count as unremarkable yet has everything.

And suddenly I know that if I could choose one destiny I would choose that one.

It's not late and I'm not tired but after a little while I duck into my own tent for the night. I told Steve the truth when I said I want to get out of here early to avoid the masses on the road. I know what I need to do. It's time I really did start fighting for something.

CHAPTER TWENTY-ONE

REN

Cate Camp bangs on the front door at the crack of dawn. Since I haven't slept much the past several days I'm awake enough to fling the door open before she manages to disturb the whole house.

"Loren." She slides right past me without being invited inside. There are no crew members straggling behind her so she must have driven out here from Consequences alone. She paces the front room with her teeth sucking loudly on her bottom lip and I get the feeling she's high on something.

"Come on in," I say with a dash of irritability. Cate Camp annoys the crap out of me. She has been in what I would politely call 'a state' ever since she heard that Oscar took off. Apparently Gary Vogel is displeased with the turn of events and holds her at least partially responsible. I can't really muster much sympathy for her career though when my heart is in shreds.

Cate stops pacing and fumbles through her vagina-sized designer wristlet. She withdraws a black e-cig and starts vaping with a vengeance. She looks me over and I think I detect a slight frown of disapproval, although with all the collagen she's pumped into her lips it's tough to tell. At any rate I haven't showered yet today and I'm probably not looking very fetching.

I plunk back down on the leather sofa where I've been reading for hours from one of August's dusty old books, *Volcanic Formations of the American Southwest.* It's captivating stuff. Either I'll end up suddenly yearning for a career in geology or I'll fall asleep. Win win.

Cate Camp vapes and fidgets and stares out the window with her e-cig pinched between two manicured fingers.

"Today will be the day," she says fearfully. "He's coming today."

"Who? The anti-Christ? Pardon me while I get dressed then."

She ignores my sarcasm. "Gary only travels out for filming if there is a huge setback. Once the pieces are in place he expects that everything will proceed smoothly."

I stare down at black and white photos of Sunset Crater. "That's interesting. Is everything not proceeding smoothly?"

Cate Camp shoots me a dirty look. "Your cousin or whatever the hell he is really fucked things up. I always thought he was a wild card. But Gary figured having him here would be useful for dramatic effect."

Slowly I turn a page. "Gary was right. It was dramatic."

"What happened out there, Loren? Oz was insufferable about following instructions from the beginning but you had been fairly cooperative. I'm not oblivious. I know you're here reluctantly but you need to remember you have a job to do."

Slowly I raise my head and look her in the eye. "It's not a job to do. It's a life to live."

She merely shrugs. "Not right now it isn't. You have a contractual obligation so spare me the self-righteous talk." Cate Camp primly returns her e-cig to her vagina purse and gives me a rubbery smile. "And I'll have you know that we have enough footage to show there was something going on between the two of you. Looks like it was shaping up into a hell of a story considering your past together. But this leaves me with a problem. A story is nothing to an audience without an ending."

"Oh. Would you like an ending?"

She practically leaps across the room. "Yes, I would like an ending!"

"Okay. It's not very exciting though. We argued about whose turn it was to feed the chickens and he, Oz that is, said he was tired of feeding chickens and he was going to return to life as a reclusive mountaineer."

Cate Camp is angry. I can tell because the bulbous collagen flaps on her face are quivering. "That is *not* what happened."

Is it sick that I find her distress amusing? I bat my eyelashes innocently. "Really? Funny, that's how I remember it. I can go in the Blue Room and discuss it in detail for the sake of posterity."

A sound erupts from her throat. It sounds like a snarl. "Gary will have something to say about this. You can be sure of it. And if you think you're saving face here you're wrong. We are obliged to edit the content however we please."

I close the book, feeling oddly detached. Perhaps I've sobbed out all my emotions already. I press my thumbs against my temples to relieve the building pressure. "Just go away, Cate. If you want a different ending then make one up. Oz is gone. He's not coming back. You'll have to live with it."

As will I.

She hisses like a reptile and stalks to the door. Before she gets there she tosses off a few words that she probably thinks are insulting. "Go hose yourself off. You look fucking homeless."

The door slams. I close my eyes and concentrate on pressure points to alleviate the looming migraine. I should go to my room and dig out some of my essential oils. When I open my eyes again my nephew is standing in the hallway with a drooping diaper and a stuffed monkey.

"Hey, sweetheart." I smile and open my arms. The best thing to come out of these last few weeks has been the opportunity to spend time with him.

Alden gives me a crooked grin and scampers into my arms. I gather up his warm little body and ask him if he's hungry. He nods eagerly and twists my hair around his fingers.

By the time I get the kid changed and settled down with a bowl of oatmeal, I glance at the clock and realize it's nearly time for the crew to show up for the day. Spencer is the only one who sleeps less than I do. He was out and about before the sun even waved hello this morning. The crew knows by now that bothering Monty before noon is not a good idea. They are likely to merely lurk around the house for a while, filming Ava and Brigitte drinking coffee and arguing about petty everyday things.

My sisters have been cutting a wide path around me and for that I'm grateful. These days I sometimes feel like I'm barely hanging on. That shouldn't be. I've lived without

Oscar for a long time and of course I can live without him again.

But something happened to me during those brief, burning moments in the desert a few nights ago. I let myself go, not caring how far we were taking it, not listening to the pitiful begging that came out of my own mouth.

Oscar had me figured out all right. He knew I was trying to scrub him out for good. Out of my mind, out of my heart. I wanted him to take it all out on me; the hostility, the bitterness, everything he must have been harboring for the past five years. I wanted him to make me forget the heartbreak of losing him. I warned him he needed to make it hurt.

And he did. My god, he did. Far more agonizing than any physical pain is the agony of the heart.

"Morning." Ava pads into the kitchen, all sleepy-eyed and beautiful with her hair flowing over her shoulders and a simple blue dress hugging her curves. Alden lights up and runs to her. She settles him on her hip and pats his back. "What are you doing up so early, baby?"

"He's been keeping his old aunt company."

Ava scrutinizes me. I know she's worried. She saw me at my worst once, five years ago. She saw me cry so hard I couldn't breathe. She doesn't want to see me like that again. "So what's going on today, Ren?"

"I don't know. I think I'll do some laundry. That would probably make a captivating episode. Oh, and Cate Camp stopped by. She says Gary might show up."

"Gary Vogel?"

"I think he's the only Gary left in this century."

She gives a short laugh and swings Alden down to the floor. "Did she say what he wanted?"

"I think he wants to yell at me for not inviting the cameras to observe my wild sexual exploits."

Ava's eyebrows shoot skyward. I hadn't said it out loud yet. Of course anyone with half a brain would have figured it out the night he disappeared and I wandered home looking fairly used and disheveled. But I hadn't admitted it. I guess it's time to admit it.

"I wish..." I whisper but I can't seem to finish the sentence. There's that good old thick knot in my chest again. It has Oscar's name on it. I was an idiot to think I could just fuck it away.

My elbows are up on the table now and my head is down, my fingers laced behind my neck. Those two words keep bouncing around the room.

I wish.

I wish.

I wish.

I'm drowning in wishes. Things I wish I hadn't said. Things I wish I hadn't done. Things I wish I *had* said. Courage I wish I could have found. Years I wish I hadn't lost.

Soft arms surround me. My sister presses her head against mine.

"I know," she whispers back.

I stay inside that comfortable hug for a full minute, holding on to my little sister and trying not to leak snot on her shoulder. When that's over I pat Alden's head and start down the hall, figuring I ought to make an effort to look slightly better than 'fucking homeless'.

But before I get to the shower I take a detour. I've been avoiding the Blue Room since my first week here, spending less than five minutes on my required self-interviews. Typically I gloss over anything that might be important and instead summarize events like the cleaning of the chicken coop or the loading of the dishwasher. Whenever Cate Camp pulls me aside for an entreaty to 'dig a little deeper' I just pretend like I don't hear her.

Since almost everything I've been doing since I got here just isn't working I make up my mind to try something else. Determinately I wind my long hair into a knot and push a few stray strands behind my ears. I'm wearing a ratty old gym ensemble, I slept very little last night, and I haven't even washed my face. In other words, I'm not classic camera material. But that will have to be okay.

I flip the camera on and settle into the papasan chair. This time, when I look straight at the lens it isn't intimidating. There's nothing to be afraid of here.

This is me. The real me.

I clear my throat.

"Hello. I haven't really let you meet me yet. I'm Loren Elizabeth Savage. Yes, of the famed movie star Savages. You probably know about my family. And you may have heard a few things about the rest of us. Some of them might even be true. But there's still so much you don't know. No matter how many cameras there are in the world there will always be a lot you can't see. I was in love once. Really and truly in love. Like what you see in the movies. Like what you read about in stories. It was as incredible as it was heartbreaking.

I hope you'll stick around and listen for a little while. Because I really want to tell you about it..."

CHAPTER TWENTY-TWO

OZ

It wouldn't make any sense for Atlantis Star to have changed in the last three days when it probably hasn't changed much in decades. But when I blow through Consequences and make the turn off down the dirt road that leads to the old movie ranch it looks different to me. Smaller somehow.

The crew's truck is parked where it always is when they're around, in the shade of an old mesquite tree about thirty yards off from the house. The leader, an amiable type of guy who goes by the unfortunate name of Rash, is tinkering with some equipment in the yard. He looks up at the sound of my truck and offers a wave.

I don't bother being discreet about my arrival. I roll right up to the doorstep of the big house. Rash has his camera on his shoulder and he's filming me now but that's fine. I'm beyond caring who might be watching what at this point.

Before I get my hand on the doorknob I see Monty Savage coming from the direction of the barn. He's got his shirt off, like he usually does, as if his thick chest is allergic to fabric or needs chronic admiration to remain solid. He stops cold when he sees me and I brace for some noise but he just lowers his head and keeps walking.

Since the front door is unlocked I stroll right on through it. A small blond tornado whips past my legs. Ava's boy, Alden. He's laughing as only kids know how to laugh.

Ava is laughing herself as she follows the kid. Her laughter dies abruptly when she sees me. She puts her hands on her hips and cocks her head, looking none too friendly.

I close the door behind me. There's no one else in sight. "Is she here?"

Ava looks me up and down. Of course I don't know what's gone on here in the last few days but judging from Ava's expression it's nothing good. I remember the deathly silence between Ren and I after we finished fucking our brains out. I remember the almost desperate look she gave me before opening the door to the truck and trudging back to the house. But at the time I thought it would be better if we just left things unsaid. I was too wrapped up in my own feelings to notice her pain.

From the look on Ava's face though, she understands her sister's pain all too well. And she's decided who is responsible.

"Ava?" I prompt gently.

"She's here," Ren's sister says. Her kid tears back into the room and crashes into her legs. She hoists him to her hip and jerks her head toward the hall. "Last bedroom at the end. Knock first, Oz. And if she tells you to leave then you should."

"Fair enough. I will."

Alden claps his hands together a few times and I give him a little wink. I just lied to his mother but that will come out soon enough. Today, I have no intention of leaving even if Ren throws a frying pan at my head.

One of the lesser Camera Creeps tails me as I head down the hall. Just before I turn a corner I see Brigitte lurking in the small piano alcove. She notices me but says nothing and doesn't move. Usually she tries to insert herself in the middle of whatever might give her camera time so it's a little out of character for her to stand down but I'll take it.

When I get to Ren's door I almost just barge through it but decide to scrape together a few manners. I rap my knuckles on the wood five times and wait.

Ren's sigh reaches me from the other side of the door. She was probably enjoying some mid morning solitude away from the cameras.

My entire body freezes when the door creaks open. Christ, I'm nervous, more than I was that first day I drove up here, weeks ago. Because back then I put on an armor of arrogant attitude. Now I'm going to face her with honesty. It's tougher than it sounds.

"Hi," I manage to say, noting the way her eyes widen. I can't read whether the look on her face is anything other than shock. Her cheeks are flushed and her eyes are slightly red. She's cried recently. Her dark hair hangs down straight and appears damp, fresh from a shower. She's barefoot, wearing a plain black cotton dress with thin straps that falls to her knees and doesn't have a speck of makeup on. She's so blindingly beautiful I can't stand it.

Ren recovers from her shock and crosses her arms over her chest. "You're back."

"I'm back."

"For how long?"

"Depends on you."

She cocks her head to the side, her soft lips slightly parted. "I don't understand."

I have to touch her. I act like I'm trying to push a piece of nonexistent hair out of her face. She doesn't shrink away when my fingers brush her cheek. But the shiver that rolls through her is involuntary. The idea that her tears were probably caused by me twists my gut into knots. If that's the case then I have a new goal. I'm never ever going to be the cause of her tears again.

My hand falls back to my side. I want to grab her, hold her, but I can't. We can't just pretend that all the agony, both fresh and old, never happened. If we're going to do this, we've got to do it the hard way. "Ren, can I come in? Or can you come out?"

Her eyes shift to the camera. I can tell she's wondering what the hell I'm up to. I hope she gives me the benefit of the doubt, whether I deserve it or not.

"Give me two minutes," she says. "I'll meet you out front."

"Take your time. I'll wait."

She still looks puzzled. After all, the tone of this short encounter is rather subdued compared to the last one, when I warned her that when I was done getting my fill she'd be nothing more to me than another empty pussy. It doesn't matter if she'd ever said or done anything to justify it. A bigger lie was never told.

The day is a rare one full of clouds. I make my way outside and stand there in the yard beside the corner of the house where once upon a time I'd held her close a few moments after our first kiss.

When Ren comes outside she's wearing a pair of brown leather cowboy boots and a wary expression. The way she looks at me it's like she's expecting a slap. Or worse. She folds her arms in front of her chest in a defensive pose and keeps her eyes on the ground as she closes in.

"I love you and it doesn't matter what time or anything else does to us. Even if the worst happens and we're ripped apart it will change nothing. I'll still love you, Oscar."

How is it possible we've come to this? Two strangers fighting the saddest, most useless of wars.

I meet her halfway and there's a highly awkward second where we face off and stare at each other. Meanwhile, a sizeable lizard breaks out of some nearby sage and scurries through the space that separates us. It's strange. Lizards don't typically abandon their shelters to get closer to humans. Somewhere I heard that lizards represent good omens. I hope that's true.

She breaks the silence. "Before you say anything, I want you to know that I'm glad you came back."

"Are you?"

Ren nods and inhales deeply, closing her eyes and then exhaling slowly. She opens her eyes and looks at me clearly. "Yes. Oscar, I never told you that I was sorry. I'm truly sorry for everything happened five years ago. I'm sorry for turning my back on you. I need you to know that I never believed anything Lita said. That wasn't it. That wasn't the reason at all. I should have said so the day you came back here but I didn't."

The lizard has paused from his journey back to the brush. He jerks his head, watches us for a split second with tiny inscrutable eyes and then darts away with lightning speed.

I shove my hands in my pockets and get closer, nudging her shoulder. "Let's take a walk."

She's surprised but she nods and her body language relaxes as we stroll beyond the yard of the big house, past the brothel, close to the cemetery. When we reach the far side of the wrought iron fence that surround the clump of fake headstones, I pause and give her a hard look.

"Ren, I *know* you never believed her. I'm not an idiot. I know that somebody probably threatened you with something and that's why you felt like you had no choice. That part's done. And we were kids. I don't blame you anymore for not knowing what the fuck to do."

We're standing close now, close enough for my body to start responding to her. Jesus, I just can't help it. She smells like cherries and vanilla. Plus she's not wearing a bra. I shift from my weight casually, trying to relieve the rising pressure in my pants.

Ren notices and a knowing smile tugs at the corners of her mouth. It's like we're both hit with the same memory at the exact same second. It seems like the moment just happened.

"Didn't know the Savages were telepathic."

"We're not. You're just transparent."

"What am I thinking about, Ren?"

Her smile fades. She hugs her arms around herself and looks sadly at the corpse-free cemetery. "It wasn't so much their threat to me. It was the threat to you. Lita said she would sick the dogs of the press on both of us and there would be nowhere to hide from the scandal she would invent. She also said she could make criminal charges stick because she'd somehow uncovered the fact that you were over eighteen."

"I could have handled Lita." My voice is sharper than I meant it to be.

"Maybe," she whispers. Then she shakes her head miserably. "But maybe I couldn't. I guess that's my biggest regret. That I never had the strength of character to really say fuck you to Lita and to every ridiculous expectation attached to this last name. Remember when you told me I'm just a shell of who I once was?"

"Ren, I didn't mean-"

"Well, you were right." She nods and looks me in the eye. "And you were wrong. I'm not tough or courageous. But then, I never was."

The wind picks up. A falcon flies right over our heads, its dark shadow briefly washing over us. The cameras keep rolling.

"I'm not asking for your sympathy, Oscar. And I don't expect it. Just know that you were once everything to me. You were everything to me for a long time, far longer than I've ever been able to admit." She looks down and her voice drops to a whisper. "That's all."

"That's all," I echo. She nods tiredly and starts to walk away. I grab her arm and pull her back a little roughly. "That's *not* all, dammit. I didn't come back here for vindication."

There's a flash of something her dark eyes. She looks down to where my hand is fastened to her arm. Ren tilts her head up proudly and challenges me. "Then why *did* you come back?"

I release her arm and stuff my hands back into my pockets where they can't get into any more trouble. "I came back because once I knew you, Loren Savage. The two months I spent with you were the best ones of my life. I could see clear into your heart and I loved you with all of mine. I came back not because I want to fuck things up for you or because I want my day in the stupid spotlight. I came back because I just want you in my life again. However I can get you."

She takes a step back and studies me. I've surprised her. We've surprised each other. Maybe we're not too far removed from the kids we were after all.

Ren presses her lips together and glances back at the house. "You know," she says. "It'll be lunch hour soon. Spence is likely to be back anytime now from delivering a restored Thunderbird to the next county. The girls and young Mr. Alden are always happy to see anything edible. And even Monty sits down at a table now and again." She pauses, bites a corner of her lip and looks nearly bashful. "I was thinking about making some barbecued chicken wings."

"I'll help you," I tell her because it was my offer the last time we had this conversation.

The day we met.

She grins. "You can cook?"

"No. Teach me."

"All right, Oz. I will."

On the short walk back to the big house I don't even try to touch her. For now it's enough just to walk beside her.

For now.

CHAPTER TWENTY-THREE

$\mathcal{REN}$

Cate Camp was wrong about Gary. He has apparently decided to take his time about showing up. Maybe once Oscar returned that was the end of the Born Savages emergency and he just didn't feel like hauling his cookies out of Los Angeles. After all, chilling on the coast is probably more pleasant than sweltering in the desert. Whatever the reason, I think I can safely say that nobody has been yearning for his arrival.

Regardless, this morning we have word that apparently he's on his way. We are told to expect him within the hour. Cate Camp is tearing around here like a bleached lunatic. The camera crew fuss with their equipment and glance fearfully at the sky, as if they are expecting the lumpy form of Gary Vogel to descend directly on their heads like a turkey vulture. Everywhere, from the brothel to the church, there is the frantic drumbeat of 'Gary is coming!' I hope Atlantis Star can handle it.

Oz is outside with the boys. There shouldn't be anything sexy about a man carrying a shovel full of horseshit but somehow he makes it look good.

Not that I'm looking.

Ever since he unexpectedly returned three weeks ago, everything has changed.

Oz is a friend now. Nothing more, nothing less. He helps in the kitchen, cooperates with the crew and joins me on twilight walks around the perimeter, pointing out creatures and rock formations of interest. We steer clear of any subject heavier than the dangers of rattlesnakes. To the rest of the family, even Monty, he is down right sociable.

Life has been quiet. Life has been pleasant.

Maybe that's Gary's problem. Quiet living makes for boring television.

But Oz and I have been getting along so well. It certainly makes no sense to consider spoiling our new friendship by running my hot tongue over the sweaty ridges of his six pack and then dipping lower to nip at that that delectable happy trail until I get to...

"Ren!"

"What!"

Brigitte manages to startle me so badly I drop a wine glass. It shatters all over the terra cotta and I curse as I gather the shards into a pile. Brigitte watches me.

"You're jumpy," she observes.

"You're smart," I mutter.

Bree pointedly looks out the window, sees the shirtless, magnificent Oz out there helping Spence repair a fence post. She grins.

"Nice view."

"It's all right."

"It's all right," she mocks. "You missed that piece of glass by the fridge." She puts her hands on her hips and bites her lip. "I suppose our visitor will be here any minute. Are you worried?"

"Are you?"

"I don't know." Bree snaps her fingers and addresses a quiet corner of the room. "What do you think, Rash? Do we have any reason to worry? Is Gary going to shut down production because we're not interesting enough? Put that camera down for a minute and tell us what you know."

"Not allowed to socialize with the talent," he answers but there's a smile in his voice.

Brigitte bats her eyelashes. "I do love being called 'the talent'. Say it again please."

"Industry term," Rash laughs. "You are all 'the talent.'"

Brigitte starts to say something but then stops and returns to the window. I hear it too. It's a low buzzing that grows closer and breaks into a rhythmic chopping sound.

"That's him," Rash says cheerfully.

I join Bree at the window and see a growing black dot in the brilliant blue sky.

"Where's he plan to land that thing?"

Bree shrugs. "Wherever he wants, I guess."

"Ladies," says Rash, setting down his camera. "It's Gary time."

By the time we get outside, Gary's descending chopper is wreaking all kinds of havoc. The chickens are flapping and trying to escape the coop. Spencer shouts an obscenity and starts jogging toward the barn to soothe the horses. Cate Camp stands rooted to a spot that looks destined to be covered by a helicopter in less than a minute. Her brassy hair whips around in seventeen directions and she's holding her arms out.

Monty and Oz have stopped whatever they're doing and are just watching everything. Mercifully, Oz has pulled his shirt back on, covering most of that tempting tanned muscle.

Just as I walk over to stand between them, Monty hisses and points to where Cate Camp stands with arms outstretched.

"Does she think she's going to catch the fucking thing?"

"Maybe." I have an uneasy feeling that we're about to witness what happens when woman and helicopter collide.

"Goddamn idiot," Monty mutters and jogs over to forcibly remove Cate Camp from a bloody fate.

Oz stands so close to me I can feel his body heat. I look up at him and find that he's already watching me. He gives me an amused little wink that sets all kinds of things in motion that I can't think about right now.

To my surprise, Gary Vogel himself is the one piloting the chopper. He lands seamlessly, without causing any damage. As soon as he climbs out of the helicopter, all spray tanned and combed over, he only wastes a split second glancing around at the barren view of Atlantis Star before heading right over to us. Cate Camp is full of whines and protests but he brushes her off.

Something touches my leg and I look down to see my nephew grinning up at me.

"Hugs?" he lisps and I hoist him up into my arms.

Brigitte and Ava are standing on the porch looking a little anxious so I offer them a smile. It will be all right. Whatever Gary came here to say or do, we will be all right.

Gary Vogel is a man who gets right to the point. He greets us all without much fuss and beckons for us to follow him inside the big house. By the time we're all indoors he's made himself comfortable on Rex Savage's morally abhorrent chair of elephant tusks. He's not smiling. He watches us file in with a very grave expression.

"Apologies for the short notice, my friends. I'm afraid I have some bad news. Your mother is dead."

Someone gasps. I think it was Ava. I'm trying to let the words sink in.

"Lita is dead?"

"Quite." He snaps his fingers and Cate Camp scurries over with a magically procured bottle of water. "Early this morning her maid found her. No signs of a struggle. A brain aneurysm is suspected although the autopsy will tell more. She was found stiff and naked on a velvet settee in the pool house." He grimaces. "Forgive me. That detail was unnecessary."

I have to wonder how in the hell Gary came by this information before we did but considering how connected

Gary is, the fact that he would hear the news first is not exactly far fetched.

My hands are clasped in front of me and I stare down at them, trying to feel something about the death of the woman who gave me both life and misery. Each of my siblings seems to be processing the news separately and none of us say a word. Oz is closest to me. It's Oz's strong hand on my shoulder, squeezing lightly for comfort. I cover his hand with my own and squeeze back.

When I look up I notice Gary Vogel is watching us. Not all of·us. Just me and Oz.

"There's more," he says.

A bad feeling is born somewhere deep inside my gut. It starts to grow. My sisters glance at me with confusion and I shrug. Monty crosses his arms and scowls. Spence appears bored.

Oz is the one who asks the question. "So what else is there?"

Gary seems slightly uneasy for the first time. "Due to your stipulations, your mother was not invited to participate in the show. However, Lita gave us an exclusive interview right before filming started. She had a lot to say. Particularly when she found out *you* were joining the cast."

He points to Oz. Oz doesn't react. I have a feeling I know what's coming next.

Gary licks his lips and begins to speak again but Brigitte steps forward and cuts him off.

"My mother," she announces, "was a fucking evil witch." She struts in front of Gary, flings her red hair over her shoulder and gives him an icy glare. "If I were you I would pay no attention to whatever she garbage she spewed in that so-called interview you're so proud of because it's bound to be the sickest of lies. And we will contradict every damn one of them."

Gary Vogel is amused. His mouth twitches and he taps a finger to his lips before answering. "I have no doubt. Nonetheless, you are aware that I am here for the same reason you are all here. To capitalize on a story. And Lita had a quite a story to tell us. In some cases the truth is, shall we say, immaterial."

I hear Oz let out a slow hiss. I feel him stiffen with anger. I'm afraid in another few seconds the 'story' will evolve to include Gary Vogel being choked half to death.

"But this is not one of those cases," Gary says quietly, his muddy eyes focused on Oz. "Did you know that my crew sends me highlight reels once a week? It's enough to get a pretty solid idea what's going on here. I know a good story when I see one. And Lita Savage has no role in it. At least not a role she would approve of."

Gary grunts and heaves himself out of the chair. He takes a long drink from the bottle of water and then holds the half empty bottle out. Cate Camp silently appears and takes it from him.

"So that is all I have to share. I wanted to deliver the unfortunate news of your mother's passing before the press comes calling. And I wanted to let you know that her last interview will never reach the public, not if I have anything to say about it. And of course I do. Naturally I could have delivered all this information to you remotely, but my new ride was begging for some sky."

Gary strolls right past us and out the door without saying goodbye. The rest of us stand around with puzzled looks for a few seconds and then we follow him outside. He has paused about ten yards away and is squinting at the Harquehala Mountains.

"My god it's fucking hot here," he announces loudly and then returns to his gleaming personal helicopter. A few short minutes and one cheery wave of his fat hand later, he is back up in the sky. Gary and his machinery quickly disappear into the west while we stand on the ground and stare.

Montgomery shades his eyes and grunts. "You think a word of that bullshit is true?"

"Yes," I answer because I'm sure *all* of it is true.

Spencer had removed his cowboy hat but now that he's back under the sun he sticks it back on his head. "Well I'll bet we'll be hearing about it real soon. Place was a circus after Dad died. Parasites will crawl out of the woodwork and beg for a statement."

Oz is still at my side. "You okay?"

I blink. I try to smile. "I am absolutely fine."

I'm not, but it has nothing to do with Lita. I just want to crawl into his arms and rest against his warm chest for a little while. Only a little while. A mere decade or two.

Despite the fact that Lita was far from beloved by any of us, hearing that your mother is dead kind of turns the mood a little somber. We all just wander around, ignoring Cate Camp's suggestions to visit the Blue Room and 'unburden the grief'.

My brothers decide to make this a special occasion and take a trip to town together in Spence's truck. It's good to see them like that. Not about to kill each other and stuff.

Ava seems the most affected by the news. She retreats quietly to her bedroom and lays down in the dark. Brigitte hangs around the kitchen and tries to eat every bit of raw chocolate chip cookie dough that I mix together. She's looking out the window, keeping an eye on Alden and Oz, who are apparently scouring the ground for interesting rocks.

The crew is filming. The crew is silent. The crew is doing their jobs. It's funny how I don't even really mind that fact right now.

Spence and Monty eventually return from Consequences with a pile of raw meat they plan on barbecuing. Even though Oz is helpless in the kitchen he's something of a master cookout chef so he takes charge of the food preparations.

Sometime later, right on the cusp of evening, when the divine smell of sizzling meat hangs heavy and we are all just doing ordinary things, it occurs to me that it all seems completely normal. Not the Savage version of normal, which was always a bit bizarre, but the everyday variety. When my sisters and I drag a table into the yard and cover it with a checkered tablecloth so we can sit outside and dine together in the twilight, it seems like the sort of thing any typical family would do.

And we *are* a family. All of us. Even if most of the time we don't seem like it.

At the table Monty relaxes and discovers a sense of humor. He talks about the grotesque trauma of prison food and about how when he was inside he learned how to knit. Who knew knitting was a popular prison pastime? I have some trouble picturing a bunch of lumbering, hardened men dressed in orange jumpsuits, frowning over their double pointed needles and asking the guy in the next cell, *"Hey, is this row knit or purl?"*

I am totally aware of the fact that Oz is beside me the entire time. As night crawls closer, Spence and Monty find some mesquite sticks and show Alden how to toast marshmallows. Bree and Ava laugh and fuss when the little boy manages to get marshmallow goo all over his face. Alden grins and smears some spare melted marshmallow in Monty's hair for good measure. I laugh as Monty struggles with being both annoyed and charmed as he scrubs marshmallow out of his hair with a napkin. I can't remember the last time I laughed so freely.

Oz and I are the only ones still seated at the table. When I lean back slightly on the wooden bench he closes in. His arms circle my waist, his chest presses against my back and his breath is in my ear.

Of course my heartbeat immediately accelerates by a factor of ten and my panties suffer an instant soaking.

"Come with me," he whispers urgently.

"Where?" I whisper back. Actually, it sounds more like a moan.

Oz pushes my hair aside and seductively trails his lips along the hollow at the base of my neck.

"Everywhere."

I'm dizzy. I might have to just stay right here because I'm not sure standing is possible.

"Right now?"

He tightens his hold around my waist. Somehow a confident finger finds its way under the hem of my shirt to stroke the skin beneath. It's not totally dark but it's getting there so we're somewhat obscured. But even if we weren't I probably wouldn't stop him if he shoved his whole hand down my pants.

"*Right now*," he says and stands up, pulling me with him.

That kind of catches everyone's attention. It's like when there's music playing and it suddenly cuts off, leaving everyone to stare in the direction it was coming from. There's some awkward throat clearing and Oz wraps his arm around me, looking everyone defiantly in the face one by one before tearing his microphone off and leading me into the big house.

When a crew member attempts to follow us, Oz stops, tosses back, "I wouldn't try that tonight," and then slams the door in his face.

I'm breathless and slightly puzzled. I'm not so dense that I don't understand what he's got in mind, but what I don't get is why we're headed into Casa de Savage. It's a place of history, and of heartbreak.

Oz knows exactly what he's doing. As soon as we're inside he picks me up without even pausing and heads down the hall.

When I say his name he stops and brushes his lips across mine ever so briefly.

"Shh, we've wasted enough time. And Loren," he frowns, "take off your fucking microphone."

My arms hold fast to his neck as he smoothly carries me to the bedroom. His skin smells of smoke and soap, a combination that strikes me as supremely erotic.

As soon as we're in the bedroom he kicks the door closed, locks it and sets me on my feet. When I get a good look at his face I shrink against the wall. Not out of fear. I could never be afraid of him.   But Oz's mild manners of the past weeks have all been exhausted, replaced by something far more primal.

Staring straight into that kind of commanding lust would make any woman weak.

I've seen what Oz is like when he's tender.

And I've seen him when he's rough.

I can't tell which side of the coin I'm looking at.

But then he cups my face gently into his palms, stroking my cheeks with his thumbs.

"Loren," he says with supreme tenderness. "I swore I'd never kiss you again. At the time, I meant it."

I swallow hard. "I remember."

How could I forget? That night in the desert I'd begged him to use me hard. We said things to hurt each other. That was what I wanted. I wanted the bad memory.

It didn't turn out how I thought it would. But then, nothing has.

My voice is the thickest of whispers. "Oz. Oscar. Kiss me now. Please."

He shuts his eyes briefly and lets out a small groan. He tips forward and presses his forehead lightly against mine. At the same time his body grinds against me with hard, urgent need. My hands travel eagerly down his strong back, craving to feel more skin.

I need more. I need it all.

If I don't get all of him soon I don't think I can hold onto sanity. I want him so bad I can't see straight.

But I want this first.

When our lips touch, it's soft, tentative, contradicting the frantic hunger ready to bust right through his pants and take me where I stand. I move my hand lower to cup the hard outline of him and he inhales sharply. Yet the kiss remains tender. His tongue slides against mine in a slow dance that's sweet agony.

The very first time he kissed me I knew that kiss would be the gold standard forever. Until this moment it was. I'm lost in this kiss and I don't ever want to be found.

But there's a more primitive part of me that can't take it anymore. My hips start rocking against him in rhythm, mad for relief. When his hands leave my face and travel between my legs I groan into his mouth. I'm grabbing at his shirt, pulling it up and running my fingers along hard, smooth muscle that never ends.

Oz breaks free and pulls back. His eyes are blazing and he yanks his shirt over his head with one fluid motion.

"Wait," he growls when my trembling fingers begin to undo my own shirt.   His hands cover mine and his deft fingers go right to work. "That's my job."

He's quick and sure, sliding the fabric down as he runs his lips along my right shoulder.

"Oz," I breathe, reaching for his pants.

The sight of his dick straining to be released is hypnotic. Every muscle between my legs twitches expectantly.   I've never needed anything so much.

Oz is in charge right now though.   He flashes a sexy, knowing grin and carries me the short distance to the bed. Once he's got me on my back he gets between my legs, circles my waist with his big hands and rolls his thumbs over my belly.

"We'll get there, Ren. But first you're going to hear this." His strong thumbs travel lower and lower until I gasp, then bite my lip, trying to compel my body to stop writhing in the most wanton manner.

He's doing it on purpose, teasing the hell out of the most sensitive place I own and stopping short of letting me get too close. I raise my hips, straining wildly against his fingers. I'm so ready I swear I could come if he would just finish sliding my shorts down. He smiles at my struggle, content to tease until *he* decides I'm ready.

Then his smile fades and his mood grows intense once more.

"A long time ago I fell hard for you, Loren Savage. I never really got up again. I don't want to rehash how we hurt each other and why. I just want us to have a future."

He holds my gaze while he slowly runs his hands up over my belly and over my breasts, gently tugging the straps of my bra down before nimbly unhooking the back.

"Our future is here," he whispers, leaning forward and lightly kissing my chest, just above my heart. "And here." He moves up to my mouth and kisses me with furious passion. When my arms pull him closer he backs off, grins at me wickedly and moves down my body. He slides my shorts off with excruciating leisure before tugging my panties down with his teeth. While I'm biting my tongue and trying to stifle the urge to buck my hips like a lust-starved nympho, he flashes me a grin that says he knows all about my desperation.

"And here," he whispers before sliding his tongue inside me for one final, unbearable torment. I nearly scream when he withdraws. But screaming won't give me what I want.

Instead, I get right up on my knees, flatten my palms against his chest and push him back. Since Oz is likely ten times stronger than I am he could stop me easily but he lets me straddle him. He also lets me do whatever I need to do to get his pants open and his dick released. We lock eyes and I bend forward. When I get my mouth on him a groan rips out of his throat and his hands press the back of my head. I lick the shaft and teasingly suck my way to the sweet spot. Slowly I slide my lips over him until the tip of his cock touches the back of my throat. That's when he stops me.

"No," he demands in a half strangled voice. "I need to watch your face, Ren. I need to watch you the entire time."

Oz lifts me with one hand while searching through his pants with the other. He extracts a condom and gets it rolled on before pulling my legs around him once more and gripping my ass, kneading the flesh.

Our bare chests press together and we stare into each other's eyes. He isn't inside me yet. I feel him; so hard, impatient, ready to enter. I'm just as impatient. I'm aching to stretch wide enough and take all of him inside.

We pause in the same breath. We are frozen together, an inch away from joining. His heartbeat is right there, right on the other side of mine.

My fingertips trail lightly along his square, rugged jaw.

"I love you, Oz. Not just for what we were. But for what we are now. For everything we're going to be."

He grabs my hand and kisses it lightly, the sexiest of gentlemen.

"I love you too, Ren. I never stopped. I never will."

Then he drops my hand, grips my hips and slides into me hard. I'm wrapped around him so tightly I can't imagine ever letting go.

We go slowly the first time. We ravage each other the second time and the time after that. We fall sleep in each other's arms.

And when we wake up we start doing it all over again.

CHAPTER TWENTY-FOUR

OZ

They are leaving. I'd be a two-faced prick if I said I was sorry to see them go. I'm not. I've been counting down to this day. Since the crew seems a little behind schedule, I join Monty in scouring the property for cameras, screwdriver in hand. Cate Camp does her bouncy-titted run over to the house, trying to stop me.

"Don't rip them out, Oz! Just cover them with something for now. Remember, Season Two is likely to start in the spring."

I ignore her and successfully remove the camera mounted on the wall behind the kitchen sink. She scowls when I hold out the electronic souvenir so I just toss it on the table and move on.

The rest of the crew really isn't so bad. They're just guys with cameras trying to get a job done. It's just that I don't like being the job.

Rash is carefully packing up the van. He waves as I exit the house and head for the barn. I wave back. We already did our handshake thing. I don't see any reason to do it again.

Sometimes I get an uneasy feeling about what's still on the horizon. After all, Gary and friends can do whatever they want with all this footage. That's what it means to be at the mercy of someone else's project. I remember scoffing to Brock that I couldn't give a wad of armpit hair what they turned me into for the sake of ratings. I feel differently now. Not because I'm looking out for *my* reputation. But because I don't want this whole thing to kill theirs. I'm not just talking about Ren. I'm talking about the rest of them too. In a roundabout way I've finally started thinking of them as my family.

Ava and Alden are out in the yard feeding the chickens. It's the kid's favorite thing to do. I stop by and throw a fist full of cornmeal in the air. It scatters everywhere, the chickens lose their peck-happy minds and Alden laughs so hard he plunks right down in the dirt. There's no other option but to laugh just as hard.

"Best sound in the world."

She has managed to sneak right up on me. She has a talent for doing that. Ren stands there on the other side of the chicken coop looking like a million gold bucks with loose hair, cutoff shorts and a peasant-style top that has just enough of a see-thru quality to get my gears moving.

"Best *view* in the world," I counter, joining her on the other side of the gate. We start walking hand in hand and when we're beyond the caretaker's house, no one else in sight, we stop.

When I get my arms around her she melts right into me. It's good. I'm holding my dream girl close and neither of us cares who knows about it. At this point I actually have a grudging kind of affection for the whole stupid show. God knows it gave me the push I needed to reclaim what I'd lost.

"Oh!" Ren exclaims suddenly and pulls away. "Gary called. He called my cell phone which I thought was a little weird but it turned out to be a suspiciously nice conversation."

"Oh yeah?" I turn her around so her back is against my chest and my arms are crossed over her body. We stare out at the mountain views while I breathe her in. "How's that?"

"He started off by telling me he'll arrange a private screening in L.A. so we can see the episodes before they air. He's expecting the show to be a huge deal. I warned him that people want scandal and dirty laundry. They don't want to see a happy ending. He just chuckled and said, 'Very wrong. That's *exactly* what people want, Miss Savage.' I don't know, maybe he's right after all. We'll find out soon enough. That screening he's talking about, that's supposed to be in August. Next month."

"Hmm, that's nice. Too bad we won't make it."

She runs her fingers over my forearm. "No? You told me that despite all the places you've been, you've never managed to set foot in California, let alone Hollywood. Don't you want to view all the decadence of our family origins up close?"

"Hell no. I want to be holed up deep in the Smoky Mountains wilderness with you, no one around for miles. I have my own plans you see and quite a few of them involve the cooperation of your body."

She looks amused. "My body would be pleased to comply. I can't quite abandon modern feminism though. My mind would like some attention too."

"You'll have it." I turn her around and take her face in my hands. When I cup my palms together her face fits there perfectly, like it was sculpted for that purpose. "I want to show you the caves and the mountains. I want to get you underground and see the look on your face the first time you get a load of the Round Room. Remember the first time I brought you into a cave, Ren? And when I'm done showing you everything I know, I'm going to take you with me and we'll explore the rest of the world together. That's a promise."

She tilts her head with wonder. "How do you do that? You make it sound so perfect."

"It *is* perfect, baby."

A shadow crosses her face. "Sometimes I think I'll wake up in my lonely Vegas apartment. Just me, my couch and my regret."

"No more of that. No more regret. Just us. You just name your destination and we'll go. You want to go to California and consort with the illuminati I'll take you there. I'll even wear a tux to blend in."

She smiles. "You are overcompensating. I thought you knew you weren't getting a red carpet kind of girl. You're getting a cotton candy on the boardwalk kind of girl."

"I can handle cotton candy and a boardwalk. I'll even join in on the carnival, take you for a ride on the Ferris wheel. What the hell is so funny?"

Ren is laughing so loudly the sound echoes across the valley. She keeps shaking her head when I ask her what is so amusing. Then she throws her arms around my neck and jumps up, her legs around my waist.

"I'll ride anything with you, Oz. But of all the plans in question I like yours the best. I want to see everything with you."

"And you will," I promise, kissing her. "We'll make every pair of lovers on earth shake with jealousy."

"Swear it," she whispers, tightening her legs around me, moving her body so that her hot center rubs so hard against my abruptly aching cock that I consider dragging her behind the nearest building to find the relief we both need.

"I swear it."

I do. She's got me. Always has, always will.

"There's no more cameras, Oz," she purrs, licking at my earlobe, nipping at my neck. "There's only us."

That's it. We're fucking doing this.

In a fitting move I carry her over to the far side of the brothel where there's a short wall forever bathed in shadow. Wordlessly I strip her shorts off, palm my cock, get her against the wall and wrap her around me in a way that lets me find the best angle inside.

It's a dirty thing to do but she loves it. I love it.

That's the way it is between us, sometimes sweet and sometimes filthy.

Sometimes it's such a powerful connection I start to doubt that being with anyone else was ever possible. It seems like it's always been her.

Ren comes hard and sighs into my ear. I follow with an explosion that sends my fist into the brittle wood of the building. We're both dusty and sweaty but it was well earned.

I would have carried her back to the big house but she hops down, pulls her clothes together, and takes my arm for the short walk.

We reach the heart of Atlantis Star just in time to see the dust cloud from the truck of the departing crew.

The only one around watching them go is Brigitte. Monty is still skulking around on a hunt for cameras, Spence ran into town for something horse-related and Ava is where we left her, having fun with her little boy.

Brigitte Savage looks kind of like a little girl, standing there in the dust wearing a plain pair of jeans and a white t-shirt, twirling her red hair around a finger. It's one of the rare times she's not getting on my nerves right off the bat. She looks up when we approach, notices our clasped hands and gives a vague smile. Then she shrugs, sighs, and looks into the distance.

"What now?" she says in a low, confused voice that I'm not sure she meant for anyone to hear.

Ren leaves my side and swings an arm around her sister's thin shoulder. "Whatever you want, Bree. Go after it. I have nothing but faith in you, little sister."

Brigitte doesn't look like she's listening but then suddenly she throws her arms around Ren and they hug tightly for a full minute. I can't hear what Bree says when she whispers in her sister's ear, but it's something that makes Ren glance back at me and blush.

When Brigitte starts heading my way I'm all prepared for something obnoxious to come out of her mouth. She stands there with her hands on her hips and gives me an arch look.

"I know you'll be good to her, Oz. Because if you're not I'm going to feed you to Monty." She giggles, grabs me for a quick hug and then bounces over to where Alden and Ava are living it up in the chicken coop.

I nod at the cloud of feathers. "What do you think Spence is going to do with all those chickens?"

Ren smiles. "I imagine he'll keep looking after them. Ava and the baby are sticking around for the time being and if Alden's pets turn into fried nuggets someone will have some explaining to do."

"Monty going back to San Diego?"

"No. I didn't tell you? In a shocking turn of events, Monty got a job. It's even legal. He's going to be bartending at a place in Consequences."

I tug on a strand of her hair, sifting it through my fingers. "So how long do we need to hang around until we're cleared for departure?"

She kisses the hollow of my neck and then smiles prettily. "We can leave tomorrow."

"Yeah?"

"Yeah."

"Hey, what did your sister ask you that made you turn all red?"

Ren smiles, bites her lip. "She asked if I was going to marry a man named Oscar Savage."

Oscar Savage.

For a long time I told myself that he didn't exist anymore because he was always an invention. That's not true. I'm not about to go strolling around and claiming to be a Savage but it would be false indeed to say he never existed.

"You didn't answer her, did you?"

"Oz. I can't answer a question that was never asked." She's teasing but the blush is rising in her cheeks.

"All right. Well, Oscar Savage will worship you for eternity. And Oz Acevedo is *asking* if you'll let him."

She stands on tiptoe and sweetly kisses my lips. "Yes. Even though eternity isn't nearly long enough."

"No. But I'll take it for as long as it lasts."

She takes both my hands in hers and our fingers lace together. "Well then, consider eternity all yours, sir."

Thank you for reading!

corabrentwrites@yahoo.com
www.facebook.com/CoraBrentAuthor
https://www.goodreads.com/CoraBrent

OTHER BOOKS BY CORA BRENT

Unruly

GENTRY BOYS

DRAW

RISK

GAME

FALL

HOLD (December 2015)

CROSS (February 2016)

DEFIANT MC

Know Me: A Novella

Promise Me

Remember Me

Reckless Point

Printed in Great Britain
by Amazon